BOOKS BY JON GODDEN

The Bird Escaped   1947

The House by the Sea   1948

The Peacock   1950

The City and the Wave   1954

The Seven Islands   1956

Mrs. Panopoulis   1959

A Winter's Tale   1961

In the Sun   1965

*Two Under the Indian Sun   1966
    with Rumer Godden*

Mrs. Starr Lives Alone   1972

Ahmed and the Old Lady   1976

AHMED AND
THE OLD LADY

AHMED AND THE OLD LADY

Jon Godden

ALFRED A. KNOPF · New York · 1976

THIS IS A BORZOI BOOK
PUBLISHED BY ALFRED A. KNOPF, INC.

Copyright © 1976 by Jon Godden
All rights reserved under International and Pan-American
Copyright Conventions. Published in the United States
by Alfred A. Knopf, Inc., New York. Distributed by
Random House, Inc., New York.
Originally published in England as
Ahmed's Lady by Chatto & Windus,
London. Copyright © 1975 by Jon Godden

Library of Congress Cataloging in Publication Data
Godden, Jon, [Date] Ahmed and the old lady.
I. Title.
PZ3.G54215Ae3 [PR6013.018] 823'.9'14 75-34932
ISBN 0-394-40297-9

Manufactured in the United States of America

First American Edition

For K.N.G.
1876-1966

CONTENTS

PROLOGUE ix

PART ONE: *First Journey* 1

PART TWO: *The Meadow* 51

PART THREE: *Second Journey* 101

PART FOUR: *At the Lakes* 139

PROLOGUE

ON A TRAINING EXERCISE in mountain warfare, a section of Indian soldiers, a corporal and six men, walked in single file along the ridge. They were several miles behind the cease-fire line between Kashmir and Pakistan and were on their way back through bleak, uninhabited country to the base camp far below in the valley.

It was a cold, bright autumn day. The sun shone from a sky of deepest blue, but frost still lingered between the rocks, and the men's breath went before them in a cloud. Down in the distant valley, the birches were gold on the lower slopes of the hills and the river ran shallow and clear. Where once the call of the great Kashmir stag resounded from the forests, lorries carrying supplies ground noisily along the new military road. Up here, there was silence, broken only by the sound of boots on rough ground. As they were supposed to do, the men kept a sharp look-out, scanning this wild, high, desolate landscape for any movement, any sign of life. The corporal, carrying a light automatic gun, was in the lead; the brown-green of their combat uniform blended with the rocks. Only the eagle soaring far above watched them go.

The path twisted and turned. Now, on their right, they passed the mouth of a narrow, rock-filled gully and looked down it to a glimpse of water, a lonely mountain lake. The corporal waved them on along the ridge path and when his back was turned again, the rear man in the file stepped aside into the gully to relieve himself. He stared down at the lake, but did not linger in this desolate, rock-strewn place longer than he needed. The last of the platoon had disappeared round the corner of the path and, hurrying, he slipped on the loose stones and fell sprawling. Cursing, he scrambled up, bent to retrieve his rifle, and saw a gleam of blue shining up at him from a cleft between two stones. It was a pin, a long, tarnished pin, crowned with a blue enamelled head shaped like a butterfly's wings. The young soldier held it in his hand, turning it to catch the light. One wing was cracked across, the other scarred and bent, but it was well worth keeping; the vivid, shining colour delighted him and he had never seen anything like it. Not troubling himself to wonder how it came to be in such a place, he quickly hid this unexpected find under his windproof smock in the pocket of his tunic and ran to catch up with the others, hoping the corporal had not noticed that he had lagged behind.

PART ONE
First Journey

I

It was on a July day over thirty years ago, in 1943, that three Scottish missionaries on holiday from a mission hospital far off in the plains of India came down a valley in Kashmir on their way back to Srinagar.

Only the two women, dressed alike in khaki smocks, jodhpurs, and khaki topees, rode on small shaggy hill ponies; the man, bearded, spectacled, and carrying appropriately a Biblical-looking staff, walked, and behind them straggled their servant, baggage ponies, and ponymen. One of the women was lean and elderly, the other young with a round, happy, dreaming face. She was at least fifty yards ahead, letting her reins hang loose and her pony amble along as it pleased.

Old Mrs. Harding saw them coming from afar and halted her pony. Her blue eyes narrowed; she frowned and her long upper lip grew longer, was drawn in behind the lower, as often happened when she was displeased. Under the large straw hat, pinned to her white hair by a hatpin whose head was an enamelled brilliant blue butterfly, her pink-and-white old lady's face took on the forbidding, obstinate look that her servant, Ahmed, had come to recognise. She would have preferred to meet no other human beings at all in this beautiful valley on this golden summer day, although the few peasants she had glimpsed working in the fields and the two children in ragged clothes who had followed her from the outskirts of the last village, running beside her pony, looking up into her face with enormous dark eyes and holding out grimy little paws, had fitted into the landscape well enough. This party, rapidly coming nearer, was a blot on the scene, alien, out of place, as it did not occur to her she, too, must be. She looked round for Ahmed; there he was, far behind, chattering to the pony-men, scuffling up a cloud of dust with the new chappals, the Kashmiri sandals, that she had bought for him. Ahmed could have done nothing, even if he had been in his proper place, walking at her pony's head. There was only one track up the valley, no way of escape; an encounter with her compatriots was inevitable; one of them, the younger woman, was almost upon her.

Leah Harding inclined her head in a bow of greeting as from one traveller to another, quite sufficient, she thought, and attempted to ride on. The way was barred: an earnest, sunburnt, and youthful face was on a level with her own. As the two ponies nuzzled each other in pony fashion, a hand was laid on her knee.

"Oh, how lucky you are to be going there, not coming back!"

The voice was far too fervent. Pale eyes, slightly protu-berant, with the wide rapt look of one who has recently seen a vision, filled with tears. "It's Paradise," the voice breathed. "You'll see—Paradise."

The hand was withdrawn, the ponies moved apart, and Leah rode on. 'Not quite right in the head, poor thing,' she said to herself. All the same, as she looked up the valley at the waiting mountains, her heart lifted, seemed to beat more quickly.

"Good afternoon." The second woman, a sensible, reti-cent person, evidently, rode past her with nothing more than a smile—and a rather searching look; unfortunately the tall, lanky man stood still and lifted his topee, baring his bald head to the sun. Leah thought him unattractive, but was forced to pause again.

"Going far?"

It was no business of his where she was going, but Leah answered politely that she was going as far as she could.

"It's another three stages up to the Meadow. That's where everyone camps. Glorious place—we have just spent three weeks there."

He was staring at her curiously and, she realised, with concern. She was not surprised when he asked, "Travelling alone?"

"You are not going *alone?*" the few people she knew in Srinagar had said; they had not added "At your age," but that is what they meant. They had said the same thing when she moved from the hotel to a houseboat on the lake. Alone, of course, meant without a companion of her own race and colour.

"I have my servant and my ponymen," she told him. "I consider them adequate. Good-bye."

He was left—looking after her, she was sure—and when, at a safe distance, she turned her head, she saw that he was talking to Ahmed, who stood before him in one of his graceful poses—a willow-wand confronting a bean-pole. 'What impertinence,' she thought, 'to question a servant,' and she called, "Ahmed! Ahmed!"

For a moment she thought that he had not heard; then she saw him sketch a salaam and come running. As he put his hand on her pony's bridle to steer it through the approaching cavalcade of laden ponies, she saw that he was frowning. His thin, eager face had a sullen look that she had never seen on it before. She said, "What did he want?"

Her words came to Ahmed as if from a great distance. The years fell away and he was a child again in the mission's infirmary. The bald-headed doctor had not recognised the grown Ahmed after so many years, but this unlikely encounter in a remote valley hundreds of miles from the mission was upsetting, to say the least. It was a bad omen. Ahmed felt that the fates were against him.

"What did he want?" Leah repeated, and Ahmed, trying to shrug off the past, as he usually managed to do, looked up at her and said, "These mission sahibs very prying, always asking questions." Then he called out to the passing ponymen, exchanging greetings, Leah supposed, in his own language, which, although she had spent the last two years trying to learn Hindi, she did not understand.

When the cavalcade had passed, leaving a cloud of dust

and a smell of cheap cigarettes on the air and the jingle and voices had died away, she said, "Missionaries? You learnt to speak English in a mission, didn't you?"

Ahmed scowled. He saw the austere, whitewashed room; the drone of the classroom was in his ears; the old rebellion rose in him as he answered, "Long ago. Yess— many, many years."

Leah smiled as she looked down at him. "When you were young?"

'How like a young goat he is,' she thought once again: lean and yet supple, chock-full of energy and guile, close-cropped black and waving hair under the black curly astrakhan hat, slightly hooked nose, bold, almost yellow eyes, and always cynically cheerful and gay. She would not have travelled even as far as this without Ahmed and, with his help and connivance, she would go further, higher and higher, up into the mountains.

"Where everyone camps," the missionary had said. Leah did not like the sound of that. She had not come all this way to pitch her tent among other tents, to be asked questions, perhaps to be stopped. . . . To Leah, who in her life had been out of England only once before, it had seemed a long and adventurous journey, especially in wartime, from Buckinghamshire to Calcutta. It had disappointed her to find that the life her grandson expected her to lead there was much the same as life in her small country town: more servants, a different climate, more leisure among much the same kind of people. Hugh had been glad to see her, although he had cabled her not to come as he hoped to be called up before long. She had kept house for him and the two friends who shared the flat with him, had worked for the Red Cross rolling bandages, but had spent much time exploring the city as best she could, something that Hugh disapproved of. When, after nearly two years, the summons had come and all three of them went off to their training depots, she had waited on in the flat, where they spent what leave they had, until Hugh's hopes were realised and he was sent overseas.

He had not wanted her to go to Kashmir. "It's too far, Grandma. If Calcutta is too hot for you and you find it boring, why not try Darjeeling? There will be people you know there." Poor Hugh, he had never understood the first thing about her. The journey to Kashmir had been long and tiresome, but all too soon Leah had found that Srinagar was not far enough, although there was so much to see. The houseboat on the lake had been a haven after the hotel, and there, until it grew too hot, she had been able to spend her time as she liked, just looking, seeing. Yet even there people had come "to make sure you are all right," to advise and show concern, as those missionaries had done. 'Bother all good, kind, interfering people,' Leah thought. 'Bother those missionaries, even the one who talked of Paradise,' and with an effort she put them out of her mind. She would have been more than annoyed if she could have known what, at that moment, they were saying.

"Rather elderly to be setting out alone, don't you agree?"

"Yes, well over seventy, I should think. An intrepid old lady. What brought her here, do you suppose?"

"I didn't like the look of that servant of hers. Shifty, I thought. I couldn't get anything out of him, not even her name. I don't like it, but I don't see what we can do."

"She shouldn't come to much harm if she goes by easy stages only as far as the Meadow. Plenty of people there."

"The Johnstons will be in camp for another week or so. Shall we send a note back, asking them to keep an eye on her?"

"We could, but she seemed such an independent old soul."

"We had better send a note—she need never know."

"Oh, Doctor—must we interfere?" the younger woman said. "Let her do what she likes. Whatever happens to her, I'm sure that she would think it worth it—just to have seen . . ."

"You exaggerate so, Sister. Just as well we're leaving, the place seems to have gone to your head. By the way, did

you notice her clothes? Not exactly suitable, such colours
—and that hat!"

Leah had taken thought and trouble over the right sort
of clothes for this expedition. Nothing she possessed had
seemed right. Knowing that she was not the age or shape
for trousers, much as she would have liked to try them, she
had decided on divided skirts, one of cotton drill—it would
be warm at first—and one of the soft Kashmir tweed called
puttoo. Ahmed had found a tailor, but the results had been
peculiar at first and much good material was wasted before
she was satisfied. She liked bright colours, and khaki, which
even Ahmed had advised, she detested, especially in wartime when there was so much of it about, and she had
chosen blue drill and a purplish tweed. Her own long-
sleeved blouses would do very well, and she had found a
broad soft red leather belt in one of the shops along the
bund and a clever leather worker who had sewed little
pockets inside it in which she could keep her money and
keys; it made her waist look even thicker, but she had always
been short and thickset, even in girlhood, and this did not
worry her. The same tailor had made her a long tweed
waistcoat, copied from the one Ahmed wore, and the thick
cloak she had brought out with her from England would
keep her warm if she managed to get far, perhaps almost
to the snowline. The snowline . . . the gleaming word beckoned her. . . .

None of her shoes were thick or strong enough and
Ahmed had suggested chappals; she had invested in several
pairs because there was no knowing how long they would
be on the march. She would have liked to wear gaiters, but
contented herself with the chamois inner shoes, or socks,
that went with the chappals. She had hesitated a long time
over the hat, a large white straw brought out from England,
too; but when she removed the trimming of roses, she
decided that it would do to protect her fine, still smooth
skin, of which she was proud, from the sun. Oddly enough,
she had found that the sun in Srinagar, at over five thousand feet, was even fiercer than in the plains. Here in this

valley between the hills that shut it in, it was hot in the early afternoon, too hot for comfort. She was growing drowsy, nodding as she rode.

Yesterday had been a long and tiring day. Leah was already tired after the effort of packing, checking her stores, and settling up with the houseboat crew, and then the early start, when the car that had brought her and Ahmed along the shores of the lake rattled over the suspension bridge, giving her a first sight of the valley's river. After a short drive, she had been deposited on the outskirts of a village of tall wooden houses, where a pile of camp equipment, sent out by lorry, was waiting with the ponies and ponymen. The noise, the haggling as the loads were apportioned, had bewildered her; while Ahmed enjoyed the commotion and fuss, darting about like a self-important dragonfly, she had felt shaken and old. She had eaten her picnic lunch under a tree, sitting on her camp-stool, surrounded by a ring of interested villagers. The flies had been terrible and she had wished that she was back in the houseboat on the wide shining lake. Almost she wished that she had not come. 'Pull yourself together, Leah Harding,' she had told herself crossly. 'This is only the beginning. You know that you will have to take the rough with the smooth if you want to get anywhere.'

When Ahmed came to help her mount her pony, a rough-looking little beast with one wall-eye and a string of blue beads round its neck, it restored her self-respect to know that she could wave him away. She had not ridden since her marriage, but what is learnt in childhood remains all one's life, as she discovered when, with some trepidation, she put her foot in the stirrup Ahmed held for her. She was pleased to find that she felt quite confident, in spite of the odd-looking saddle, as they moved off.

That first day—was it only yesterday?—after all that commotion, they had made only a short march, setting up camp early at one of the recognised camping sites. She had not liked the place, which was near the track and too far from the river. "Always first camp here," Ahmed had told her, and she had been too tired to protest. Until the sun set behind the hills, the flies swarmed everywhere; people passed up and down the track and paused to stare. Unaccustomed to a camp-bed, she had found it difficult to sleep, and when at last she dozed off, she was woken by the snores of the ponymen, whose tent was pitched too close. She had lain awake wondering if she had been wise to ignore Colonel Baxter, who, with his wife, had been so kind to her in those first weeks at the hotel, when he advised her to go to the well-known contractor he recommended for her camp equipment. "Much dear," Ahmed had said. "Leave to me, Memsahib."

At least she had had the sense to insist on going with him to inspect everything provided, not that she knew anything about tents. Ahmed, who, of course, had his cut from the contractor—she was not so green that she did not know that—had sulked when she had tried to cut down, refusing more than one camp-chair, more than two tables, refusing to take the large wooden commode. "How Memsahib manage?" he had wailed, but had given in gracefully, as he always did when she insisted, and an enamel chamber-pot had been added to the growing pile of boxes and bundles. Although Ahmed had seemed to think it unnecessary, she had also added a length of clothes-line, being sure that they would do their own washing in camp, and had asked for clothes-pegs, which had not been forthcoming. There had been another battle over tinned food; this she had lost. "We shall live on the country," she had said, and the contractor, who, she had then discovered, was Ahmed's uncle, had joined in his nephew's protestations: "Verree poor country. Verree poor people. Perhaps little atta flour, perhaps some eggs, nothing more." It seemed that a runner had already been engaged for her, a man who would make the journey between her camp and Srinagar once a week and carry back all she needed.

She looked round at the straggle of ponies behind her. It seemed absurd that one woman should need so much. Surely she had more ponies in her train than the three missionaries had done? There was, of course, the cook tent, where Ahmed slept, and the tent for the ponymen. Feed for the ponies had to be carried, too, yet this valley looked so green, so prosperous, with its fruit, poplars, and walnut trees, its richly brown earth; those children had been ragged, they had not looked ill-fed. How did such beauty and poverty exist side by side? In her own country, poverty was grey, drab; here it seemed all the colours of the rain-bow. . . .

Leah was dozing off again, clutching the pony's mane. Perhaps if she walked for a while she would manage to keep awake. Her watch, a flat gold half-hunter that had belonged to Geoffrey, her husband, hung from a chain round her neck. It was only three; they had started later than they should have done; the stage that day was fourteen miles. 'I have come far enough for today,' she told herself.

Her pony, as if it knew, stopped of its own accord. Ahmed, who had dropped behind again, came hurrying up. "Not far now, Memsahib," he said.

A little path, made by goats, or sheep, wandered off the road across a flat grassy stretch of ground towards the river, which she could hear and see.

"We'll go down there," she told Ahmed, pointing with the peeled willow-wand he had cut for her as a whip. "We'll camp close to the river."

He objected, as she had known he would. "Proper camp place only few miles. Good water, village . . ."

The village, of course, was the attraction. Muslims, she knew, were not supposed to drink alcohol, even the mildest rice beer, but there was always a tea-shop even in the poor-est village. Leah had had enough of flies and inquisitive peasants, and Ahmed—looking up into her face, which, although she did not know it, had taken on its stubborn, mulish look—gave in. Leaving him to argue with the pony-men, she turned her pony on to the path.

In all the valley there could not be a more perfect place to camp. A small stream ran crystal clear, bisecting the greensward that ended only at the pebbly edge of the river, which, racing past, filled the air with its cool sound. Beyond the river, the tree-covered hills, shimmering in the golden afternoon, rose into a clear sky. The track seemed a long way off. Far ahead, up the narrowing valley, were only trees and a glimpse of thatched roofs—the village, she supposed, but blessedly far off, too.

Having pointed out to Ahmed—or, rather, to Nabir, the head ponyman—exactly where she wanted her tent pitched on the river's verge, Leah was content to rest on her camp-stool under the single tree, which grew at exactly the right spot to give her shade without obstructing the view, and to watch camp being made. Nabir, a bearded, quiet middle-aged man who yesterday had kept in the background, now asserted himself and for the most part ignored Ahmed. Canvas was unfolded, tent-poles put together, ropes stretched, and wooden tent-pegs hammered into the ground. In what seemed to Leah an incredibly short time, the tents rose and soon all was ready. The unloaded ponies were hobbled and turned loose to graze on the short grass, starred here and there with small, bright flowers. Smoke rose from a newly lighted fire. Presently Ahmed set up a table and her comfortable folding chair under the tree and, a few minutes later, brought tea on a tin tray covered with a clean napkin.

He had discarded his waistcoat, and his pink shirt hung down over his loose white cotton jodhpurs. The shirt was not particularly clean; as he put the tray down on the table beside her, she saw that there was a grey rim inside the open collar—which was not surprising considering the dust and heat. She had always found Ahmed a pleasing sight; he was something of a dandy and liked to cut a dash. The black hat was worn at an angle and there was a red flower tucked behind one of his neat, small ears. Geoffrey had left her well-off, but Leah was by nature careful over money, a throwback to her frugal Quaker ancestors; all the same, she had given Ahmed a tweed jacket, two pullovers, blankets, as well as the new chappals. His eyes had sparkled as he stroked the good tweed of the jacket. Soon after she had

engaged him, he had asked her to provide him with nee-
dles, cotton, and darning wool and had produced, at his
own expense, a little bag to hold these sewing things. "Ahmed's job darn Memsahib's stocking and sew on buttons,"
he had said, which had amused her, although she knew that
in Kashmir, at least, it was the men who did all the embroi-
dery and sewing and that Hugh's servant, until she arrived
in India, had done his mending as a matter of course. Later,
on one of their shopping expeditions from the houseboat,
which she and Ahmed had so much enjoyed, she had given
him a watch, and when he persuaded her to buy an expensive, fitted picnic basket as well as a small satchel to hold
her spectacles and anything else she needed on the march,
she had seen him eyeing a large knapsack, a real climber's
knapsack, and, in a moment of weakness, had bought it for
him. Ahmed, when she first met him, had possessed nothing except the shabby clothes he had worn.

As she looked up at him, Leah thought that, after nearly
four months with her, he was at last beginning to put on
weight and fill out. That first time, when she had seen him
waiting on the verandah outside her hotel room, he had
been too thin, almost gaunt, his high cheekbones too
prominent under the odd, yellow-brown eyes that were not
merry then, but anxious, pleading. How Ahmed knew that
she needed a servant to replace the man Hugh had sent
with her—his own personal servant, who, after a few days,
had wanted to go back to Calcutta—she never discovered.
Colonel Baxter had disapproved of Ahmed from the first
and had been almost disagreeable when she had engaged
him instead of the reliable middle-aged man the Colonel
had recommended. "What's wrong with Ahmed?" she had
asked, and had shown the glowing letters of recommendation from Ahmed's previous employers. "An excellent servant, honest, clean. Speaks English. Can cook." "Good
chits don't mean much," the Colonel had said. "These
were very likely stolen. Never trust a mission boy."

Well, she had been right and the Colonel wrong.
Ahmed had proved a treasure. His English, if breathless,

with many essential words left out, was fluent and he had a surprisingly large vocabulary. He was not, perhaps, that excellent servant, being slapdash, too enthusiastic, too original, but he suited Leah; he understood her, knew what she wanted almost before she knew it herself. As eager to leave the hotel as she was, he had found a houseboat and crew and arranged to have it poled out to a mooring on the lake before she had even told the Baxters or anyone else what she intended to do. As things turned out, it had been an expensive move but, to Leah, well worth it; she had been able to leave everything to Ahmed and to spend her time as she wanted, exploring, finding out. . . . It was Ahmed who took her down the Jhelum River to the Third Bridge —the third of Srinagar's seven bridges—where the embroiderers, jewellers, and carpet sellers had their treasure trove of shops. He had not seemed put out when she bought very little; could he have realised that she only wanted to look, touch, marvel, not to possess?

Ahmed had gone with her to the Mogul pleasure gardens across the lake and had waited patiently for hours while she wandered through the pavilions, watching the fountains play, or watching the picnic parties in their gaily coloured clothes sitting on the grass round a steaming samovar, which was lit, as far as she could make out, by dry leaves and grass. She had bought a chased-silver samovar for herself, but Ahmed had not encouraged her to use it and had managed to leave it behind on the houseboat.

He had engaged a private shikara for her, a long, flat-bottomed, cushioned, and canopied boat paddled by six men, in which she explored the waterways of the water-bound city, and every island and inlet of the lake. It was Ahmed who, when the lotus flowered all over the lake and the mosquitoes and heat began to bother her, suggested it was time to move up into the mountains. "One month, two months, three—as long as Memsahib want, then come back to houseboat in cool." Mrs. Baxter, on one of the Baxters' innumerable visits, had suggested that she should go with them to Gulmarg, a high and beautiful place, Leah had heard, but a summer resort complete with wooden chalet-like houses, a club and golf-course, a polo ground. "You would be more comfortable and safer with us, dear Mrs. Harding." It was kind of the Baxters, although why they, and almost everyone Leah met, found it necessary to worry about her, she could not imagine, and she had refused, perhaps with too much firmness.

"Ahmed," she said now, as he poured out tea for her, something he had not done before—could he know how tired she was? "I like it here. We'll stay here all tomorrow and tomorrow night."

At first she thought that he was going to object. He frowned and hesitated, considering. The frown cleared and he smiled. "Atcha—very good—Memsahib," he said. "Yess, good place, good water. I go tell Nabir. He go village tonight, make arrangements, fix wood and grazing for ponies. Memsahib have to pay—not much. Tomorrow religious day for Muslims. If Memsahib give one lamb for feast, ponyman much pleased."

"A lamb? And where will you find a lamb? I thought you said this was such a poor valley we would not be able to buy anything."

He was not in the least disconcerted. "Verree poor place," he agreed. "All same, get chicken last night, get lamb tomorrow. Ahmed get, you see."

Leah laughed; she could not help it. Even if he turned out to be a rogue, there was something disarming about Ahmed, a confident gaiety, a sweetness . . . but that was going too far. "Very well," she said. "Have your lamb. Come for the money after dinner."

When Ahmed had taken the tray away, Leah took off her hat, laid it on the ground beside her, and sat listening to the river and letting the light breeze flow over her. Her tent was ready and waiting, the flaps put back, showing the foot of the bed that Ahmed had already made up. In a moment she would move, unpack, make herself comfortable. There was no need to hurry. Time was hers to spend exactly as she liked. Tomorrow she would go for a long leisurely walk beside the river. This evening it would be wise to recoup her forces, do nothing, simply rest.

The ponymen were gathering round their own fire, perhaps preparing their evening meal. With them she could see the skinny little sweeper boy Ahmed had pronounced necessary to the camp, although all he did, so far as she could see, was to sweep the ground inside her tent before the thin blue-and-red striped cotton carpet was spread and, she supposed, empty the chamber-pot; although it was warm, he was already wearing the new red pullover she had given him. Ahmed was in the cook tent, unpacking the stores that were carried in wooden tea-boxes or in kiltas—tall, lidded baskets covered with leather. She hoped he was thinking of her supper. It seemed a long time since her rather frugal breakfast, and all she had eaten since had been a sandwich, washed down with a drink of lime-juice and water from her water-bottle, a real cloth-covered bottle of the kind carried by soldiers and explorers. "Start early," the Colonel had advised, "and wait to eat until the day's march is over and you have made camp; never set out after a heavy meal. Never drink from a stream, however clear and tempting, unless you are sure there is no house or village anywhere near." The houseboat had had its own cook, quite a good cook, who had offered to go with them on this expedition—a needless extravagance, she had thought then. Judging from the dinner Ahmed had produced last night, "Can cook" had been a misstatement. Perhaps it was not fair to judge so soon. Tomorrow she would inspect the cook tent, see what he had to contend with—everything had tasted strongly of woodsmoke. She was not a large eater, but particular, and she liked good food.

Ahmed's voice roused her. She must have fallen asleep in the chair. The light had changed; the gold haze had thickened; the sun was low in the sky.

"Bath ready," Ahmed was saying. "Hot bath. Memsahib feel better after bath."

When Leah struggled up, she found that she was stiff after long hours in the saddle. As she hobbled to her tent, she saw the sweeper boy carrying two kerosene tins of hot water hanging from a pole laid across his shoulder. Such tins, pierced for rope handles, were, it seemed, an indispensable part of life on the houseboat or in camp, perhaps of rural life generally.

The white, double tent had a lining of yellow cotton patterned with a small black design; as Leah passed under the tightly stretched canvas that made an awning over the entrance, she thought how cosy and welcoming it looked. Ahmed had unpacked her night things, leaving the canvas bags holding the rest of her possessions against the opposite side or wall, and had put a hurricane lamp on the table beside her bed, with a box of matches, her small folding mirror, a glass of water, and another glass holding a few wild flowers; she wondered if the Colonel's man, or anyone except Ahmed, would have thought of the flowers. Her camp-stool stood just inside the entrance; there was no other furniture but on each side of the tent, above her bed and luggage, were several loose pockets in the lining in which there was plenty of room for clothes and books. Ahmed had hung her waistcoat above her head across the rope that stretched from tent-pole to tent-pole; there, too, she could hang her skirt and blouse. It was all most convenient and comfortable.

Standing up, she parted the back flaps and looked into the minute space that served as a bathroom. A tin tub of steaming water with a bucket of cold water beside it took up most of the room. The bathmat was a slatted board and the tin mug was for pouring water over herself, she supposed. Standing on a bamboo tripod was her enamel basin, fitted with a leather cover for travelling, in which she kept soap and face flannel, all her toilet things; Ahmed had told her that this ingenious piece of camp equipment was called a chelumpchi. There was also the chamber-pot, thoughtfully placed on an upturned box.

Leah closed the tent flaps, although there was no one to see her as she undressed, nothing except the river and the hills. The tub was about half the size of the one in the houseboat's bathroom and it was with some difficulty that she inserted herself into it; the brown water, smelling strongly of woodsmoke, was still almost too hot and silkily soft. As she poured water over her shoulders, Leah could hear voices and laughter coming from the direction of the cook tent, and a pony's neigh. She chuckled as she thought, 'If I were anywhere else, I would think this too primitive for words; here it is luxury, all I need!' It was impossible to stand upright without touching the canvas, but what did that matter? A towel hung from the tripod—Ahmed had forgotten nothing.

When she was dressed again in a housecoat, socks, and slippers, Leah sat on her camp-stool at the entrance to the tent and watched evening come. The colours of the hills deepened and then withdrew, as if a purple veil had been drawn over them; the sound of the river was loud on the now cool air. A sense of great well-being filled her; her stiffness had gone and she was comfortable, clean, and relaxed.

A breeze was blowing up the river, the evening gorge breeze, and presently she got up and fetched her woolly shawl. When she sat down again, she saw that a camp-fire was being made: logs were carried and piled on the grass between the tent and the river. As the first flames rose among the smoke, Ahmed came towards her followed by a man wearing the skull-cap most Kashmiris wore. He, it appeared, was the woodcutter, recruited locally. "Always have woodcutter if stay more than one night. Cheaper than buy wood in village." The man had a grizzled beard and the light grey eyes of many Kashmiris, which Leah still found disconcerting in a brown face. Nabir had just such eyes and just such a cap.

Nabir was waiting in the background; she could see him standing in the half-light by the fire. As the woodcutter salaamed and retreated, Nabir came forward and stood silently beside Ahmed; he was, she had already discovered, a silent man. Ahmed had lit the hurricane lamp and placed it on the ground in front of the tent; the gold light shone on Nabir's red shawl, worn over his shoulder like a Highlander's plaid, and lit his face from below. It was a proud, even a noble, face. Colonel Baxter had told Leah that she was very lucky to have Nabir and his ponies, as he was much in demand. "He's been with us on several treks and my wife and I swear by him—you can rely completely on Nabir." Leah had noticed that even Ahmed now treated the head ponyman with respect. They had come, it seemed, for the money for the lamb.

Her money was safely stowed in the belt hanging with her clothes over the tent rope. Even though she trusted both of them, it seemed foolish to fetch it under their eyes. "After dinner," she told Ahmed.

"Nabir going village now."

"After dinner," she repeated, more loudly, and added, "You can bring dinner when it's ready, the sooner the better."

She was looking directly at Ahmed and did not see Nabir leave as silently as he had come. Ahmed's gathering scowl vanished and he was all concern. "Memsahib sit by fire and rest—look, chair ready. Ahmed bring little drink, small whisky do Memsahib good. Dinner soon."

Among the stores there was a precious bottle of whisky, so difficult to get in wartime India. Geoffrey would not have approved: a glass of sherry, a little wine on special occasions, was what he had considered appropriate for a female. The whisky had been brought for possible emergencies—exhaustion at high altitudes had been in her mind—but tonight was really the first night of her adventure, she refused to count last night, and she would celebrate, wish herself luck.

"Very well, just this once, Ahmed," she said and, gathering her shawl about her, walked over to the chair placed near the fire with its back to the breeze, fainter now that darkness had come.

Leah watched the flames spring from the dry wood and the sparks streaming up and out into the night. The warmth was pleasant on her face and knees, as was the smell of woodsmoke in her nostrils. If she turned her head, she could see the lights of the camp, the lantern burning in front of her tent and other lights, and the glow of other fires. The camp sounds, voices, the chopping of wood were drowned by the sound of the river, rushing past in the darkness only a few yards away.

Ahmed was beside her again, setting a tray down across her camp-stool. The sharp, clean smell of whisky mingled with the blue scent of woodsmoke.

"No soda," Ahmed said as he put the glass carefully into her hand. "Verree sorry, only water."

"That's the right way to drink whisky," she told him, "neat or with water." How often had she heard Geoffrey say that? She saw her husband clearly for a moment, sitting in his armchair, a paper on his knee, a glass in his hand, as he had sat before dinner all the evenings, it now seemed, of their married life. How handsome he had been even in his old age! How wonderfully good-looking when she had first seen him! She had married him for his looks, his romantic, dashing air. No one had ever known how deeply he had disappointed her. What would he, the least adventurous of men, the most conventional, say if he could see her sitting here? Leah sighed and then smiled to herself in the firelight. He had never known—she had been a good and loyal wife. There was little she could reproach herself with, and now she was free to go where she liked, to do as she wanted, to live at last.

She was almost asleep, dozing with the half-empty glass still in her hand, when Ahmed came to tell her that dinner was ready. The laid table was waiting just under the awning, at the entrance to the tent, the hurricane lamp standing to one side on the cloth. She was reluctant to leave the fire and, as if he knew what she was thinking, Ahmed said, "Not good stay here. Dew come, much dew." This was true; the wooden arms of her chair were damp, so was her hair. Leah found it an effort to stand up; her stiffness had returned. The tent was only a few yards away, but she wished she had a stick—she must remember to ask Ahmed, or Nabir, to cut her one tomorrow, a good stout stick like that missionary's staff, which she could use all the journey. Ahmed came behind her, carrying chair and glass, and settled her at the table, facing the river. As she finished the whisky, she realised again how hungry she was.

The gold beam of the lamp, standing between her and the river, was bringing a host of winged creatures hurrying out of the night; until Ahmed had moved it, setting it on the ground at a safe distance, it was impossible to eat.

He had made last night's tough chicken into a casserole. "That's better," she told him when he came to take the plate away. How did he manage to cook and serve even such a simple meal by the light of a fire and two hurricane lamps? Ahmed must be used to camp life, have been on many such treks. It was strange that there had been no mention of this in his "chits." When her turn came to write him a recommendation, she would certainly put, "A very useful servant in camp. Made me most comfortable. . . ." Something like that. Tomorrow she would ask him about his travels—perhaps she would find that he had been to this valley before. Tonight all she wanted was her bed.

The tent was awash with pale, milky light when Leah awoke. Without moving her head from the pillow, she could see the moonlit hills and sky framed in the darker triangle of the entrance. She lay in drowsy contentment listening to the river and wondering what had woken her.

The silent peace of the night was broken, shockingly torn apart, and Leah started up in bed. Screams, cries were coming from the direction of the cook tent. Was someone being murdered in his sleep? She threw the bed-clothes back, pulled on her dressing-gown, and, on bare feet, ran out of the tent and turned to look at the sleeping camp. Nothing was moving, and she stood by the dying glow of the fire, wondering what she ought to do.

The hoarse, babbling cries came again, and now other voices were raised, protesting sleepily, enquiring. Then she saw Nabir emerge from the ponymen's tent, his shawl round his shoulders, a stick in his hand. Before he reached the cook tent, the sound stopped, as if a dreamer had been rudely shaken awake. The sweeper boy crawled out of the tent and stood gesticulating, looking up at Nabir. For a moment she did not know what to think; then she saw that Nabir was laughing. Ahmed, bare-headed, wrapped in a blanket, joined them; even at that distance he looked sheepish. She saw Nabir clap him on the back and turn to shout explanations to the roused camp. There was derisive laughter and some shouted comments, probably rude, before Nabir and the boy went back to their blankets, leaving Ahmed crouched over the ashes of the cook fire. No one, apparently, had seen her standing there in the moonlight and she was glad that she had not called out or demanded to know what was happening. Ahmed had been having a nightmare, had screamed with fear in his sleep, that was all. But why should a dream keep him sitting there, hunched up, wretched, wide awake, when everyone else had gone back to sleep? There was nothing she could do for him, and reluctantly Leah went to her tent. As she found her warm bed again and pulled the bed-clothes up over her shoulders, she thought, 'Poor Ahmed, it must have been a horrible dream.'

Ahmed sat on by the still red embers of the fire, his knees drawn up under his chin, his thin brown hands clasped round his knees. Although the night air was mild, he was shivering uncontrollably. His nightmare was still with him; there was no escape from the memory of that accursed hut. The walls, dimly lit by a wick floating in a saucer of oil, were closing round him again. He heard the clink of heavy jewellery and felt the cold knife thrust into his hand. Again he smelt the blood.

The sane light of dawn was in the sky before he crept into the tent and pulled the blankets over his head.

II

It lay contentedly in the crook of Nabir's arm: a black lamb covered with short, close curls, whose blackness had a blue sheen in the sunlight. Sunlight shone through the semi-transparent, too big ears, showing their delicate pink lining, the same pink as the hoof, not much bigger than a walnut shell, that dangled over Nabir's arm. The yellow eyes, still faintly misted with infantile blue, were regarding her with a confident, innocent gaze.

Nabir and Ahmed were waiting. She had given them the money last night. What did they expect her to say? Leah looked from the lamb to the radiant morning sky and said, "No."

It was difficult to convince them that she meant what she said, that she refused to allow the lamb to be killed. At first they thought she considered it in some way inferior, not worth the money. Placing the creature on the ground in front of her, they pointed out how plump it was, how tender: "Still full of mother's milk," Ahmed said. She was invited to feel its ribs, while Ahmed assured her that there was enough meat on it to feed the whole camp with some left over, that it would be impossible to find a better lamb anywhere in the valley. When she agreed that it was an excellent lamb, a beautiful lamb, adding incautiously, "Too beautiful to die," he stared at her as if she had gone out of her mind. How could she expect them to understand her when she did not understand herself? She had never been sentimental about animals and had eaten meat all her life; she knew that she was being not only illogical—one of Geoffrey's favourite words—but foolish. Why risk antagonising everyone in camp at the start of her journey? Why could she not say, "Very well, then, take it away"? She could not say it, not on this golden morning, not having seen the lamb. . . .

Leah looked at the two uncomprehending faces and, drawing herself up in the chair, putting on her most forbidding expression, frowned and said, "No one is to touch this lamb—it's mine. Get yourself another lamb; I will give you extra money for your trouble. Get a sheep, if you like, but don't show it to me."

Ahmed stared at her incredulously; she could see that he was not only angry but ashamed of her, but she met his eyes with a cold stare of her own, and he was the first to look away. As the lamb, folding its legs under it, collapsed with a small, plaintive bleat and went to sleep at her feet, he shrugged and turned to Nabir. Withdrawing a few yards, they talked together in low voices, Ahmed doing most of the talking, until she saw Nabir smile; he glanced towards her, salaamed gravely, and walked away.

When Ahmed came back, she watched him suspiciously. All trace of his annoyance had gone; he seemed unduly pleased with himself and he, too, was smiling. "What's that for?" she asked in alarm as he took a piece of string from his pocket and tied it round the lamb's neck. He looked up at her with eyes as yellow and, seemingly, as guileless as the lamb's, and said in his most soothing voice, "Memsahib finish breakfast. Ahmed look after lamb. Take now and tie to post or it run away. Make bed for lamb, bring food."

"What can it eat?" she asked. "Perhaps it's too young to leave its mother."

"Not too young," he said promptly. "You leave to Ahmed."

He set the lamb on its feet and, making encouraging coaxing noises, tried to lead it at the end of the string. It refused to move, digging in its tiny hooves and bleating piteously. Ahmed laughed. "Doesn't want to leave Memsahib," he said. Gathering the creature up in his arms with surprising gentleness, he carried it away.

'You have been a fool,' Leah told herself. 'What do you

want with a lamb, what will you do with it?' Fool or not, she felt a glow of satisfaction, of increased well-being. 'Time will show,' she thought vaguely as she watched the river racing by. Her coffee was cold by now; she set the cup down and walked slowly to the tent to put on her hat and get ready for her walk. She would give Ahmed time to clear the breakfast things away and then, before setting out, would inspect the cook tent and at the same time make sure that the lamb was safe and well cared for. She refused to have doubts, to worry about anything, on such a day.

The camp, at first sight, seemed deserted except for the lamb tied to a post near the cook tent and fast asleep on a pile of grass. Somewhere, someone was chopping wood; it was the sweeper boy, squatting with a hatchet beside a pile of firewood. She heard voices and laughter coming from the direction of the river and saw that many of her retinue had taken advantage of a fine and idle morning to do their washing downstream; the bushes that grew along the bank were spread with drying clothes.

The cook tent, when she peered inside, was smaller than she had thought and made smaller still by boxes of stores and two bedding rolls. This would not matter, in fine weather anyway, because the cooking was obviously done outside on the ground. She looked down at a wooden chopping-board, complete with wicked-looking knives, a blackened frying pan, and a stack of the handleless aluminum saucepans, known as dekchis, shining silver in the sun—scoured, as Ahmed told her later, with river sand. She was examining a hole in the ground, edged with clay and stones and covered with an iron grid, in which a fire was still smouldering, when Ahmed appeared.

He was carrying a basket of crockery—washing-up was evidently done in the river—and he must have bathed at the same time; his curly hair was wet and the shirt that had been hastily pulled on when he saw her clung to his still wet back. After he had fetched his astrakhan hat from the tent and put it on at the usual rakish angle, he was delighted to show her everything and to answer questions.

The iron grid, it seemed, was carried from camp to
camp and on it all cooking was done and water heated over
a fire of sticks and a little charcoal. For roasting he used his
largest covered dekchi, and for baking a big square biscuit
tin, in which improvised oven he proposed to bake bread
when the loaves they had brought with them from Srinagar
were finished. Leah was so intrigued with these arrangements, with Ahmed's toasting fork, tin box of condiments
and spices, that she stayed longer than she had meant and
forgot to ask him where and how he had learnt camp cooking and camp ways. When, at last, carrying her water-bottle
and small satchel, she set out, following the path along the
river bank, Ahmed came running after her with the packet
of sandwiches she had forgotten.

He had been shocked and disapproving when he realised that she meant to go alone and would not let even a
ponyman go with her, "in case Memsahib want anything."
Memsahibs, it seemed, did not go for walks alone. What
would any villager who happened to meet her think?
Ahmed, as leader of the expedition—although Nabir, of
course, was the real leader—would lose face. Leah had cut
his protestations short by turning her back on him and
walking away up the path.

Ahmed watched her go, an odd, foreshortened little
figure under the big hat. His thoughts were confused. He
felt both irritation and admiration when he thought of the
old lady on whom he was pinning all his hopes. That she
was game for anything he had discovered almost at once,
but it was a pity that she was so old. He must look after her
carefully, nurse her strength, which was difficult with one
so obstinate; never before had he met such mulish ob-
stinacy in a woman, not even in his mother. The only thing
to do was to let her have her own way as far as possible—
or to make her think she was having her way. The business
of the lamb, for instance—he had settled that cleverly, as
even Nabir had admitted. Boasting, as he often did, perhaps to keep up his courage, Ahmed said to himself, "You
can settle anything, Aziz, if you keep your head."

Aziz was his real name—a better name, he thought, than Ahmed, which was written on the chits he had bought in Lahore from an elderly man who, having seen his employer off to the war, was returning for good to his village. Many sahibs were leaving in this manner, as his, Aziz's, own sahib had done. With luck, many of them would not survive to come back and ask awkward questions about their former servants. It had been a pity that he had had to destroy several glowing recommendations because they were dated when he was a child—clever of him, though, to have thought of it. The chits had been expensive, had used up nearly all the money he had nerved himself to take that night in the hut. Perhaps it was just as well; he had felt better, less tainted, when it was out of his possession. . . .

Ahmed backed away from that thought and, instead, thought of the coming night's feast. There was much to do before then. Nabir had already left for the village and he must finish his work and hurry after him. He did not wholly trust Nabir, and anyway it was his duty to see that his employer was not cheated. "A religious day for Muslims," he had told her, and she had believed him, being as ignorant as all women are. For that matter, every day is a religious day for a true Muslim, such as he. Ahmed laughed and, with a last look at Leah's retreating form, hurried back to camp. As he bounded along in the sunshine, he first hummed, then sang his favourite little love song. His cares were forgotten; he was his gay, unthinking self once more.

By mid-afternoon Leah had only reached the bend where the river turned towards the village and the road; the camp was still in sight, her tent a spot of white in the distance. She sat down on the grassy verge in the shade of a clump of trees, her feet on the river's strip of pebbly beach, and opened the satchel. She had been too absorbed in all she saw to think of stopping to eat; there were many wild flowers, birds she could not identify, butterflies; a lizard sunning itself on a stone had kept her motionless for minutes on end, watching the pulse beating in the pale throat, the diamond-shaped eyes, the flickering tongue. The river with its changing blues and greens, its varying surface, running smooth and shining in one stretch, broken and foaming in another, had accompanied her slow wander.

'What have I been doing all my life?' she asked herself as she unwrapped the sandwiches. 'What missing?' This power of seeing, really seeing, was something new to her. It was as if this land, so far from her own, had jerked her awake, pulled the veil of ignorance and indifference from her eyes, making her look, see, as she had never done before.

At the bottom of the satchel, under her spectacle case, was a letter from Hugh. It had arrived at the houseboat as she and Ahmed were leaving; she had read it, of course, in the car on their way, had put it in the satchel, and then had forgotten all about it, poor Hugh! And yet she was not an indifferent, careless grandmother. She loved Hugh with a deep, if often exasperated, love. Her son Paul, her only child, had been killed in his twenties in that other war, and his poor little widow had died in the flu epidemic, as so many had done, leaving the three-year-old boy to her and Geoffrey's care. She had devoted herself to Hugh, had hoped much of him. . . .

As he grew up, he had become more and more like his grandfather; in character, that is. In appearance he took after her, which was a pity; if it had been the other way round, would she have loved him more? She would certainly have liked him better, love and liking being very different feelings, as she had found. "How good your grandson is to you," her friends had often told her. "How lucky you are to have such a good steady boy!" Leah had, of course, always smilingly agreed, but sometimes she had found herself almost wishing for a bad grandson, a wild, gay, handsome, reckless grandson who would be exciting, interesting, even if he made her anxious, someone who would need her help and protection. Leah sighed and, putting on her spectacles, read the letter through again. It had been heavily censored, told her little. She knew, though, that Hugh was somewhere in North Africa and safe so far.

It was only when she came to Kashmir that she had been able to put the war out of her mind and she would not think of it now. "Why can't they all look, just look at the world, and enjoy it instead of destroying themselves and each other?" she asked the river and the hills. There was so much to see—a lifetime was not enough. . . .

Something was moving in the leaves above her head; she looked up as she heard the familiar cheerful notes. Small brown-crested birds such as these, bulbuls, with shining white cheeks and yellow undertails, had haunted the willows and orchards near the houseboat, even flying into the rooms. As she had expected, this pair readily took the crumbs she threw for them, only flying off when she went to wash her hands at the river's edge. The water was ice-cold even in the shallows; the colours of the submerged pebbles gleamed up at her.

The Baxters had told her that they had once taken a fishing beat on this same river, and now, for the first time, she wondered if she had a right to be here. When she and Ahmed had crossed the suspension bridge, she had seen a camp downstream and had glimpsed a fisherman casting a fly. Suppose such a fisherman should now appear on the path? She looked anxiously towards her camp. Was there someone coming up the river bank, someone tall, wearing a tweed jacket and a tweed hat, someone in waders, carrying a rod, a creel on his back, a landing net slung from his waist? It was Geoffrey, of course, as she had so often seen him, fishing the Scottish rivers he loved. Every spring or summer they had gone north and she had spent the long days as he expected and wished her to do, watching him fish.

The path was empty. She did not want to think of him or of her grandson. Surely she had earned the right to think for a while only of herself? As she walked on slowly, following the river upstream, and looking to the mountains at the head of the valley where tomorrow she would be journeying again, she remembered something she had read in the days soon after she arrived in India. It was something about the Hindu belief that in the last stage of life it is right and proper to forsake the world and concentrate on the soul's salvation—"to seek the Forest." Hinduism had defeated her—all those gods and goddesses and their innumerable names. Her mind was too direct and simple to grasp its convolutions and, she suspected, the core, the inner truth and meaning, had eluded her; but those words had remained in her mind, giving her a sense of peace each time she repeated them to herself. Well, in her way, that was what she, Leah, was doing—seeking the Forest—though she was not interested in the state of her soul. She was interested in this world, the physical, ever-present, many-coloured, natural world. More time on earth was all she asked.

Lost in her thoughts, she did not realise that the path had left the river until she found herself walking into a willow grove beside a narrow slow-moving stream. She hesitated, looking back, and saw that, behind her in the sunlight, a plank bridged the stream; if she crossed it, she could follow the river again. The thin shade of the willows was inviting after the glare of the bank; the path wound between their grey trunks, following the course of this deep, silently flowing stream, beckoning her on. Leah decided to explore it, to see where it led.

It was cooler in the willow grove, cool, grey-green, striped with filtered sunshine, and yet oddly breathless and close. The willow fronds hung without a tremor, the stream ran almost imperceptibly and without a sound. There were no birds, as far as she could see. The path rounded yet another bend and ahead, looming up among the willows, was the dark shape of a building, wooden, thatched, tumbledown, leaning over the stream; it was, she saw, a mill, its wheel silent and at rest. Leah stood still, staring up at it; in the muted sunshine of the grove, it seemed to her too dark and sudden. It looked deserted, and yet she thought for a moment that she had heard voices, at least two people talking or whispering together, and a stifled laugh.

As Leah retreated a few steps and paused again, a trout rose almost at her feet; its blue-grey back turned in the water, leaving a green ring of ripples. She drew back, hoping to see another rise, and almost collided with someone running down the path from the mill.

It was a girl in a hurry, a young girl wearing a faded reddish-pink pheran and carrying a basket in one hand and a short-handled hoe in the other, who paused in mid-flight to stare at her with great, astonished black eyes. Dishevelled black hair, long and lustrous, flowed under the once white head-cloth; heavy silver earrings framed a flushed perfect face, rosy as a peach or a ripe apricot. Seldom, if ever, had Leah seen a girl as beautiful, or as dirty. The pheran—the loose, open-necked Kashmiri gown with wide turned-back sleeves—was stained and filthy, the slim hands and bare feet and ankles caked with dried earth. For a moment they stared at each other. Leah had time to admire the small straight nose, the full red lips parting in an amazed smile; then the girl, with a glance back down the path, a stifled exclamation, was gone, silver anklets flashing, veil flying, as she bounded like a stag through the grove, dodging between the willows towards the open fields.

Leah watched her go, then turned to see what had caused this precipitous flight. Someone else was coming down the path from the mill, a bent old woman flourishing a stick. It seemed almost a profanation that her pheran, head-cloth, and silver earrings should be much the same as the girl's when she was so hideously different; the contrast was so great and sudden that Leah gasped. It was not the poor creature's fault that a goitre hung beneath her chin, or that she was so wrinkled and beak-nosed, but no old woman—one probably not as old as Leah herself—should look so full of spite and anger.

She stood her ground as the other came nearer, waving

the stick and talking as she came. Leah was being asked a question, that much she gathered; black eyes, once perhaps as large and lovely as the girl's, searched her face, but she could not understand the words that poured from the toothless mouth.

"No, I haven't seen anyone," she said firmly.

The old woman glared at her with such malevolence that Leah recoiled. Then she spat on the ground at Leah's feet and, wheeling round, hobbled back the way she had come.

Such ugliness following hard on the heels of such beauty distressed her—the beauty itself seemed shadowed and dimmed. She was no longer at ease in the willow grove; the old dark mill was sinister; she did not like this unnaturally silent stream. Leah turned and walked back as quickly as she could towards the river.

Once out in the sunlight again, she stopped to look at her watch. She must have forgotten to wind it that morning, for it had stopped; she had no idea what the time was but the sun was still high. Leah decided not to go on across the plank, but to rest beside the river and then to make her way back to camp, which seemed a long way off. If she could, she would find a patch of shade and a bank to lean against.

The exhaustion that sometimes came over her unexpectedly was, she had found, one of the disadvantages of old age, and one she usually tried to ignore. Even the short walk to the trees, only a few yards, was almost too much for her and she sat down thankfully with her feet once more on the pebbly strip of beach. There was no sign of the bulbuls, but a gentle breeze was flowing up-river, setting the leaves moving over her head and cooling her hot face. Leah folded her hands in her lap and fell asleep at once, her bent head nodding forward under the wide straw hat.

Someone close at hand was speaking to her, urging her awake. Unwillingly she opened her eyes and looked up.

Ahmed was standing beside her, a dark shape against the blue of the sky. What was he saying? She felt heavy and stupid, and did not understand a word.

"Where have you sprung from?" she asked, interrupting him.

He gestured impatiently in the direction of the village, and now, as she looked at him more attentively, she saw that he was breathing hard, as if he had been running. His shirt was unbuttoned and his hair ruffled, his black hat at the back of his head, his thin young face wet with sweat, and his eyes were shining.

"What have you been up to?" she asked suspiciously. "Where have you been?"

He was talking about a fish, an enormous fish, urging her to come and see, to be quick, or it would get away.

"A fish?" she repeated as she struggled to her feet and straightened her hat and pulled down her skirt. "Did you say a fish? Where?"

"Great big fish, big as this!" Ahmed held his arms wide apart and Leah could not help smiling. "Memsahib come, come quick!" He was as excited as a child, as excited as Hugh had been when he caught his first salmon.

He turned and ran back down the path, looking to see if she was following, and as Leah, her tiredness forgotten, hurried after him, she heard the plank rattle under his feet. When, moving more cautiously, she crossed the stream in her turn, she saw him kneeling on the path peering into a ditch, an irrigation ditch, perhaps, that ran between the path and a field planted with maize; above the ripening cobs, she could see the roofs of the village against their backdrop of blue mountains. The late-afternoon sun gilded the scene as, almost unwillingly, she knelt down and looked where Ahmed was pointing.

There was water in the ditch, evidently an overflow from the mill-stream, and someone—Ahmed, probably—had made a dam of stones, forming a shallow pool in which something was moving. As she looked more closely, she saw that it was indeed a fish, a big fish, but not as big as he had said, swept here from the mill-stream on a sudden spate and left half-stranded.

"Memsahib kneel here," Ahmed whispered as if the trout could hear and understand. "Splash hard in water when Ahmed tell. Stop fish going that way."

Taking her co-operation for granted, he lowered his hands cautiously into the water. Why she did as he asked when she would have liked the fish to escape, Leah did not know, unless his excitement, the hunter's lust for the chase, which is in all young men in some form or other, was catching. There was a sudden commotion, a threshing and splashing, and as Ahmed yelled she thrust both hands into the water and splashed as vigorously as she could.

For a second she felt the fish move against her hand, then Ahmed had it. Standing knee-deep in the ditch, he held it up by the gills and laughed triumphantly.

It was a fine trout, every ounce of six pounds, she thought, looking up at its shining, still-moving length. For a moment she felt triumphant, too—Ahmed could not have succeeded without her; he must have been hurrying to the camp in search of someone to help him. Then she cried, "Put it in the river, let it go!"

She might have known that he would ignore this, would pretend not to understand. "Then kill it, kill it at once, do you hear?"

Ahmed laughed again, showing his white teeth. She feared that he was going to disobey, to let the poor creature thresh and gasp, and she sighed with relief when he lowered the fish on to the grass and took the stone she held out to him. While she had stared up at him, seeing him against the pure blue of the sky with the sun shining full on his face, the thought had come to her that he might have his dark side, something hidden. But Ahmed was not cruel, of that she was sure, or no more cruel than any other careless, unthinking young man. When a trickle of blood ran out on to the grass, she saw him wince and look away, and he flung the stained stone out into the river with unnecessary violence.

As Leah watched him wash the dead fish carefully and, squatting down beside her, take a piece of string from his pocket and thread it through the gills, she saw that a long black hair, too long and lustrous to have come from Ahmed's head, was tangled round one of his waistcoat buttons. She remembered the whispers and stifled laughter coming from the old mill. . . .

What Ahmed did, or did not do, in his spare time was, Leah decided, none of her business—unless it caused trouble in camp. She got stiffly to her feet and led the way back.

III

NEXT MORNING and all that day, the track, still following the river, wound up between steep hills into another world; as they journeyed, always climbing higher, the gentle fields and willows, the fruit and walnut trees were left behind. Here was a wilder, grander valley of dark firs and pines, steeply wooded hillsides, rocks, boulders, waterfalls. The river was a mountain torrent hurling down its narrow gorge.

When Leah, turning in her saddle, looked back, she saw her cavalcade strung out behind her along the stony winding path. She could see the black lamb, safely secured between two bedding rolls on the leading pack-pony; Nabir, a minute figure in the distance, distinguishable by his red plaid, brought up the rear, and Ahmed walked at her pony's head. He was unusually silent that morning, had not said a word for nearly half an hour, a long time for him. Leah, looking down at him, saw that he was deep in thought; he smiled to himself as he walked; the smile faded and he frowned. She wondered what he was thinking.

Ahmed was thinking that he had been a fool again. Curse all women! Would nothing teach him to leave them alone? The girl had been luscious indeed, and young— unlike that other—yes, a succulent sweet peach, an unexpected and juicy treat there by the mill-stream, but hardly worth, in the circumstances, the risk of stirring up a hornets' nest against him. It all depended on that hideous old crone. Had she glimpsed him or had she not as he slipped away among the willows? He had half expected that the camp would be invaded by a band of outraged husband, brothers, and cousins and, even after that heavy feast, he had not slept a wink. Nothing had happened that night, or when they passed through the village early in the morning. His luck had held again. All the same, he would feel more at ease when there were many, many miles between himself and the willow grove.

Always there was something, trifling or not, to keep him on the move, to act as a spur that gave a light prick—or a painful jab. When he had reached Srinagar, he had thought that the hut and what it held were miles enough behind him, hundreds of miles. He had thought that he could forget it and all that had happened there and start a new life. His mother had insisted in the cold dawn after that terrible night that he must learn by heart the address of her brother, whom she had not seen since her marriage. She was a Kashmiri, and it was from her that he had inherited the good looks that made him, to his undoing, attractive to women. This long-lost uncle had turned out to be a useful relative, for a time at least. A fairly prosperous contractor for camp equipment, he had accepted his unknown nephew Ahmed for his sister's sake, had taken him into his house, in spite of the cousins' protests, in exchange for a little touting for the firm until Ahmed could find regular work. Ahmed might have stayed on, insinuating himself into the old man's favour, if it had not been for those cousins, who —jealous, of course—had been determined to get him out. When the memsahib took him on as her servant, he had thought that he could relax for a little, but one day, while he was enjoying a little free time to himself, wandering through a rather shady part of the bazaar, evil chance had brought him face to face with Dost Mohammed. Although neither had liked the other and they could not be called friends, they knew each other well and, until their sahibs went off to the war, had worked for years in the same block of flats in Delhi, had smoked and gossiped on the same back staircase, and, Muslims though they were, forbidden by their religion to gamble, had often played cards together for money.

Ahmed had pretended not to recognise him, but that

had been no use. Dost Mohammed—Old Two-Ways, as he was called because of his fearsome squint—had seized his arm, hailing him as Aziz; luckily no one who knew him was nearby. Dost Mohammed, it seemed, had come to Kashmir with his new employers, an American couple, who were on a short holiday and, with luck, would soon be back in Delhi; promising that they would meet again for a good long yarn, Ahmed had managed to shake him off, but that had been a painful jab indeed. It was fortunate that his own mem-sahib had already left the hotel for the houseboat. Ahmed had decided that in future their shopping expeditions to the city must be discouraged. Another move, as soon as possible, had been the answer, a move up into the mountains. The further they went, the better for him.

For the moment, Leah had forgotten Ahmed; she, too, was busy with her thoughts. How much further today, she wondered. In spite of the feast, which, to judge by the sounds of revelry that had reached her tent, must have gone on for the best part of the night, they had set out soon after the sun rose. This was a long stage; tomorrow's would be much shorter; many travellers did the last two stages before the Meadow in one, but she had decided to take her time until she was more used to riding and camp life. Everyone seemed to think that once she had reached the Meadow, she would be content to stay there until the time came to return to the houseboat, but she had every intention, after perhaps a week or so, to go further, much much further and higher.

All her life she had longed to travel, to see strange lands and people, to go far. Well, here she was, travelling as she had never thought to travel. If it had not been for the war, she might have decided to see Europe first, before going out to India where she would probably have thought it right to spend her time with Hugh. She might never have seen Kashmir, never have seen this valley—or might have seen it with him, which would have meant not really seeing it at all, not in her way.

Leah looked across the river, up, up the opposite hillside of closely packed dark trees, and saw, high against the blue sky, in which a few white clouds were floating, patches of brilliant grass-green among the rocky peaks; these, she knew, were alpine meadows where the wandering tribes took their flocks to graze in summer. That was where she would like to go, so high that there were no trees, only rock and grass, and the small bright alpine flowers that came when the snow had gone. In the long winter, snow must cover these hills, powdering the trees. Ahmed had told her that in late spring and early summer anyone using this track would have to cross several ice bridges that spanned the gorge. He must have had this information from Nabir; she knew, because she had questioned him last evening, that Ahmed had often worked in fishing and shooting camps, but that he had never seen this valley before.

Her pony shied across the road, nearly unseating her. As she clutched at its mane, four men carrying a litter passed at a jog-trot. On the litter of rough pine branches lay a man half-covered with a blanket. Leah looked down and saw, before she could look away, that under a cloud of flies and a blood-soaked rag one side of the head had gone and was a gaping, bleeding wound from scalp to chin. Ahmed, seizing her pony by the bridle, called out as they passed, and one of the men grunted an answer. Then they were gone.

"What happened? What did that?" she asked when she could speak.

"Bear got him," Ahmed said. "That man woodcutter, perhaps. Perhaps come on bear when bear asleep. Verree dangerous, bears."

"How horrible! Where are they taking him?"

Ahmed shrugged. "Perhaps to village near bridge. Maybe dispensary there. Maybe find lorry to take to hospital in Srinagar."

"But that village is miles and miles away—we have taken nearly three days."

"They do it in one, perhaps few hours."

"We should have stopped them, tried to do something." She shuddered, and Ahmed said with his usual cheerfulness, "Not make any difference. Probably die soon anyway."

He walked on, leading her pony, and Leah was silent. The sun still shone, but the brightness had gone from the day.

"Memsahib tired?" Ahmed asked, looking up into her face and putting his hand on her pony's neck. "Stop for lunch soon?"

She shook her head. "I'll wait until we make camp. Let's get on—how much further is it?"

"Two hours, perhaps three. No need make camp to-night. Bungalow there."

"A bungalow? What bungalow?"

"Forest bungalow. Only two bungalows in all valley. This one verree nice, verree comfortable, Nabir say. Hope no Forest Sahibs already there."

"Forest Sahibs? What are they?" Leah asked, and did not listen to Ahmed's answer. There was nothing she could have done for that poor man; she must try to put him out of her mind and not allow a shadow to be cast on her day. At her age, every day was precious.

A forest bungalow, Ahmed had said. That had a pleasant sound, but Leah did not want to spend a night in any bungalow; although she had slept for only three nights in her tent, she had become used to it; as time went on, she would probably become as attached to it as a snail is to its shell. The whole camp would be against her: no one would want the unnecessary labour of unpacking the tent and setting it up for one night. She was being selfish and self-willed, but why should she not have her own way? Were they not, Ahmed, Nabir, and the ponymen, employed to do what she wanted? And at once she felt ashamed of that thought.

"I'll wait and see," she said aloud, and Ahmed, looking up at her again, said, "Memsahib?"

The roof of the bungalow showed above the trees from some way off. When they reached it, she saw that it was set back above the track on a flat patch of ground on which a white goat was tethered. Behind it and its fringe of out-houses was a steeply terraced field of maize and then the trees began again. It was a brown wooden building and she had to admit that she liked the look of it. Her pony, whose name she had learned was Lallah, turned off the track and climbed the path that led to the verandah steps.

An old man with a wisp of a beard and the usual drab clothes and skull-cap, was waiting there, as if she were expected. He salaamed and moved to hold the pony.

"Chowkidar," Ahmed said. "Caretaker."

They both helped Leah to dismount; she climbed the steps and sank down thankfully into the basket chair the old man pulled out for her.

It was good to be out of the strong afternoon sun, good to be in a chair and not in a saddle. She unpinned her hat, laid it with her riding gloves on the wooden plank floor, and, leaning back, closed her eyes. The pack-ponies were arriving. She listened to the hubbub below as they were unloaded on the worn grass beyond the steps. There was a jingle of harness, snorts, neighs, shouts, and cries; every-one seemed to be talking at the top of his voice; she could smell the dust and sweat. 'What am I doing here, alone with this set of noisy, arguing scallywags?' she asked herself, and at once corrected her thought. Nabir was no scallywag, of that she was sure—an absurd word to use of Nabir. Leah sighed and wondered why she had singled out Nabir, a comparative stranger, and not Ahmed. . . .

She was too tired to think clearly and, for the first time, she allowed herself to wonder if this mode of travelling would prove too much for her at her age. Always she had disliked being reminded of her age, as she so often had been by well-meaning people, and now here she was, ad-mitting to herself that she was old—that would never do. 'You can go anywhere, Leah Harding, if you want to, really want to,' she told herself and sat up straight in the chair, refusing its sagging comfort. Where was Ahmed? She would feel better after a wash and tea.

There was no one on the verandah or, she felt, in the room behind it; she got up to make sure. The central room had a smoke-stained, rough stone fireplace, a table, and several chairs, and the two small bedrooms were complete with bathrooms, holding the usual wooden commodes and tin tubs. The furniture was sparse and made of wood, as the whole building was except for the stone chimney pine that gave out a faint, disinfectant, but pleasant smell. Her bags had been put in the bedroom nearest the tree-clad hillside and her bedding roll laid on the bed, a bed of stretched webbing instead of springs. Of Forest Sahibs, or anyone else, there was no sign.

The turmoil below had ceased when she came back to the verandah. The confusion of packs and bundles had miraculously disappeared, and there was nothing to be seen except the caretaker's goat and a few hobbled, grazing ponies. Voices came from the direction of the cook-houses and a smell of woodsmoke mingled with the prevailing pine. Leah went back to the basket chair, and soon, as she had known he would, Ahmed appeared with the ever-welcome tea-tray.

"What have you done with the lamb?" she asked as he put the tray down on the table, which was clean, if covered with other people's distasteful traces, round marks made by damp glasses and cigarette burns.

"Lamb fine. Tied up near cook-house."

"I'll come and have a look at it when I've rested a bit."

"Memsahib not trust Ahmed?"

"No further than I can see you," she retorted, and he laughed delightedly, as if she had said something witty.

Leah had spoken lightly, smiling at him; when he had gone to make her bed and see to her bath, she wondered why she had said it; he had never given her any real reason not to trust him, though she knew that he could lie fluently when it suited him and then gaily admit the lie. She liked Ahmed for his youth and gaiety, his eagerness to please. He seemed to her the least complicated of beings, but she had known him for only a few months. She had to trust Ahmed if she wanted to get anywhere. There was no one else.

Soft footfalls sounded on the wooden floor behind her and she swung round. It was only the caretaker holding a lit lamp with a round glass shade, which he set down carefully on the table before going as silently away. The soft gold light dispelled the gathering darkness, and when other lamps appeared in the rooms, the bungalow no longer seemed to her depressing, or even slightly sinister, or haunted, perhaps, by shades of long-departed travellers. Leah reminded herself that she did not believe in ghosts, and went in to the central room where, until her bath was ready, she sat looking into the flames of the wood fire that Ahmed, without being asked, had caused to be lit.

After dinner, the caretaker appeared again, with Ahmed, to ask her to pay for the night's lodging, oil, and wood, and there was a book for her to sign. She turned the pages curiously, reading the names and dates; those of the State's Forest Service men predominated. The first entry had been made many, many years before, and the last two days ago: "Dr. and Mrs. Macleod, Miss Dora Mackenzie," she read. Those missionaries, of course.

Leah roused with a start from a half-doze. She had found it difficult to sleep. The bed was hard after her camp-bed, the small bedroom too large and lofty after her tent, and now there was a flickering red light moving across the walls and ceiling. At first she thought that it was the reflection of the fire in the other room; then she heard shouts and cries. Was Ahmed having another nightmare? Or was the place on fire?

Seizing her dressing-gown, she hurried onto the verandah. There was no one there and no sign of flames or smoke; the noise was coming from the outside, from the back.

When she looked out the bedroom window, she could

not see the outhouses; she was looking up at the maize field, lit now by flaring torches carried by dark figures moving up towards the trees. Last evening she had noticed a small, raised, rickety-looking platform set amid the crop and had wondered why it was there. She could see it now in the flame light, and on it stood another dimly seen figure, who appeared to be beating a tin with a stick. Some wild animal must be raiding the crop. A leopard? Leopards surely do not eat maize? A deer? As the shouting and cat-calls increased and a torch was hurled, she thought she saw a dark lumbering shape moving through the tall stalks and making for the trees. Could it be a bear?

Leaning as far as she could out the window, Leah called, "Look out! Take care! Take care!" No one, in that din, could possibly have heard her and she drew back feeling foolish.

Whatever had been in the maize had gone. The dark figures were returning, chatting and laughing; all the torches except one were extinguished, and that smouldered above the platform where the watcher over the crop must evidently continue his vigil until dawn. She turned away, almost regretfully: she would have liked to be sure that she had really seen a bear; it would have been something to tell Hugh in her next letter. Leah went back to bed and fell asleep.

IV

LEAH WAS ANGRY.

While she was at breakfast that morning on the verandah and the pack-ponies were being loaded on the steps for
an early start, Ahmed, having refilled her coffee cup, had
announced, "Lamb gone."

"Gone? What do you mean?"

"Bear take it."

She had glared at him. "I don't believe it."

Ahmed had been reproachful. "Bear come in night for
corn. See lamb tied to post. When Ahmed wake, lamb gone.
Everyone make much noise, chase bear with sticks and
lights. No use . . . bear go back to trees, lamb all eaten up
by now."

When Leah, too upset to speak, glared at him, Ahmed
had met her angry blue eyes, betraying uneasiness only by
shuffling his feet. "Do bears eat lambs?" she had asked at
last, in her most forbidding voice.

"Oh, yess! Eat anything. Memsahib ask Nabir, ask anyone."

"You are all in it together," she had told him furiously.
"Greedy, ungrateful, cruel . . . Go away! I can't stand the
sight of you."

Ahmed's large eyes had filled with tears, but she had
remained unmoved, and after a moment's hesitation he had
obeyed her. She had been too angry to finish her coffee,
and presently the old caretaker had come cautiously with a
tray to clear the breakfast things away.

They made camp that evening on the only flat patch of
ground that Leah had seen all day in the steep and narrow
wooded gorge, and Ahmed moved about his duties in a

mournful, reproachful way and now she was filled with an unreasonable sense of guilt. What was a lamb to Ahmed? Food. This was India—what did she, Leah, know of poverty and hunger? She was sad for the lamb, but it was Ahmed's stupid, palpable lie that had enraged her. Did he really think that she was naïve enough to believe it?

The sense of guilt increased when Ahmed came to tell her that her bath was ready. All water, as she had seen while she sat in comfort, had to be carried up an almost sheer path from the river; it should have occurred to her to tell him that she could do without a bath that evening. 'You are a spoilt, selfish woman,' she told herself. 'Arrogant, taking everything for granted—you ought to apologise.' Apologise to whom? The sweeper boy, helped by a ponyman, had carried the tins of water, not Ahmed.

Her heart hardened again when, for her supper, he had the effrontery to produce a stew that, she had to admit, gave out a delicious smell, onions, vegetables and, unmistakably, meat.

"What's this?" she asked, peering into the dish he held for her in the lamplight.

"Meat stew. Verree good."

"Meat? What meat?"

"Is goat, young goat, tender. Ahmed get caretaker sell enough for Memsahib's dinner. Much money, but do Mem good."

Leah looked up at his bland, solicitous, smiling face, gold-brown in the lamplight. His dark yellow eyes, ringed with curling lashes that would have graced any girl, were wide and candid, unblinking. For a moment she could not trust herself to speak.

"Memsahib not well?" he asked.

"Ahmed, you make me sick!" she exploded. "Take it away!"

"No dinner?"

Leah controlled herself. "You can bring me a boiled egg," she said, "and cut some bread and butter."

"Bread finished. No time to bake. Ahmed bring two eggs?"

"Bring what you like," Leah said wearily. "Only take that away at once."

There were no alarms or disturbances that night; no one called out in his sleep, and yet Leah again was restless. The tumult the river made, so close, almost under her tent, was enough to keep anyone awake, and for much of the night she lay in the darkness considering Ahmed.

After he had cleared her supper away, he had come back to stand in the shadows beyond the circle of lamplight, waiting until she asked him tersely what he wanted. He had come, it seemed, to make his peace with her. He did not say as much but, approaching the table where she sat, put a small bundle down in front of her—one of the dishcloths she had given him, no longer clean, wrapped about something hard and knobbly. Intrigued in spite of herself, she had undone the knots and spilled the contents out onto the table.

"Crystals?" she had asked wonderingly, forgetting her determination to say as little as possible to Ahmed. "Are they crystals?" The semi-transparent stones, which might have been thick clouded glass, sparkled and shone in the lamplight; they were an inch or two long, of varying shapes and sizes, a few stuck immovably together, but all apparently cut into sharp-edged planes and many-sided facets.

"Where did you get them, Ahmed? Who cut them?"

"No one cut. River cut. Ahmed found all in river."

This was, in part, the truth. Leah was to discover later that such stones, cut and shaped by the action of the water, were found in many mountain streams; she was to find some herself. She was not to know that Ahmed, foreseeing trouble ahead, had bought them that morning for a few pice from a small boy met on the march.

"Memsahib like? Present for Memsahib."

Although she had tried not to show it, Leah had been

pleased and touched. "They are beautiful," she had said slowly. "Thank you, Ahmed."

She had heard him give a small, relieved sigh. Was her pleasure, or displeasure, of such importance to him? Whatever he did, or did not do, she could hardly dismiss him until they returned to Srinagar. She was dependent on Ahmed for everything.

The night passed slowly and she was glad when dawn found the whole camp stirring.

V

THE SUN WAS not yet up above the mountains when a start was made on what everyone except Leah thought would be the last day of travelling for a long time. By midday the gorge was left behind and the valley broadened into a mountain-ringed upland plateau. The laden ponies were to take the long way round, following the winding river to a bridge and passing Nabir's village, still hidden by a wooded spur, while she and Ahmed, with Nabir and a ponyman carrying her picnic basket, forded the river, shallow and broad here, and took a steep short cut up through the pines.

Emerging suddenly from the trees, they came out onto the Meadow and Leah took a deep breath; she let her reins fall on the pony's neck and sat unmoving in the saddle, transfixed by what she saw. That fervent young woman, that missionary, had not exaggerated when she had talked of Paradise.

PART TWO

The Meadow

I

THE CLOSE GREENSWARD of the Meadow was an immense, gently rolling expanse lying between wooded hills on one side and immediate, towering snow and rock peaks on the other, and ending only at a quick glacier stream backed by steep pine woods. Was it the silver dazzle of snow against the deep blue sky, the sharp contrast of the sheer rock faces, the dark of pine and fir against the brilliant grass, or was it the height, the crystalline clearness of the light, the pure thin sparkling air, that made the Meadow seem set apart, out of this world, celestial? After weeks there, Leah still felt this, although she had soon discovered that even in this place there were drawbacks.

The camping sites were far apart, set tactfully in the borders of the trees, and the tents, for all their whiteness, were unobtrusive, overwhelmed by the vastness round them, but for Leah there were too many of these small encampments; she would have liked the whole Meadow to herself. On that first day, it had been a shock to find that she was expected, that one of the sites had been booked for her at the same time that Nabir and his ponies were engaged. She had objected at once to the allotted site, although it had a fine view of the snow peaks, because it was too near another group of tents. When the ponies arrived, she would not allow camp to be made and Nabir had to go down to the village, which was a mile away, to fetch the Kashmiri known as the Collector who was in charge of the camp-sites and their rents. After more delay, much riding to and fro, she had chosen the loneliest of the vacant sites, one with a less fine view, set at the edge of a pine wood near a spring; from it she could just see the small hill near the entrance to the Meadow on which the rest-house—another bungalow—was perched, but luckily the building was completely hidden by trees.

Life on the Meadow, once she had settled down, was almost too comfortable, too civilised. Workmen appeared to lay a wooden floor in her tent as, she gathered from Ahmed, was always done; without asking her, he arranged that a small shamiana, a shelter of four wooden posts roofed with sweet-smelling pine branches and complete with a rough-hewn table and bench, should be made to serve as a dining and living room; the awning and poles they had brought with them from Srinagar would have done as well but, she had to admit, been less pleasing to the eye. Milk was delivered to the camp every day, carried by an uncouth-looking boy, and transferred from his covered pail to one of her jugs under Ahmed's watchful eye. Ahmed had been right about her clothes-line, which remained unrolled at the bottom of a kilta; the Meadow had its own resident washerman, or dhobie, who collected her laundry every week, loading it with similar bundles on his donkey and returning it punctually, washed in a stream, beaten clean on its stones, and spread out on the grass in the sun to dry; how the ironing was accomplished she never discovered.

A postman, with his bag slung on his back, made the round of the tents every day, almost as if they had been houses in suburbia, and in the village there was a post and telegraph office where it was possible to buy stamps and even to read a typewritten sheet of the latest war news; there was also a telephone, although the line to Srinagar was precarious and often down. It was difficult for Leah to feel that she was living out of the world, at the back of beyond, as she longed to do.

After the first day, Nabir, leaving only her own riding pony Lallah—Lallah, she found, meant Tulip—and a ponyman to look after it and to help about the camp, went back to his village, but Ahmed assured her that she would have first call on Nabir and his ponies when she needed them;

Leah, although she said nothing to Ahmed, resolved in her own mind that this would be soon. Meanwhile a camp routine, a pattern to her days, was established, which she enjoyed, even if it sometimes seemed, once she was used to living in a tent, rather tame, even ordinary.

Soon after five, Ahmed, bringing Leah her early-morning tea, always found her awake. The mornings were so fresh, so sparkling, so blue and gold, that it was impossible to laze in bed; she was up and dressed by six o'clock. For the first few days she did little except potter about the camp, arrange her tent to her liking, or sit under the pines, taking deep draughts of the scented air. She was acclimatising herself to the height, as the Colonel had advised her to do; the Meadow was over nine thousand feet above sea level and she was determined to be cautious. After breakfast, she inspected the cook tent and talked over the day's food with Ahmed. Food required much thought and planning; almost everything had to be brought from Srinagar, as there was little to buy in the village; a chicken, perhaps, dried apricots, sag—which looked like spinach. Sometimes she would do a little cooking herself to show Ahmed how to make a sauce, or to bake a special cake. The spring, which bubbled up between two boulders fifty yards or so away among the pines, was a constant source of delight; the water was so cold, so clear, so soft, with only a faint taste of iron; she liked to take a jug there and fill it herself. The pines hid the stream that she could hear rushing down its deep wooded ravine not far from the camp, the same stream that bordered the Meadow under the snow peaks and was now on its way to join the river far below.

Every day, Leah dutifully read through the last batch of newspapers the carrier had brought, setting one aside for each day of the week, but the outside world was of little interest to her and the war might have been waged on another planet; it was only at night, when she could not sleep, that she felt a nagging anxiety for Hugh. For much of the day, she would sit and dream in peace.

In the afternoons, she would sally out on Lallah, that

small surly animal supposed to be Nabir's best riding pony, who had not responded to her friendly advances, merely snatching at any apple or sugar she gave it and then putting back its ears. Followed by the ponyman, a silent, obliging, bow-legged, simple creature called Gaffur—it was rather like being followed by a large shaggy dog—she would explore the Meadow, avoiding the other encampments, and always going a little further. Evening was perhaps the best part of the day. Leah would sit in the fringes of the pines, looking out across the Meadow, watching the lengthening shadows on the grass, the changing colours. The overhanging snow peaks took on a rosy glow as the sun went down, and the shadows up there were violet. Too soon the warm colour went, leaving an icy blue, and a little breeze would spring up from nowhere, rustling through the pines.

It was cold when the sun had gone, and she would retreat to the fire that the sweeper boy lit in front of the shamiana, a huge fire of logs and pine-cones that burned far into the night. As darkness fell, she would see the lights of other camp-fires shining like fireflies round the perimeter of the Meadow; their ruby glow was warm and friendly, a remote companionship that, all the same, she could have done without.

Leah could certainly have done without the Johnstons. On the very day after she had arrived at the Meadow, they had walked into camp, a tall middle-aged couple, grey-haired, lean, who at first sight looked much alike. They introduced themselves without delay, seeming confident that she would be glad to see them, and she learned that they were Eric and Iris Johnston, both doctors—not medical doctors, apparently, but schoolteachers who ran a mission school somewhere in the North-West Frontier Province. They had come, they told her, to see if she was well and comfortable and to find out if there was anything they could do for her—which, if kind, she thought a little presumptuous. How did they know that she had arrived at the Meadow? How could they know that she existed? When, bluntly, she asked them this, they had looked at each other and smiled. Everyone in the Meadow, they assured her as they sat drinking the tea she could not, without being rude, have avoided offering them, knew everything about everyone else; servants gossipped down in the village, for one thing. Before they left, Eric Johnston had asked her to ride over to their camp the next day, which was luckily on the far side of the Meadow, an invitation she had refused, pleading tiredness after her journey. "We'll be back," they told her as they took their leave. "We'll drop in from time to time, just to see that you are all right."

It was good of them to spend even a few hours of their hard-earned holiday with an unknown old woman; they were kindly, admirable people and they could not know that all she wanted was to be left alone. Soon she—or, rather, Ahmed—found a way of circumventing them. As if he knew how she felt, he would appear at her elbow and say, "Mission sahibs coming," giving her time to vanish into the pine woods if she felt that she could not face another visitation. Did he, at likely times, post a look-out, Gaffur or the sweeper boy? Anyone approaching across the expanse of the Meadow could be seen from a long way off. She did not ask; her complicity with Ahmed was a silent one.

Most of the visitors to the Meadow kept themselves to themselves. Sometimes on her rides, Leah would see a strolling couple or meet a climber returning to camp with his knapsack on his back, and these would pass her with a nod and a smile, but unfortunately a few were good, interfering people like the Johnstons. They must have spread the word among their fellow missionaries: "Poor old lady, all by herself; how lonely." Two small English children appeared one morning, bringing a bunch of wild flowers and a note asking her to come to tea next day at some camp or other. Ahmed's dislike of missionaries, it seemed, did not extend to their children. He had brought them to her, leading them by the hand and smiling all over his face. Leah had given them some biscuits, talked to them for a minute or so, and sent them off on their ponies with a note of polite

but firm refusal. She had not come all this way to take tea
with her compatriots.

Leah did not know that, in her big white hat and brightly
coloured blouses, she was becoming, as the days went by,
a well-known figure on the Meadow, or that people smiled
when they saw her and wondered about her; but she began
to feel, when she left the shelter of her camp on foot or
even on her pony, that eyes were following her, and she
said to herself, 'Time I moved on. The sooner I go, the
better.' When she dropped a few vague hints about future
journeys to Ahmed, he was not, at first, as co-operative as
she had expected.

Ahmed was content to stay where he was. For the time
being, at any rate, this was far enough. Tucked up here, in
this remote place, with the pine woods behind him and the
wide green view in front, he felt secure for the first time in
months. He had begun to relax, although he still kept an
eye on all new arrivals at the Meadow. There were sahibs
from all over India holidaying here, and many had brought
their own servants, among which there might, by evil
chance, be another who had known him in his Delhi days;
he had no desire to be hailed again as Aziz. As for the dead
man's two sons, whom Ahmed had never seen, he was sure
from all he had heard of them, from their dead stepmother
and his own mother, that they would not hesitate to avenge
their old tyrant of a parent if they knew where to look and
whom they were looking for. They could not know, and yet
the thought of them—Ahmed always pictured them as
large, bearded, formidable—kept him awake at night and
still gave him bad dreams.

Except for these lingering fears, life in camp was pleasant and easy with only one old lady to look after and cook
for; the sweeper boy and that dimwit Gaffur did any hard
work there was. As Ahmed lazily tidied the mem's tent, he
sometimes found himself thinking of his last sahib, now
gone off to this war, for whom he had had an off-hand,
slightly contemptuous affection because he was generous
and careless with his money. That sahib, although forced

to spend much time in his office, really thought of nothing except shooting and fishing. He, Ahmed—or Aziz, rather—had found life strenuous in many jungle camps, but at least all he had learnt there of camp life and ways had proved useful. His old mem was not perhaps as easy to please as the sahib, but she was not too demanding. Life, stuck up here, was dull, of course; the only excitement was the weekly arrival of the carrier, the only diversion a visit to the tea-shop in the village. As far as he could see, there was no chance of a woman; the village was out of bounds in that respect, as he could not risk getting up against Nabir, who was the village headman as well as the best-known guide and ponyman for many miles around. The village was a poor place, depending for what prosperity it had largely on the summer visitors to the Meadow and in winter moribund under a pall of snow. There were shacks along the river, a walled serai for travellers and their beasts, the post office, and the tea-house where one could sit and watch the traffic, such as it was—mules, ponies, people walking—on the road or track that went on down the valley and eventually on to Leh, Ladakh, Tibet. There was also a policeman, the sole representative—in his khaki uniform, badge, and red turban—of the law for miles, as far as Ahmed knew. He gave the man a wide berth, but did he really believe that the police, here or anywhere else, were interested in him? There was nothing, absolutely nothing, to connect this "Ahmed" with that small, lonely homestead of four huts standing like an island in a sea of cultivated fields.

Only his mother knew. Although, on that night, that fatal night, he had tried to make no sound, she had heard him creep in out of the darkness and, starting up, had lit the lamp, only to extinguish it at once when she saw the state he was in. Wasting no time, she had stripped the blood-soaked clothes off him, then hurried him into the courtyard and poured bucket after bucket of water over his shivering body. When she had wrapped him in a blanket and, pushing him down on her bed, had given him a little warm milk to drink, his Ma, his Mouj—the Kashmiri word for mother, which he still used—had soon had the whole story out of him, told through chattering teeth in a whisper. They had argued for what had seemed hours, and when she realised that nothing would make him stay, that his only idea was to get as far away as he could, she had suggested that he should take advantage of the Government's enlistment drive and join the army. "Many young men from the villages are soldiers now—good pay, good food," Mouj had whispered. "Razia's Abdul has already sent fifty rupees home." He had snarled at her, "Don't be a fool, Mouj. Me, in the army, doing 'left, right, left right'—ordered about!" She should have known that the thought of such discipline, all those shouted commands, enraged him. At last they had agreed that he must change his name and try his luck with his uncle in Srinagar. They had not given a thought to his wife, that useless stick, asleep in the inner room; even if Jasmilla had heard or seen anything that night, she was too stupid, too cowed, too much under Mouj's thumb. Ahmed lay with her when he came home every year to see his mother only because the old woman insisted. The girl was still young; even after five still-born babies, there still was a chance of a live son.

Surely the police, if ever they had been after him, had given up the chase by now. It was nearly six months since that dawn when Mouj had made sure that there was no one stirring in the still dark deserted village street before he slipped past her and slunk away, carrying his shoes until he was clear of the houses, and then hurrying between the silent mist-wrapped fields towards the distant railway station.

Now, as Ahmed flicked a duster in Leah's tent, he was thinking about his mother, something he rarely did. The memsahib reminded him of her, although in appearance no two women could have been less alike—one a plump, well-fed white pigeon, the other a lean, bright-eyed hawk—but both were forceful characters, always determined to have their own way, obstinate and courageous. To many Muslims, such as he, women were soulless chattels, fit only for childbearing and hard work, yet for these two he had an unwilling respect and of his mother he was still a little afraid. He had been a good son to her, sending her money when he could, standing up to her in-laws when he was old enough, setting her up in a house of her own, and marrying the girl of her choice, but he had always borne her a grudge. In his heart he had never forgiven her for taking him when he was five years old to the mission. When his father died so suddenly, far from his village, she should have managed somehow to have taken them both to her own people in Kashmir. In her homesickness she had often talked to him of the Vale, of the hills and lakes she longed to see again; then why had she submitted to staying on in the plains as an unpaid drudge in her brother-in-law's house and handing him, Aziz, over to a discipline he had not understood and had detested?

In her childhood, she had once been treated at the famous mission hospital in Srinagar and had always remembered the missionaries' kindness and care. Finding herself widowed, at the mercy of her husband's relations, she had taken her son to the nearest mission in Pratapur, the small town ten miles away, walking the whole way because she had no money, carrying him when his short legs could go no further.

The boy, Aziz, had been accepted by the missionaries, fed and clothed and taught. No one had been unkind to him, no one had let him go hungry; on the contrary, he had been treated for a time as something of a pet. There had been, of course, a great deal of what he still called "Jesus talk," but he had let it flow over him. It was the discipline he had rebelled against, but the dullness, the lack of colour and noise had oppressed him. Twice, in the first year, he had run away and Mouj had taken him back. It was when the mission was training him to earn his living as a house servant, as his father had done, that he had run away for good to the city, where he nearly starved before he found work, and would have starved if it had not been for the charity of various ladies of easy virtue who found his fifteen-year-old good looks to their liking. The very thought of those lean days made Ahmed hurry now to the cook tent where he crammed a handful of rice from the pot into his mouth.

If lean, those days had at least been colourful and as crammed with life and movement as the narrow teeming streets, the jostle of the bazaars, had been. For Ahmed, anything was preferable to the quiet, ordered, contained life of the mission. He shuddered even now at the remembrance, and to him, as perhaps to Leah, the chief drawback of the Meadow was that there were many missionaries on holiday there. If Leah had realised the extent of Ahmed's aversion to these admirable, though annoying people, she might have rebuked him, pointing out that there was nothing to set them apart from the other visitors except a true kindliness and an unselfish concern for others. Ahmed would have answered that he could recognise a missionary from afar, that the very sight of the Johnstons walking in their purposeful way across the grassy slopes reminded him of his childhood and set his teeth on edge. "Bad luck coming," he would mutter to himself, and hurry off to warn Leah. To his annoyance, she did not always respond as he expected. It was possible that she would put her book down and, instead of slipping into the pine wood, leaving him to inform the intruders as impertinently as he dared that the mem was out walking and he had no idea when she would be back, she would tell him to get tea ready, say perhaps, "Put out that cake we baked yesterday."

Another missionary, a Dr. Phoebe Warren, came to the Meadow, riding in one evening with her modest retinue from a trek into the neighbouring mountains.

Leah had heard much from the Johnstons about Dr. Warren before she met her the next afternoon, when they brought her with them to the camp at their usual "dropping-in" time. As she rose to greet this woman who, according to the Johnstons, was famous throughout North-West India and—to them, at least—something of a heroine, Leah's first feeling was one of disappointment. The doctor was small, pale, colourless, with mouse-coloured hair parted in the middle and done up in an untidy bun. She was wearing badly cut khaki drill trousers, a white shirt, and a grey cardigan too big for her. It was difficult to imagine this insignificant-looking little person riding in her doctor's white coat, which was her passport and protection—not even the most trigger-happy Pathan would fire on the white coat of a mission doctor—into the tribesmen's rocky fastnesses where she would treat their women and children and even do operations. Leah longed to ask the doctor about her work—the words North-West Frontier conjured up an exciting, wild, mountainous, desert land where anything could happen—but there was no chance while the Johnstons were there.

Having introduced their friend—who, Leah gathered, belonged to the same Anglican order of missionaries, an order with missions all over India and whose hospital was near their mission school—they seemed determined to keep her up-to-date with the Meadow's latest news and gossip. An officer in the R.A.F. camp had died of a heart attack the day before, after a long climb among the peaks; his body had already been carried back to Srinagar.

"They will overdo it at this altitude," Eric Johnston said. He looked at Leah through the horn-rimmed spectacles, which, she thought, gave him the look of a solemn and rather pompous owl, and added, "And this poor fellow was young, Mrs. Harding."

His wife, knowing that Leah resented any well-meant attempts to curtail her riding and walking, interrupted him, rushing into an incoherent account of the behaviour of a couple of recent arrivals. "Their tent was pitched out in the open, slap in the middle of the Meadow under everyone's eyes, and they disappeared inside and, after three days, they are still there—food is carried in by their servants."

"Iris, you're exaggerating as usual."

"I'm not, Eric. They haven't come out once, even for a look round or a breath of air."

As Iris subsided, a flush rising in her sallow cheeks as it always did when she realised she had gone too far, Dr. Warren laughed and said, "If that is all they want, why come all this way? They might as well have stayed in a hotel in Srinagar."

She had a pleasant laugh, young and infectious, and a quiet, pleasant speaking voice. So far she had said little, but sat drinking her tea, listening to the Johnstons. Her grey eyes, surrounded by many fine wrinkles that came, Leah was sure, from dry winds and too much sun—the doctor, she knew, was not yet forty—went from face to face, calmly, consideringly, resting longest on Leah. She was evasive when at last Leah managed to ask her a few questions about her work, yet willing, even eager, to talk of her latest trek into the mountains—a short journey, it seemed, only three marches from the Meadow and back again.

"I meant to go further, much further," the doctor said, speaking directly to Leah, "but when I reached the lakes, I stayed camped beside them for days. I couldn't tear myself away. You cross the Pass, a terrific winding pull up with a glacier at the top, and then look down this incredibly green valley—nothing but grass for miles and miles, grass and a winding stream and, on each side, bare rocky hills, rocks and snow. There are no trees, it's too high for trees, but everywhere in the grass are flowers, millions upon millions of flowers; I saw magenta-coloured primulas growing up out of the snow. And then at the end of the valley, lying under the mountains that shut them in, are these two little lakes, so clean, so high, so blue. There are icebergs floating in the lakes, real true icebergs!"

She looked at Leah and said, "You should go there and see for yourself, Mrs. Harding, you really should," and added, as Eric Johnston started to expostulate, "There was no one there. I met no one all the way, except the Gujars."

The Johnstons were both talking together: "That Pass

is over fourteen thousand feet and the way is very rough."

"They say that if it rains the path down becomes impossible—you could be stuck up there for days."

"Mrs. Harding would be extremely foolish at her age even to think of such a journey."

"How could you make such a suggestion, Phoebe?"

Phoebe Warren smiled and said nothing, but Leah, when she could make herself heard, said, to change the subject, meaning to come back to it when she could manage to get the doctor to herself, "The Gujars? You said Gujars, didn't you?"

Eric Johnston turned to her eagerly and launched at once into what was almost a lecture, on one of his favourite subjects. It was evident that she could not have asked a question that pleased him more. The Gujars, she was told, were a nomad people who, every spring, drove their herds of goats, buffaloes, and ponies up to the high mountain alps and pastures in a great exodus. They would spend the summer months in small tribes and clans, living in tents or the log huts they had left the year before, while their flocks grazed on the rich grass; when autumn came with its first frosts, the Gujars would return the way they had come, the flocks augmented by new foals, calves, and kids, to winter in the Vale and the plains of Kashmir until spring came round again.

"They are an almost Biblical people, with their flocks and herds," Eric said, "and they have Biblical-sounding names: Davood, Jossoof."

"They are supposed to be one of the Lost Tribes, aren't they?"

"That's nonsense, Iris," he said testily. "There's absolutely no evidence."

Leah sat back on her bench under the shamiana, folded her hands on the table, and did her best to listen attentively. Soon her attention wandered. Eric could make even the Gujars seem dull. Dr. Warren, as guest of honour, was installed in the only camp-chair, Iris Johnston perched on the camp-stool, while her husband had to put up with an upturned stores box—poor man, with those long legs of his he must be uncomfortable. Perhaps she ought to ask Ahmed to have some more wooden benches made. Not worth it, she decided, when she would soon be off on her travels again.

Dr. Warren was growing restless as Eric droned on, and, interrupting him without any more compunction, said, "The women wear the most beautiful clothes, Mrs. Harding. Enormously full trousers and floating veils. It's a sight to see them on the march, swinging along, fierce and proud, with their babies on their backs and their cooking pots in nets on their heads, their fierce dogs at their heels. On my way back I stopped at one of their encampments. It's not far from the Meadow; you could get there easily."

"It's a stiff climb," Eric said. "It's on the way to your lakes. You cross the river at the bridge and take the path up the mountain. Very steep . . ."

Iris Johnston said eagerly, "I rode when we went there a few weeks ago. It's a beautiful place when you get there, such a view, and there's a marvellous camping site. Gujars will soon swarm round, the children to sell you wild raspberries, and the women to ask for medicines."

"Your day there must have been something of a busman's holiday, Phoebe. Did you take your famous black bag with you even there?" Eric asked.

"Ever since I had to operate here with a pair of nail-scissors on one of the summer visitors who had a miscarriage, my bag goes with me everywhere, although I hope I won't have to open it."

"It was no use our telling the Gujars that we were not doctors," Eric said. "Even one of their Elders came for aspirin. They elect Elders, you know, to govern each clan, not always old men. . . ."

Iris, perhaps fearing another lecture, said quickly, "This one was old, with an enormous red turban. When they discovered from your ponyman that you were a doctor, Phoebe, you must have been besieged."

Dr. Warren smiled. "Luckily they are a healthy people on the whole, beautiful and hardy."

"And dirty! They can never wash."

"Only on their wedding nights, I believe," Eric Johnston said. "And the new-born babies are washed, those born on the march, in an ice-cold mountain stream. No wonder they are hardy."

For the time being, at any rate, Leah had had enough of the Gujars. She said, "It's all very interesting—I must certainly go to see that encampment. Next week, perhaps. I must send for Nabir."

Ahmed, too, had decided to see Nabir as soon as possible. As he had brought first the cake, then more hot water, then cleared the tea-things away, he had listened to every word that was said. He had seen the expression on Leah's face when the doctor miss sahib talked of the lakes. He knew by now what that eager look meant. He must ask Nabir about this Pass and the way to the lakes; it sounded to him an arduous journey. When the camp's three guests stood up to say good-bye to their hostess, he made himself scarce but kept within hearing distance. He heard Leah say, as she held Dr. Warren's hand for a moment, "Come again, please. I would so like to talk to you."

Dr. Warren came again and, after her second visit, came almost every day, staying perhaps for a few minutes, usually for an hour or more. How Phoebe Warren managed to evade the Johnstons, whose camp was near her own, Leah did not ask, but she always came alone, usually in the morning, never at tea-time, which was the Johnstons' time, and often after dark when she would join Leah by the fire and they would sit together watching the flames and talking until it was time for dinner. Phoebe, who always refused an invitation to a meal, would then slip away as quietly as she had come. This refusal irritated Leah until she realised that it was made out of consideration for herself, food being both difficult to come by and expensive at the Meadow. Coffee and tea Dr. Warren and the Johnstons accepted, probably because they could not resist such a treat, both coffee and the good tea Leah provided being beyond the means of frugal missionaries.

For the most part, it was Leah who talked while Phoebe listened. Usually a reserved, silent person who had always found difficulty in expressing herself, Leah found that she could talk to this woman as she had never talked to anyone before. When she came to think of it, she realised that she had never had a close woman friend. Since she had been the only girl in a family of boys, her world had been from early childhood, when her mother had died, a male world, of father, brothers, husband, son, and grandson, which made this new and sudden friendship all the more precious.

Is mutual attraction between two human beings rare when it is sexless, unseeking, unadvantageous to both, and unlikely? Leah only knew that she was fortunate in her old age to experience such kinship twice in such a short time. She knew that what Ahmed and she felt for each other, a genuine liking—unwilling, perhaps, on his part and certainly not unadvantageous, and, on hers, often tinged with exasperation and a faint doubt—was on a very different level to the feeling that existed between her and Phoebe Warren. Towards the end of their time together, Leah said gruffly, as she was inclined to be when embarrassed, "I like you, Doctor, I do indeed. How lucky I am to have met you." She did not add, because she considered it too flowery, "I can open my heart to you," but that was what she meant.

"And I like you, dear Mrs. Harding," Phoebe replied. It would not have occurred to either of them to use Christian names in the few weeks they knew each other, but she put her hand over Leah's and said, a little awkwardly as if she, too, found it difficult to put her feelings into words, "I think it a privilege to have met you. I shall never forget you." And this was true. Often, for many years to come, as Phoebe Warren went about her work, a vision of the small, stocky old woman, of the blue eyes and soft pink-and-white cheeks above the determined chin, would rise in front of her.

They did not always agree and sometimes found a gulf opening between them that took an effort on both their parts to bridge.

For instance, Leah was surprised to find that Phoebe had not taken to Ahmed, that his good looks and winning ways made no impression on her. He was never anything except deferential to the doctor, but she would look at him coldly if he came near, and if she had to speak to him, it would be briefly, in his own language. When Leah assured her that Ahmed was invaluable, that she was wonderfully looked after, Phoebe said in her dry way that she was glad to hear it and, after hesitating a moment, asked, "You don't know very much about him, do you?"

Leah was disturbed and annoyed, and showed it. "Why do you say that?" she demanded and asked, as she had asked Colonel Baxter, "What's wrong with Ahmed?"

Phoebe Warren hesitated again. "Well—he's inclined to be cheeky, for one thing."

"Cheeky! Ahmed! He's never cheeky to me. What else?"

"Nothing, as far as I know."

Leah looked at Phoebe and frowned. "Ahmed was brought up and educated by missionaries—he's mission-trained. Doesn't that mean anything?"

"Not very much, I'm afraid. You see, we so often get the riff-raff."

"Ahmed is not riff-raff!"

"I never said he was." Looking at Leah's flushed face, Phoebe said gently, "Don't be angry with me, Mrs. Harding. Don't look at me like that. I'll say no more about your paragon—I really haven't anything to say. I don't know anything, it's just a feeling. . . . No, let's change the subject."

Leah had been reading that morning before Phoebe came. Her few books were arranged in a neat pile, among them a bird book and the books she read over and over again: the *Collected Works of Robert Browning;* Trollope's *Dr. Thorne;* a shabby Bible, very much worn, was open in front of her. The shamiana looked out on the sunlit pine glade and the bright warm air carried the cooing of wood-pigeons. Now Leah's face softened; she could not be angry with Phoebe for long and she said, "Very well, best not to discuss Ahmed. Tell me, does your mission make many converts?"

Phoebe Warren smiled at this abrupt question and then sighed. "Very few, I'm afraid."

"But there are many Christians in India?"

"Yes, indeed, several million—about five, I believe. That sounds a lot, but not when you remember how many hundred millions of Indians there are! Christianity is very old in India, you know. Christian communities flourished in South India from very early times. St. Thomas, perhaps the first great missionary, founded the Church of Malabar in A.D. 52. The Nestorians . . ."

Phoebe, looking at Leah, laughed and said, "I sound like Eric, off on one of his favourite subjects. When I get back, I'll send you a book on Christianity in India, better than a lecture from me."

"Ahmed is a Mohammedan," Leah said. "I've seen him praying with the ponymen, standing and kneeling, facing towards Mecca."

She glanced at her friend and said slowly, "Moham-medan, Hindu, Christian, and Buddhist, of course—surely all are right in their own way, all acceptable to God?"

It was the Doctor's turn to straighten herself and look severe. "Christianity is the only true religion," she said. "The others are all—shall we say, incomplete?"

Leah sighed and, watching the small, gentle, yet im-placable face so near her own, knew that it was useless to persist. She had forgotten for a moment that this woman, if a doctor first, was also a missionary—or was it the other way round? Before she could think of anything to say, Phoebe drew the open Bible towards her. "You are a Chris-tian, Mrs. Harding?" she asked.

If anyone else had asked Leah that question, she would probably have answered, "Of course I am," or even have

said in her gruff way, "Surely that's my own business?"
Now she said, consideringly, slowly, trying to make her
meaning clear to Phoebe and to herself, "Yes, I suppose so
—in a way. I was christened, at my mother's wish, but I'm
not a religious person. I'm not interested, not in any religion. I love this world too much, I suppose—life, everything living. And life is so terribly short."

Phoebe said nothing; her face was expressionless, but
her eyes were kind, and Leah went on, a little desperately
now, "I'm not clever, not good at reasoning things out—
I'm not sure that I even believe in God. When I look at a
bird flying or at the markings on a butterfly's wing, I do, but
when I think of this war, of all the stupid suffering and hate,
I can't . . . I can't believe in anything."

As she turned the pages of the Bible, rustling the thin
paper, Phoebe said, "And yet you travel with this in your
luggage and I find you reading it."

"That Bible belonged to my father and he left it to me.
He brought his children up on it and I still know bits of it
by heart. I have not opened it for years and years, but now,
since I came to the Meadow, I do as he did and read a few
pages every day—quite why, I don't know, unless it's because this is such a heavenly place!"

"You have been reading the Psalms, I see. There's a
bookmarker, a pigeon's feather, marking the hundred and
twenty-first."

"I began at the beginning, at Genesis, and I'm going
right through, not skipping a word, but I often turn to the
Psalms—they suit this place, don't they?"

" 'I will lift up mine eyes unto the hills'?" Phoebe
pushed the Bible back across the table to Leah. "Keep to
those few pages every day and you'll arrive at the New
Testament again. Something may come of it—you never
know."

Getting up, she said briskly, "Well, I must be off. I'm
supposed to be meeting the Johnstons."

.   .   .

Near the end of Phoebe Warren's holiday, she and Leah met by chance in the village.

Word had come from the postmaster that Leah's weekly registered letter from her Srinagar bank had arrived, and, followed by Gaffur, she had ridden down to collect it soon after breakfast. Such registered letters, which everyone, including the post runner, knew contained money, were never delivered to the camps, but had to be signed for in front of the postmaster. This had seemed to Leah a cumbersome, if wise, arrangement when it was explained to her by the bank manager in Srinagar. "Never have more money with you than you need for a short time," he had advised. "It's a temptation for poor people." Looking at her hands, at the old-fashioned half-hoop of big diamonds, her engagement ring, and at the sapphire Geoffrey had given her when their son was born, he had added, "If I were you, Mrs. Harding, I would leave those rings in the bank's safekeeping. There are plenty of rogues here, as everywhere." Leah had not followed this last advice; she had worn both rings for so long that she would have felt undressed without them.

If there were thieves among the simple people of the valley, it seemed odd to Leah that the post runner was not robbed on the way, but this, it appeared, never happened. Ahmed, when he advised her to pay all her bills directly the money came, had used much the same words: "Many bad mans, many wickeds about." He had advised her to settle with the milkman, the dhobie, the woodcutter, and to pay Nabir for the pony's hire and Gaffur's wage at once, outside the post office, if possible, "Where everyone see. Everyones know not much money left. Not worth coming to rob Memsahib then."

Leah was standing outside the post office, settling her account with Nabir, when Phoebe rode up the village street and dismounted beside her.

Phoebe, too, had come to collect a registered letter, and Leah waited for her in the shade of the post office's jutting eaves. They had agreed, as it was such a fine day, to ride together beside the river and to return to the Meadow by way of the ford and the winding path through the pine woods. Nabir waited, too, his arms folded under his red plaid. Leah had seen his grave, dark face light up when he salaamed to the doctor miss sahib and stepped forward to hold her pony's bridle until her own ponyman ran up. The Johnstons had told Leah that Phoebe had once helped Nabir's wife through a long and dangerous confinement, managing to save the long-awaited son.

"The postmaster asked me to give you these, with his apologies," Phoebe said when she joined Leah. "They arrived yesterday and he forgot to include them in the postbag. He must have put them in the wrong pigeon-hole, because they were with my letter."

Leah took the two letters from Phoebe and, after a brief glance, put them into her waistcoat pocket; one was from Hugh and the other looked like a Srinagar bill. "They will keep until we get back to camp," she said. "Let's start—it's such a lovely day."

It was indeed a radiant day, even for the Meadow. The snow peaks far above them were dazzling against the sky and the woods shimmered in a gold haze. As they jogged along the dusty, empty road, followed at a distance by Gaffur and the other ponyman, Leah felt, as she had so often felt, that it was good to be alive. It was her eightieth birthday and she felt young.

"What a pity that you have only a short time left here, Doctor," she said.

"Only two days more; then the Johnstons and I go back together."

"You spend all your holidays in Kashmir, don't you? I mean, instead of going back to England?"

"I have no close ties in England and I've known the Meadow and this valley for many years, long before the war. It's not so very far from my mission, as distances go in India, but it might be in another world. The Meadow is so green, so rich, so flowery—it refreshes me as no other place could."

"Does Nabir go with you on all your treks into the mountains? Did he go with you to those lakes?"

"Nabir organises most of my expeditions and I hope always will, but, being such a reliable guide and having the best ponies, he's much in demand with the camp contractors in Srinagar. When I went to the lakes, I had to put up with his brother, as Nabir had gone down the valley to meet you."

"I didn't know he had a brother."

"Oh, yes, his second-in-command, but not a patch on Nabir. He has a name, of course—Mustapha—but he's always known as Nabir's brother."

"I hired my tents and everything else from Ahmed's uncle. He engaged Nabir and his ponies for me."

"Ahmed is a Kashmiri, then?"

"His mother was a Kashmiri, I believe, but he comes from somewhere in the plains—where, I don't know. From his chits he seems to have worked chiefly in Lahore. He never mentions his family—I suppose he must have one."

"Most probably a wife and children are living in his village; they marry so young, you know. All over India where the land can't support so many, it's the custom for some of the men to go to the cities to find work. They seldom, if ever, take their families with them, but send their wages home and go back themselves, perhaps every few years, to beget yet another child."

"It seems an odd way of living."

"Dictated by necessity; the best Ahmed and others like him can do."

They had crossed the wooden bridge and Leah halted her pony and, looking back, pointed her whip to where the valley stretched as far as she could see to the range that guarded the passes to Tibet; a few billowing white clouds lay upon the surrounding mountains.

"Have you ever been that way?" she asked.

"I've been as far as Leh, years ago."

"Could I go?"

"Not without a permit," and Phoebe Warren halted her pony, too, and turned to look at Leah. Across the river was the pine-covered hill crowned with the rest-house, and to their right the side of a mountain towered above them. As the ponies grazed side by side along the verge and the ponymen, glad of a rest, squatted down and exchanged news, Phoebe said, "Mrs. Harding, look the other way at that path going up and up as far as we can see. It starts at this road and goes up the mountain to the Gujar encampment we talked about. It's rough and stony, very steep, but I think you could manage it with a pony to help you. That, though, is only the first stage, the first march to the lakes. The next, to the foot of the Pass, is even rougher; you would have to walk part of it. The camp-site below the Pass is at over thirteen thousand feet. I had a terrible headache all the night I was there and the next day I was very short of breath on the climb to the top."

"When you get to the top, there's a glacier to cross, I know."

"The glacier is nothing—you just walk across it—but the path down on the other side is very dangerous when it rains, so slippery that it becomes impossible for man or pony."

"Why should it rain at this time of the year?"

"It rained here for two days a week ago, didn't it? And it wasn't very pleasant even in a comfortable camp on the Meadow, or have you forgotten?"

Leah was silent. She had forgotten, or preferred not to remember, those two grey, cold, miserable days. The shamiana had leaked and she had stayed, bored and restless, in her tent, venturing out only for a short damp walk under one of the big black cotton umbrellas that the Colonel had advised her to buy. "Take a ground sheet as well, tents can leak," he had said. Watching Ahmed splashing between the tents, looking like a huge black mushroom with two stalks, Leah had been glad that she had listened to the Colonel.

"Of course I know it rained," she said a little impatiently. "All the less likely that it will rain again. And after the Pass, once safely down, what then?"

"Then it's all plain sailing—or, rather, riding—along a grassy valley to the lakes, but . . ."

Leah looked searchingly into Phoebe's face. "You don't think that I should go there, do you?" she cried passionately. "I can see that you don't."

Phoebe was silent and then, as Leah turned her head away and fumbled in the pocket of her skirt for her handkerchief, she said gently, "The ford is quite close; let's cross it and find a comfortable place under the pines where we can sit and talk this over."

It was pleasantly cool under the pines after the sunlit, dusty road; the river flowed past, almost at their feet. Leah had put her hat down on the pine-needle-strewn ground and had leant back against the rough bark of the tree trunk whose branches, high above them, included her and Phoebe in their thin shade.

"I believe in people doing what they want to, really want to, if they possibly can," said Phoebe, "but, since you ask me, I think now that it would be too much at your age."

"My age! Why should the old be careful of themselves? They have so little to lose. It's the young who should be careful."

"They seldom are, I'm glad to say!" Phoebe put her hand on Leah's arm and said, "Mrs. Harding, please listen. Don't turn away. You must realise that if it did rain when you had once crossed the Pass, you might be marooned at the lakes for days, even weeks. No one could get to you. It could turn very cold up there, and you would run short of food—not only you but your servants and ponymen. Why not wait until next year when we could come back here and go to the lakes together?"

"I'm old, remember. I might not be alive next year. No, it's now or never."

Leah's blue eyes lifted beseechingly to her friend's face as she said, "I'm going to tell you something I've never told anyone before. It's something dark that's always been there, like a shadow. If I tell you, perhaps I can get rid of it."

"Are you sure you want to tell me?" Phoebe sounded alarmed.

"Yes, please. Please listen. My husband . . ."

She could not go on and, after a moment, Phoebe asked, "Did you marry young?"

"At twenty-two, partly to get away, and because Geoffrey was so handsome, so romantic and dashing—I thought."

Leah laughed, an abrupt, mirthless sound, unlike her usual chuckle. "It was a bitter disappointment when I found that he was dull—staid and dull. That he was also the best of husbands, kind, generous, sweet-tempered, only made it worse. No one could help loving him and there I was, caught in a trap. You see, all my life I've longed to see new places, to travel, to go far. As a child, I planned to be an explorer—an explorer, I! I never had a chance to go anywhere. Then . . ."

"Then?" asked Phoebe.

"Geoffrey had been ill, very ill for a long time; we all knew that he couldn't get better. We had agreed, he and I, that when he died I should go out to India, to Hugh—my grandson. This was at the awful time of the war, just before the fall of France, and I knew that soon no one would be allowed to leave England, that I might be stuck there for years, which, at my age, might be forever. Geoffrey lingered on and on, poor man—in a coma, they said. I was tired and strained, I suppose, and one afternoon, when the nurse was out and I was sitting with him, I found myself praying that he would die before it was too late for me. That was bad enough, but I even wondered if there was anything I could do. . . . For a moment, only a moment, I thought that if I held a pillow over his face . . ."

Leah glanced at Phoebe and looked away at once. "It

was a terrible temptation; I saw everything I wanted slipping away from me. It's all there in the Bible: 'And the devil, taking him up into a high mountain, showed him all the kingdoms of the world in a moment of time. . . .' Am I being blasphemous? Is that what you are thinking? But it was like that—I saw all the lands, all the places, in a moment of time. I didn't do it, of course. I drew back, put it behind me, but the thought had been there, to shame and horrify me ever since."

As Phoebe Warren, moving closer, took the old lady's hand in hers, Leah said, "I should have been punished; I expected to be punished, but I wasn't. Geoffrey died the next day, peacefully, in his own time. It was a near thing, but I got away from England and, what is more, we had to go all the way round Africa, the ship calling at interesting places I should otherwise have never seen, like Cape Town and Durban."

Phoebe laughed; she could not help it. Leah's face showed such conflicting emotions—shame, sorrow, and a rueful glee; the blue eyes were full of tears and yet the old twinkle was back.

"I'm sorry," Phoebe said. "It's nothing to laugh about but, dear Mrs. Harding, surely when it comes to it, it is the deed that counts, not the thought."

"Is it? I'm not so sure. Anyway, I've told you and it's gone—the shadow, I mean. Can you still like me, Doctor?"

"Of course, perhaps more than ever. I understand you now. It's one thing, though, to understand and quite another to agree. I still think an expedition to the lakes is too risky. Doesn't it ever occur to you that if anything happened, if you were taken ill up there, it would cause a lot of trouble and bother?"

Leah got slowly to her feet and, keeping her back turned to Phoebe, stood for a few moments by the water, gazing across the river. In spite of herself, her eye was caught by a small black-and-red bird with a shining white cap, moving busily from stone to stone in the shallow water, jerking its tail as it searched for insects. There was no need to consult her bird book—she knew him: the white-capped redstart, a bird of mountain torrents, found at high altitudes. 'At sixteen thousand feet,' she thought. From here she could just see the path winding up the mountain side, going up and up, as Phoebe had said. Leah sighed and, kneeling down on the narrow beach, dipped her handkerchief in the shallows and washed her flushed tear-stained face. The water, here in the shade of the pines, was stingingly cold and as clear as glass; specks of mica gleamed up at her from the sand between the submerged pebbles; among them something larger shone like a huge diamond. Rolling up her sleeve, reaching out as far as she could, Leah grasped it and sat back on her heels to examine her find. It was a crystal, more perfectly shaped and jewel-cut, a purer white than any of those Ahmed had given her weeks ago. She held it to the light, turning it this way and that; all the colours of the rainbow flashed from its angled planes as a ray of sunlight caught it.

Smiling and delighted, Leah turned to Phoebe, holding the crystal out on the palm of her hand. "Look!" she cried. "A birthday present from the river—I call that a good omen."

"Your birthday?"

"Yes, I'm eighty today."

"Eighty!" Phoebe said as she helped Leah to her feet. "I had thought you seventy-five or six, as had the Johnstons. You are wonderful, but if you're really eighty, which I still find difficult to believe, that's all the more reason . . ."

"To be cautious, not to go? If you only knew how tired I am of being told to be careful!"

Phoebe laughed and, still holding Leah's arm, said, "I do know, and I won't say it again, but before you decide, let me examine you, check your heart and blood pressure and so on, find out as far as I can just how fit you are. My ponyman can ride over now to fetch my medical bag"; and when the man had ridden off on her pony, "Come, let's go back to your camp," said Phoebe. "I'll hang on to Lallah's tail up the steep path through the wood."

Leah put her hat on, pinned it in place, and looked at her watch. "It's long after twelve," she said. "Ahmed will be wondering what has happened to me."

When Leah, with Phoebe walking beside her, rode slowly into camp, Ahmed ran to meet her.

"Anything wrong, Memsahib?" he asked. "Is Memsahib ill? Ponyman just now brought Miss Sahib's black bag—Ahmed much worried."

"I've never felt better," Leah told him, touched by his concern. "There's nothing wrong with me as far as I know. The Doctor Miss Sahib is going to examine me to make sure, that's all."

As Ahmed helped her down from the saddle, Leah said, "Hurry now and see if you can find something special for luncheon, Ahmed. You will stay, won't you, Doctor, just this once? My stores came yesterday and it is my birthday."

"Thank you, of course I will," Phoebe said, "if you promise me to have a good long rest this afternoon. You still look tired."

"I'm not—" Leah began and, as Phoebe smiled, checked herself and said, "Very well, I won't argue. I'll do as you say. Now let's get this examination over; then we can eat in peace."

"You are in very good shape for someone of your age, Mrs. Harding." Phoebe folded her stethoscope and closed her bag. "You tell me that you have had only one serious illness in your life, soon after your son was born, and that you have always been strong and active. You are a lucky woman, beginning only now to be slightly deaf, and still only needing spectacles for reading. Wonderful indeed, but what is more important is that your heart, lungs, blood pressure seem quite normal, as far as I can tell. I still don't think, though, that you should attempt the lakes. Go as far as the Gujar encampment if the weather seems set fair, not on to the high lakes." But she saw Leah set her lips.

'That's for me to decide,' Leah said to herself as she led the way to the shamiana where Ahmed was laying the table.

"Aren't you going to open your letters? I believe you've forgotten all about them!"

Leah had forgotten—what must Phoebe, who could not have failed to see the Forces letter, think of her? She took the letters from her pocket and laid them beside her coffee-cup.

"Don't mind me," Phoebe said, "if you want to read them now."

"I'll just make sure that Hugh is all right."

There was nothing much in Hugh's letter at a first glance—she would read it again when Phoebe had gone. Leah slit the other envelope and looked with surprise at the thin pages covered with spidery black writing.

"Pratapur?" she said. "I don't know anyone in Pratapur."

Phoebe looked up. "Yes, you do. Those people you met on the road, the Macleods, came from Pratapur. There is a Scottish mission there, with a school and a hospital. Eric was talking about it only the other day."

"Why should they write to me?" Leah turned the envelope over. "Oh, I see—it's for Ahmed, not for me. Ahmed Mohammed. Care of Mrs. Harding."

"Perhaps that was the mission Ahmed went to."

"Let's ask him."

Ahmed was washing up in front of the cook tent but, dishcloth in hand, came running when Leah called.

"Memsahib?"

"Here's a letter for you, Ahmed. I opened it by mistake."

He took the letter gingerly—almost as if it might burn him, Leah thought—and turned it over in his hands.

"Memsahib read Ahmed's letter?"

It was said accusingly.

"Of course not. I put it back in the envelope at once. I only saw the address."

Phoebe, looking up into his tense face, said, "Did you go to the mission school at Pratapur, Ahmed?"

He stared at her blankly, and when he spoke, his voice was rough and much too loud. "No, no! Ahmed's mission far, far away—why you want to know? Missionary always spying. . . ."

"Ahmed!"

Ahmed swung round to glare at Leah. "Yess, spy, spy! You don't know. Ahmed know. Missionary, they all the same. Jesus talk, Jesus talk, but always dirty spying!"

Backing away from the table, flinging the dishcloth down, Ahmed turned and rushed out of the shamiana across the sunlit glade and disappeared among the pines.

"Well," said Phoebe calmly, "what do you suppose all that was about?" But Leah was distressed and shaken.

"I'm sorry, Doctor," she said. "I can't think what came over Ahmed."

"Ahmed was terrified—why?"

"He will apologise to you, directly he comes back," Leah said, but Phoebe was not listening. "Pratapur," she said slowly. "I wonder . . ."

Ahmed's hands were shaking as he took his letter from the envelope where Leah had put it. The envelope, he saw, was addressed in his cousin Salim's writing, but there was also a line written in a different hand: "Brother, pray forward this to my son."

His face took on the yellow-grey colour of fear as, crouching on the ground under the pines, he read those words. Knowing his mother as he did, he was sure that she would not take the risk of trying to find him unless she had something of the utmost importance to tell him, or a warning to give. She could not be sure that he had reached Srinagar, and she did not know his assumed name. Even if it had occurred to him to write to her, he would not have done so. His mother, his Mouj, could neither read nor write; she would have to ask someone in the village to read any letter from him or go to a professional letter-writer in Pratapur, as she must have done when she felt impelled to write to him. That she had put simply, "my son," showed that she had kept her wits about her. All the same, it was a pity that she had written this letter. Now there was a link between his mother and himself, a trail that could be followed, a trail that led from Pratapur—what did that pestilential doctor miss sahib know of Pratapur? Why had she asked him about the mission?

At first he found it difficult to read the letter, written in a spidery, flowing hand in very black ink on paper of the cheapest kind sold in every bazaar, and the meaning was far from clear. "Dear Son. As I do not know your present whereabouts, I am enclosing this in another envelope and asking your uncle to send it to you." That much was plain but the rest was not so easy. The flowery, formal English used by the letter-writer as he translated the dictated words was complicated by Mouj's attempt to put what she had to say in a roundabout fashion that she must have hoped only he would understand. "The one in the house" meant, of course, his wife. Only after re-reading the letter many times did he grasp what Mouj was trying to tell him.

Ahmed looked down at the thin pages and groaned. Now he understood, only too well. Reading between the lines, he could fill in the details. His wife, Jasmilla, that despised, unconsidered creature, had not been asleep that night; she must have watched and waited for him to come in, and before the lamp was extinguished, spying through the cracks in the partition, she had glimpsed his blood-stained clothes—"the red garments you wore." That she had heard anything of the whispered talk between Mouj and himself he doubted, but it was clear now from this letter that Jasmilla had seen him leave at daybreak.

It had taken the slut a long time, nearly six months, to make up her mind to betray him, to bite the hand that had at least fed and sheltered her, as a scorpion, having crept into the house to shelter from the rains, turns on its hosts. Evading Mouj, she had at last slipped out of the house and —driven by spite and jealousy or, perhaps, by an added insult or an unkindness that had proved the last straw—had gone to the wife of one of the village Elders, who, of course, had told her husband. "The thing is known," the letter said. "The sons know, but so far there has been nothing from the red-turbanned ones." That last sentence meant, only too clearly, the police. What must the letter-writer have thought?

Doubtless the village women pitied Jasmilla for her still-born children and miscarriages, and for her sharp-tongued mother-in-law, but, luckily for him, the police were not popular with anyone. The two sons might go to the police if they could see no other way of avenging their father. Was there anyone in the village who knew of Mouj's connection with Kashmir? Her brother-in-law and sister-in-law had died many years ago, and it was unlikely that she had talked of her childhood to Jasmilla—or was it?

Putting his head in his hands, Ahmed rocked himself backwards and forwards. He groaned again as he tried to think. He could not think; his mind was too dazed with shock and fear; all it held was a vision of his mother waiting at the crossroads beyond the village for a bus that would take her the ten miles to Pratapur. He saw her clearly, wearing the Muslim woman's black burkha, that all-enveloping garment that allowed only the ankleted feet and the dark eyes looking out through the latticed face-screen to be seen. Having made up her mind to embark on this venture, she would be muttering impatiently to herself at the bus's lateness. He knew that bus. It arrived, heralded by a cloud of dust, early in the morning, and returned in late afternoon. It was always late, and always full, its shining, if shabby, painted silver sides bulging with humanity, its roof top-heavy with boxes and bundles, crates of chickens and vegetables. Mouj could be trusted to fight her way inside, using her sharp elbows, and to make a place for herself among the other women. She would sit out the discomfort of the journey, silent and withdrawn, ignoring the chatter round her, staring out at the passing fields, bare and colourless in their winter stubble. . . .

Winter? What was he thinking of? It had been winter, the cold weather, when he had last seen the familiar countryside under its high clear sky. In August there would be an expanse of green under the warm rain, and Mouj, lean and spare as she was, would be sweating in her burkha. All the same, it was in pale winter sunshine that he saw her descending from the bus, picking her way along the crowded street, squatting in her black cotton folds in front of the letter-writer's small wooden portable desk in which he kept his pens, ink, paper, and stamps. Ignoring the traffic of the busy pavement behind her, she would make her meaning plain with emphatic gestures of her still slim, though gnarled hands; he could see those hands protruding from the black garment, and the thin silver-braceleted wrists that were so strong.

The letter-writer, like all his kind, would be slow and painstaking, not to be hurried by a mere woman, and Mouj would be fuming with impatience before, at last, the outer envelope was addressed and stamped and the agreed price counted out in small coins from the cotton bag that his mother always kept stowed away about her person, its mouth drawn up tightly with a piece of string. Knowing her as he did, he was sure that she would take the letter into the post office at once, and hand it over the counter to make sure that it was properly stamped, that the letter-writer had not cheated her. Mouj had done her best to help him, although it might have been better if she had done nothing. No—at least he was forewarned.

Ahmed picked up the envelope. Had his uncle or cousin

read the letter and stuck the envelope down again? His uncle's English was poor, but his cousin Salim, who saw to the firm's correspondence, spoke and wrote English well— far better than he, Ahmed, did. Salim did not like him. It was because of Salim that Ahmed had haunted the hotels, looking for work that would make him independent of his relations. To repay his uncle who, for his sister's sake, had accepted her son, taking him in and not asking too many questions, he had advised the old memsahib where to go for her camp equipment. What would his uncle and Salim do if the dead man's sons, by evil luck, managed to reach Srinagar and came asking for him? What would they do if the police came?

The letter, he now saw, was dated ten days ago; his uncle, or Salim, had taken his time in forwarding it! Had his mother written at once when she knew what Jasmilla had done? Most probably she had delayed, unable to make up her mind if it would be wise to write at all. How long would it be before the police traced him here?

Ahmed lifted his head and looked across the Meadow. Perhaps even now the constable down in the village, having been told of a telegram from Srinagar, was putting on his turban and badge and taking up his staff before setting out to make sure that he, Ahmed, was still in camp.

Tears of self-pity came into his eyes. Was he to be hounded from place to place for the rest of his life, never able to feel secure, always driven on and on? It wasn't fair. He, Aziz, Ahmed, was no murderer. It was the woman's fault—she had put the knife into his hand. What else could he have done except defend himself when the huge, fierce old man bore down on them, brandishing that wicked dag- ger? Defending himself, as anyone would have done, he had used the knife blindly and then, as anyone would have done, he had jumped aside. . . . It was not his fault that the woman behind him had taken the dying man's last thrust in her breast. If ever an unfaithful wife deserved to die, that one did. She was the old man's second wife and, luscious though she was, not young. Why had he, Ahmed, taken the risk? Unfortunately, he had been bored after two weeks in his village, and Jasmilla was enough to drive any man into the arms of the first willing woman he came across; it was Ahmed's bad luck that it had been this one. He had passed her on the road as she was walking home, keeping, as a good wife should, a few paces behind her husband. She had lifted her head-scarf and, taking in at a glance his youth and handsomeness, had given him an unmistakable sign. . . .

That old man could never have satisfied such a one, but she must have been desperate indeed to take a Muslim as a lover; desperate and bored, too, from being marooned out there in that lonely hamlet surrounded by its neat, carefully irrigated plots. Of the four huts, three were deserted, as Ahmed had confirmed when he made his first cautious reconnaissance. Everyone in the village, a few miles away, knew that after his second marriage the old man's temper was such that he had quarrelled with his sons, whose wives refused to live any longer near their new mother-in-law. Everyone knew, too, that once a week the old man took his vegetables by bullock cart to the market in the town, staying the night, for the way was long, and that he usually took his wife with him—a wise precaution. On that night and, perhaps on other nights—Mouj had hinted that he, Ahmed, was not the only one—the woman had pleaded illness and her husband had left her behind, securing the door with a strong padlock, not knowing that she had had the foresight to acquire a second key that could be pushed out from under the door. "It's quite safe," she had said. "The old devil won't be back until late tomorrow morning." They had not even bothered to bar the door or put out the lamp. . . . Ahmed shuddered.

He had wiped the handle of the knife and had put it into the dead woman's hand. He had taken time to look round with care, to make sure, as far as he could in the dim gold light, that he had left no telltale traces. He had thought that surely, when the bodies were discovered, it would be assumed that the couple had killed each other. That was what he had hoped; Mouj, though, had been doubtful. She had berated him for taking the money, not only what the old man had on him from the market but the notes and small coins that, after a frantic search, Ahmed had found hidden in a jar of grain. He had been certain—although the family savings were probably invested in the heavy silver jewellery the woman always wore, which shone up at him in the lamplight from the sickening welter of blood—that there must be ready money somewhere, a cache against hard times. . . .

Slowly Ahmed got up. On that dreadful night, in that hut, he had managed to keep his head, to think and plan. Surely he could do so now?

It was late afternoon when Ahmed came back to the camp. Perhaps the wide, awe-inspiring sweep of the Meadow culminating in the serene aloofness of the snow peaks, at which he had been gazing unseeingly for so long, had had a calming effect on him without his knowing it. He was almost himself again and his mind was working busily. He would have to apologise to the doctor miss sahib, he supposed, and then the memsahib must be persuaded to set out as soon as possible for the high pass that led to those lakes. Surely he would be safe up there from any possible pursuers, for a time at least, and he would ask Nabir what lay beyond the lakes—perhaps the way to a far country where no one would ever find him.

That afternoon, Leah did as Phoebe had asked and rested in her tent for longer than usual. She had decided, as she was tired and so upset over Ahmed—what in heaven's name could have made him behave like that?—to forgo her evening ride. Having read Hugh's letter through again with the usual sense of disappointment, she lay dozing on her bed, listening to the wood-pigeons and letting the warm, sweet air flow over her. Every now and then, she would open her eyes to look sleepily up at the yellow-gold cotton tent lining, through which the sun seemed to shine, and idly trace the small black geometrical patterns as she had often done before. The tent, which now seemed large and luxurious, almost too big for one person, pleased her; she wondered if she would ever feel at ease in a room again. Leah could hear the familiar camp sound of someone chopping wood; that and the pigeons cooing were the only sounds. Peace and contentment filled her, or would have done if she could have forgotten Ahmed. 'At least I can laze here on my bed for as long as I like,' she thought drowsily. 'There is nothing I have to do—though I must make Ahmed apologise, sometime. . . .'

"Memsahib, Memsahib!" Ahmed's voice roused her from a confused, pleasant dream. Leah sat up, frowning. 'So he's come back,' she thought; but it wasn't only Ahmed. She heard another voice, only too familiar. Iris Johnston, perhaps both Johnstons, had dropped in once again.

Surely Ahmed would tell them that she was sleeping and they would go away; Leah put on her shoes and sat on the bed, waiting. Now she could hear a child's voice and she frowned again; they were not going away and it was no use waiting here. At the entrance to the tent she almost collided with Ahmed.

"Johnston Memsahib come," he told her, smiling as if nothing had happened, "with two babas. Two babas and dog, pup dog."

"A puppy? What next?" Leah said crossly.

Iris Johnston, her long, thin face alight with some new plan or idea, her grey hair an untidy halo, hurried to meet her, talking as she came.

". . . so glad, thought you might be out . . . no time . . ." Leah heard from afar and, nearer, "Eric said I shouldn't come but I knew you wouldn't mind."

"Mind what?" Leah asked as she took the hand held out to her, and she wondered once again why such a vague untidy woman always shook hands in this formal fashion when arriving or departing. She herself much preferred the Indian form of greeting, both hands joined together, palm to palm and raised towards the face, as being dignified and sufficient and avoiding contact.

"It's the Mayhew children," Iris Johnston said. "Poor little things, they're so distressed about their pet. One of their ponymen gave them a stray puppy from the village when they first came, and now Mr. Mayhew won't let them take it when they go back tomorrow. I thought of asking you."

The two children, the same two, a boy and a girl, who had come with flowers and an invitation weeks ago, stood together in front of the shamiana, with Ahmed standing protectingly behind them. They were unattractive children, Leah considered, being stolid, freckled, with almost white hair and pale eyes. Neither looked in the least distressed and took no notice of the brown, ambling pup with too big paws who was exploring the table legs in the shamiana and trailing its rope behind it.

"You want me to have that dog?" Leah asked. "Why me?"

"Well, you see, there's really no one else." Iris Johnston sounded apologetic, as well she might. "I tried the R.A.F. camp and they said it was impossible with so much coming and going. I would like to take it myself but Eric absolutely refuses, impossible on the journey he says, with everything so difficult and crowded in wartime, and Phoebe agrees, but then she doesn't care for dogs."

"Neither do I."

"I can't believe that, dear Mrs. Harding. You're so kind to everyone, so generous. You are staying on in Kashmir for some time, you said. A dog would be a companion—a guard, too. You wouldn't be lonely with a dog."

"I'm never lonely," Leah said, and she wondered why, when it came to it, it was impossible to be rude, or to say what she thought. Looking up at Iris Johnston's troubled face, she said, as reasonably as she could, "Why did the Mayhews let the children have a puppy in the first place?"

"I suppose they didn't think."

Leah snorted. "And now, I suppose, if I don't take it,

they'll abandon it? People like that ought to be abandoned themselves! They call themselves Christians, I presume."

"Ssh—the children will hear."

"Let them hear," Leah was furious now, thinking of the few wretched curs she had seen slinking round the village. "This is blackmail. Either I take it or it starves."

"I shouldn't have asked you. I shouldn't have interfered. Eric was right, as usual."

Leah liked Iris Johnston in spite of her scattiness or perhaps because of it, while she could not help disliking Eric, a kind and good man, she knew, but also a pompous bore. It would please her to show that for once, at least, he was wrong.

"Well," she said, "I must ask Ahmed; he will have to feed the creature. Hindus think a dog unclean, don't they? What about Muslims?"

"Not dogs—pigs, I think," Iris Johnston said in her vague unsure way, although, after so many years in India, surely she should know? "Yes, I think that for Muslims only pigs are beyond the pale."

"Ahmed cooks bacon and sausages for me," Leah said. "Poor Ahmed, I should have thought . . ."

They both turned to look at Ahmed, now squatting beside the children as he showed them how to turn a dish-cloth into a hare with pricked ears. It seemed that for Ahmed two children outweighed one missionary. The three faces, so close together—one dark and thin under the jaunty black hat, two round, pink, and freckled—were equally absorbed. Could this be the same Ahmed who had been so beside himself a few hours ago?

"It seems a pity to disturb them," Leah said, "but I want my tea; I overslept and now I'm thirsty. If you have had yours, please have some more."

The ritual of afternoon tea she had always found sooth-ing and she knew how much Iris Johnston enjoyed the expensive tea, the best obtainable in Srinagar, as a treat after the cheap bazaar "dust," which was all the missionar-ies could afford. Without waiting for an answer and before calling Ahmed to attention, Leah went to the shamiana and tied the puppy's lead firmly to a table leg, a gesture she hoped would be taken as a sign of acceptance without any more talk.

As Ahmed hurried to the cook tent with the children running after him, she said, "Let's sit out here in the sun. I'll have the camp-stool and you take my folding chair. It's comfortable and you look tired. You have been worrying about this wretched puppy, haven't you? You shouldn't look tired at the end of your holiday; you should go away refreshed."

"I shall, of course I shall!" Iris said in her quick, impulsive way. "Who could help being refreshed by this place? 'A taste of Heaven,' I said to Eric. He thought I was exaggerating, but I was not. How lucky you are to be staying on for some time yet."

Leah was reminded of the young Scottish missionary she had met weeks, which seemed months, ago. If she had known at that encounter with the Macleods what she now knew of these dedicated, selfless, often tiresome and irritating people, of missionaries in general and in particular, she would not have been so scornful then, almost rude.

"You know the Macleods, don't you?" she asked. "Dr. and Mrs. Macleod. They camped here for some time and I met them on the road, a party of three."

"Yes, I know you did. . . ."

Iris Johnston stopped short, biting her lip as she always did when she had let some indiscretion escape her.

"Know? How could you know?"

"Well, you see . . . Well, they were rather friends of ours. Dr. Macleod sent a note back by a runner, asking us to look you up when you arrived, just to make sure—well, to make sure that you were comfortable and well looked after."

Leah frowned. "Very kind of them but quite unnecessary. A little officious, perhaps."

"Please don't be annoyed. They didn't mean you to know. It's all my fault." Iris Johnston's troubled face brightened as she cried, "I'm glad they were officious, as you call it; otherwise we might never have known you, and that would have been a pity. Eric and I think you are wonderful."

Leah was touched. As she hesitated, not knowing what to say, Ahmed, followed closely by the children, arrived with tea. Having set the tray down on the camp table, in front of Leah, he seated the children on the ground on the other side of Iris Johnston and well away from herself, Leah noted—how did he know that she had taken a dislike to these two?—and handed each a half-glass of milk, which meant that there would probably not be enough for her breakfast coffee. "Some biscuits left, enough for babas," he told her as he put the plate down in front of them. "Would Memsahib like Ahmed make scones? Not take long."

She knew he was trying to placate her and, "That won't be necessary," she said curtly. "There's enough of this cake for Johnston Memsahib and me." As he still hovered, watching the children cram her precious biscuits into their mouths, she said sharply, "That will do, Ahmed. Go away."

Ahmed's shoulders drooped as he turned to go, and Leah called after him: "Ahmed!" He turned back, his eyes pleading, but all she said was "You'd better find some food —meat, I suppose—for that pup. It's our camp dog now."

If she expected any reaction, she was disappointed. He looked past her at the pup, now straining at its lead as it saw the biscuits disappearing, and only said, as a well-trained servant should, "Atcha—very good—Memsahib."

That evening, after dinner, Leah sat on in front of the camp-fire with the pup curled at her feet. Beyond the warm circle of firelight, darkness, flowing up from the ravine, pressed upon the camp, held at bay only by the flames, although the lantern burned steadfastly in front of her tent and further away was the glow of the cook fire. The night breeze sighed in the pine branches, an eerie sound; as Leah drew her shawl more closely round her shoulders, the pup whimpered in its sleep.

'Poor little wretch,' she thought. It would never take to

her, never become devoted as a dog should be. Its small heart was already given to those unfeeling children. How it had howled as they rode off across the Meadow without a backward glance! The girl, though, had shed a few tears when told to say good-bye, tears quickly dried by Ahmed when, as a parting gift, he put one of Leah's crystals in the child's fat pink hand. The puppy's name was Rex, it seemed, a most unsuitable name for a rough-coated, rat-tailed mongrel with outsize white paws and yellow eyes. It did not answer to its name, did not respond to anything that she said to it, and only stopped the whimpering, which had begun to get on her nerves, to empty the bowl of rice studded with a few pieces of meat which the sweeper boy had produced. That it had eaten at all was a good sign; perhaps, eventually, it would accept her. 'I'll call it Rab, or Rob,' she thought, 'once it has settled down, if it ever does settle down.'

Leah sighed. After her long sleep she was wide awake, but depressed and uneasy. She tried to see herself accompanied on her future walks by a large brown faithful dog, and failed.

When Iris Johnston had gone, Leah had called Ahmed and said, "Before I speak to you, you will go and apologise to the Doctor Miss Sahib. Then you can apologise to me." She had feared for a moment that he would refuse to obey her, but he had said promptly, "Atcha, Memsahib." Now Ahmed materialised suddenly out of the darkness, dragged another log onto the fire, sending the sparks flying, and then stood waiting beside her.

"Ahmed, have you done as I said?"

"Yes, Memsahib."

"What did the Doctor Miss Sahib say?"

"She verree kind. Ahmed verree sorry, Memsahib."

Leah looked up at him. "Ahmed, what is the matter?"

"Nothing, Memsahib. Memsahib, where pup sleep?"

The old jauntiness was back. She knew that it was no use asking; he would not tell her, not now. Glancing down at the sleeping pup pressed against her feet, she said after a pause, "It can sleep in my tent. See if you can find a spare blanket or a piece of sacking for its bed."

As Ahmed turned to go, she said, "Wait a moment, Ahmed, there's something I want to ask you. You love children, don't you? I can see that you do—you are so good with them. Have you any of your own?"

The firelight lit Ahmed's face from below, turning it to a red-gold mask with deep shadows. The whites of his eyes gleamed—were they suddenly wet with his easy tears, or was that her imagination? He squatted down by the fire, poking it with the heavy stick kept for that purpose, sending the flames leaping higher and higher. His voice was as light and cheerful as usual as he said, "No, Ahmed got no babas."

"Are you married?"

"Ahmed married long time, many years. Wife no good. Five babies all born dead."

"Oh, no! How terrible!" Leah was shocked, and also amazed. She had thought of Ahmed as being almost a boy —he looked so young; he was young. The custom, she knew, was to marry young; it must have been in his early teens.

"Poor Ahmed," she said, and added uncertainly, "and poor girl."

"Memsahib not worry. Wife not worth worrying about. She no good, no good for anything."

The bitterness in his voice startled Leah; he sounded vindictive, not like the Ahmed she knew. His face in the firelight looked almost grim.

He must have sensed her surprise, felt her instinctive recoil. He looked round at her and grinned his wide, impish, disarming grin and said, "Ahmed get new wife soon— make plenty of babas."

Leah could not help laughing; he sounded so outrageously cheerful and matter-of-fact. "And where is your wife now?" she asked severely, to bring him down to earth. "Is she in Kashmir? Who is looking after her?"

Ahmed stood up. His voice changed, became elusive

and vague, as he said, "She far, far away. Ahmed's mother look after," and to forestall any more questions, he said, "Memsahib want anything more? Ahmed go make bed for dog, see to water. Is late."

Leah sat where she was a little longer, watching the fire die down, then struggled to her feet. The pup did not want to leave the warmth; she had to bend down and stand it up and coax it to follow her at the end of its lead to the tent. On the way she was glad to see that it had the sense to relieve itself.

The puppy collapsed onto the sack bed prepared beside her own and curled itself into a ball again. 'It's tired out, poor thing,' she thought. 'It will be quiet now.' All the same, she tied the rope firmly to the tent-pole in case it took it into its silly-looking head to run back to the children in the night.

When she had undressed, Leah put the tent flaps back and set the lantern outside on the ground, a little to the right so that the light would not shine into her eyes when she was in bed. The first night in camp, she had blown the lantern out and next morning Ahmed had protested, "Better leave burning all night. Keep wild animals away."

"Bears, I suppose," she said teasingly, but all Ahmed said was "Memsahib leave light."

Now, as Leah got into bed, the pup began to whimper, a pitiful, irritating sound that she tried to ignore. "Lie down," she said. "Be quiet," but the whimpering went on until she untied the rope, dragged the pup onto her bed, and pushed it down against her feet. "Lie there, then, and go to sleep," she told it and was at last obeyed. 'Perhaps I'll make a proper dog of it yet,' she thought as she fell asleep herself.

Hours later, Leah sat up in bed. The lantern must have gone out, because the tent was dark—only a faint greying in the darkness showed where the entrance was. Something was in the tent, near the foot of her bed. She smelt a rank, unpleasant smell. As she shrank back, clutching the bedclothes, the pup shrieked once.

Leah seized her torch. Its dim light shone for a second on two green eyes. She screamed and the eyes vanished. A half-seen yellowish shape melted into the darkness. Something had taken the pup. There was no warm weight against her feet.

Brandishing her heavy walking stick, Leah ran on bare feet into the night, moving faster than she had done for years and screaming as she ran. In her haste she had managed to drop the torch, and only a faint glow from the dying fire showed that the thing was still there, hampered by the weight of the heavy puppy but making for the trees. 'A dog,' she thought, 'one of the village dogs, how dare it!' And, yelling with all her might, she hurled her stick.

Whatever it was, it turned and snarled at her, and as answering shouts came from the cook tent and the light of a lantern and Ahmed's torch bobbed through the trees, it dropped its prey and vanished. When Ahmed, followed by Gaffur and the boy, reached her, Leah was holding the still warm puppy in her arms. Its head lolled over her arm and she knew that it was dead.

"Memsahib! Oh, Memsahib!" Ahmed cried, and shone the torch on her. As she laid the body on the ground, she saw that her hands were covered with blood.

Now they were all crowding round her, talking at once. "Memsahib hurt!" Ahmed cried as he saw her hands and he fell on his knees beside her. "Quick, fetch Doctor Miss Sahib! Gaffur fetch Doctor Miss Sahib!"

Gaffur did not respond; his eyes rolled as if in terror at the thought of crossing the dark Meadow. The boy set up a shrill wailing through which Leah heard Lallah snorting and trampling at the end of her tether.

"Be quiet, all of you," she said. "Don't make such a fuss. Gaffur must see to the pony before it breaks loose—give him the lantern. I'm all right, Ahmed, it didn't touch me. The poor pup . . ."

Ahmed turned the torch onto the small brown huddle at her feet. "Is dead," he announced and, jumping up, cried, "Praise Allah, Memsahib not hurt! Thanks be to

Allah! Brave Memsahib, much brave. Quick, make fire! Not come back for pup if fire burning."

Leaving the sweeper boy to make the fire, Ahmed darted into her tent and came back with Leah's dressing-gown and slippers. For the first time, she realised that she was wearing only her nightgown.

"I must wash my hands," she said, holding them out in front of her.

"Ahmed bring water, Memsahib sit here."

The camp-chair was brought, into which she was thankful to subside. Ahmed knelt and, in the light of the lantern, put her slippers on her feet and held the enamel basin and towel for her. All the time, he kept up an agitated chatter to which she paid little attention. The fire roared up as Gaffur and the boy threw more wood on it. Now it was a bonfire that could have been seen miles away.

"That will do," Leah protested. "You'll set the camp on fire, or burn down a tree."

"Must have good fire. Maybe bagh come back." Ahmed was beside her again, holding a glass.

"Bagh?" she said as she smelt whisky. "What do you mean? It was a dog, a huge dog from the village."

"Was leopard. Ahmed saw."

Now she began to shake and tremble—ridiculous when the danger was past—but she could not stop. Leah reached for the glass and Ahmed had to guide her trembling hand to her mouth. The neat spirit helped her; she was able to look up at the three concerned faces staring down at her in the light of the flames. Gaffur had fetched Lallah, who stood quietly now at the end of the rope, so the leopard, if it had been a leopard, was nowhere near.

"Cover the pup up with something—use my towel," Leah said. "We'll bury it in the morning. Now, perhaps, we had better go back to our beds."

No one moved. "Stay here by fire," Ahmed suggested. "Everyone stay. Morning come soon."

And stay they did. Leah, wrapped in a blanket, dozed in her chair, rousing only when more wood was thrown on the fire. Ahmed crouched beside her while Gaffur and the boy huddled together, with the pony standing behind them. The dead puppy, decent now under its covering, was there, too, in the circle of the firelight; it had been thought too dangerous, too tempting to anything lurking out there in the darkness, to move the body further away. Dawn found them there, huddled round the still-burning fire.

Leah roused herself from a half-sleep. A grey light was seeping through the trees. She looked round the camp, which, at that moment, seemed a sad and melancholy place, at her huddled sleeping companions, at the pony standing with drooping head. The tragedy of the pup was a small one, would soon be forgotten, but—for the time being, at any rate—it had spoilt the camp for her.

Throwing her blanket off, Leah stood up with some difficulty, waking Ahmed as she moved. 'I don't care what anyone, even Phoebe Warren, says,' she thought. 'I'm going to those lakes.'

"Ahmed," she said as he sprang to his feet and straightened his hat. "Bring some tea to my tent, then send for Nabir."

PART THREE
Second Journey

I

ENTHRONED ON her folding chair, Leah looked far over the Gujar encampment at the widest, the most enormous view she had ever seen. Far, far away, beyond a jumbled confusion of rocky hills and a glimpse of a pale thread of river winding along the valley floor, towers and pinnacles of white cloud rested as lightly as swansdown on the slate-coloured mountains.

Never before had she been able to look down from such a height or see so far. Only one short, if steep, march lay between her and Nabir's village, and the Meadow was somewhere below; she might have looked down on the rest-house if it had not been for the rising ground on her right that hid all that was familiar except for the tips of the snow peaks—yet she felt as if she had already reached another world. As her eyes followed a dark speck that was an eagle, circling and soaring untiringly in the limpid air of the void, she felt dizzy and she held on to the arms of her chair; it seemed as if her own neat little camp, perched on the side of the wooded hill, might at any moment take off of its own accord and follow the eagle into that huge blue emptiness. It was a relief to turn her eyes on a small, close, busy human scene.

The ground sloped abruptly in front of her and levelled out into a green saucer-like depression across which a stream meandered to form a pool where women were filling their waterpots. The Gujar huts stood close together in the shelter of the ridge she had followed yesterday at the end of the march; although lived in for only a few months each year, they were solidly built of round, untrimmed pine logs, the cracks stuffed with earth and moss; blue smoke of cooking fires escaped from under the flat roofs on which were large stones, a protection against winter's blizzards. The encampment was some way off but in this thin bright air, Leah could see it quite clearly, even without the aid of the binoculars that now lay in her lap. She had used the binoculars to pick out the eagle, but it had seemed to her that it would be bad manners to turn them on the scene below, to bring these people, who, so far, had politely ignored her presence, nearer to her than she was to them. Yesterday she had not taken much notice of her surroundings when her tent was at last pitched. Now, after a night's rest, she was alert and eager to see all she could of the Gujars, and she was glad that she was to stay here for another night before tackling the next stage to the Pass. To her surprise, Ahmed had not been pleased.

She had thought that after their strenuous packing and sorting, followed by the stiff climb up to the Gujar encampment, where they had arrived as it was growing dark, he would be glad of a day's rest; instead he had wanted to press on, to waste no time, and had been almost rude again, lapsing into sulks when she refused.

Ahmed was becoming unpredictable. Far from being reluctant to leave the comforts of the Meadow, as she had expected, he had been only too eager to go. When, at dawn yesterday, standing by the still-smouldering fire, she had remembered that Nabir was to take Phoebe and the Johnstons down the valley to the suspension bridge, Ahmed had urged her to send Gaffur at once to fetch Nabir's brother. "Maybe leopard come back," he had said. "Memsahib go today," and when Phoebe, followed shortly by the Johnstons, had hurried over to make sure that she was unharmed and then to argue, to try to persuade her, he had hovered near, listening openly.

They had begged her not to go, or at least to wait until she was over the shock. "If you must go, of course Nabir will go with you—we can manage with his brother," Phoebe had said, "but please wait one more day." Phoebe had been oddly insistent on that one day, but Leah had made up her mind not to spend another night in the camp, which to her had become a desolate place.

The sweeper boy, in disgrace for forgetting to fill the lantern, had had a beating from Ahmed, and his sobs, had been heard all over the camp, getting on her nerves. They had buried the pup early that morning out in the pine woods, and she had been incredulous and distressed when Ahmed advised her not to wrap the poor little body in a towel. "No use, Memsahib," he had said. "Someones come and dig up again. These poor people, think wicked waste good towel."

"This camp no good," Ahmed had told her when Phoebe and the Johnstons had gone. "Water no good, air here not good, Memsahib right to go." Thinking now of the Meadow's crystalline air, pure as the snow, redolent of herbs and flowers, and of the sweetness of the water that gushed from the spring among the pines, Leah could not help wondering as she remembered the earnest, dramatic way he had said those words. What Ahmed's real reasons were for wanting to leave the Meadow, she would probably never know. Relieved that he had fallen in so eagerly with her wishes, she had not attempted to find out.

Leah could not be bothered now with the unpredictability of Ahmed; this would probably be her only chance of watching these strange and fascinating Gujars going about their daily affairs. As she gazed down, she tried to remember what Eric Johnston had told her about the tribes, of their great migrations in spring and autumn to and from their summer pastures. Here, in front of their solid huts, they looked settled, almost tame. How she would have liked to see them on the move, driving their vast flocks with the high, bird-like whistling calls he had described and she had yet to hear. She would have liked to see the women swinging along, carrying their household goods on their heads, the plodding buffaloes, the enormous herds of goats fanning out over the hillsides, and the ponies, the long-maned shaggy ponies, that only the men rode.

Here, this morning, she could see only women and old

men, and children too young to be of use; most of the men and older children must be out with the herds. An old man was smoking a hookah in a doorway; a buffalo calf was tethered to a post among the playing children; a woman was squatting in the sunshine with the head of a younger woman in her lap, searching the long black hair—probably for lice. The women at the pool filled their waterpots, balanced them on their heads, and walked towards the huts with proud, bold strides. The black-and-crimson clothes they wore swung as they moved, silver anklets flashed under the sun. In comparison, the few men about in their homespun jackets and untidy turbans seemed colourless, almost ordinary. "The women wear the most beautiful clothes," Phoebe had said. 'I must go down there,' Leah thought. 'I must see the women close to. . . . Perhaps this afternoon . . .'

There was no need for Leah to move from her chair. The women, or some of them, soon came to her. She watched them climb the ridge towards her, moving with the proud, almost animal grace she had already admired. As they drew nearer, she saw that their leader was an old woman, lean, dry, fierce-eyed, and incredibly wrinkled, yet as straight-backed and with as magnificent a carriage as had the four younger women following her. They gave her no greeting, simply settled themselves on the ground a few yards away and stared at her with frank curiosity.

Leah stared back. The young women were remarkably handsome, with pale, smooth skins, fine hooked noses, and large dark eyes. Their jewellery was as handsome as they were: heavy silver earrings, anklets, bracelets, and the old woman, perhaps the matriarch of the tribe, had three rows of large silver beads round her throat and, below them, flat on her chest, what looked like a huge heavy silver horseshoe, polished and smooth. Leah thought their clothes not only beautiful but comfortable, light and free and flowing; above enormously full pleated trousers caught in at the ankle, they wore open-necked tunics, several tunics on top of each other, some weighted round the hems with a trimming of small pearl buttons. The colours were exquisite; the purplish reds and rose, were mellowed, made soft and rich by a patina of smoke and dirt. Their black hair, thick with grease and done up in innumerable small plaits, was crowned under the black veils that hung down their backs by caps of a vivid blue, each no larger than a bracelet. As Eric had said, they were extremely dirty and they gave out a ripe, smoky, cheesy smell that was not wholly unpleasant. Two of the women had bright-eyed babies slung on their backs and the babies wore cherry-coloured peaked and padded caps pulled down over their ears.

The women had come to look at Leah, and evidently, from the young ones' giggles, found her an unusual and curious sight, as, in her divided skirt, gay blouse, and large straw hat, perhaps she was. The hat was necessary: the sun, whose rays seemed purer and stronger the higher she went, beat down on this hillside terrace and on the camp. The women had also come to ask for medicine, as Phoebe had warned her they would do; Nabir and Ahmed had both appeared at her side to act as interpreters.

"Tell them I'm not a doctor," Leah said to Ahmed. "Tell them I have no medicines."

Eric, in his lecture, had not mentioned what language the Gujars spoke; whatever it was—Kashmiri, Urdu—Ahmed evidently knew it well enough to translate her words and, at the same time, to eye the women, something, she suspected, that he could not help doing. One in particular seemed to have caught his attention: a young girl seated among the others, her head modestly bent, who returned Ahmed's look from under her eyelashes. For a moment, Leah was reminded of the girl she had seen in the willow grove, although there was nothing soft or luscious about this high-nosed, slim, wild young creature. Then Nabir stepped forward, and she saw that his usually impassive bearded face above the folds of the red plaid showed that he was annoyed. He glared at Ahmed, who, his black hat perched at a more acute angle than usual on his wavy black hair, his jacket no longer new but worn with an air, looked insufferably cocky and sure of himself. Nabir never spoke to Leah in English, but she knew that he understood it and was now sure that he had meant to act as interpreter this morning and that Ahmed, pushing himself forward, had forestalled him. Why could there not be a universal human way of making oneself understood? She would have liked to talk alone to this grand old woman, as one old woman to another. She was sure that there would be much to say.

The black eyes, still bright and sharp under their hooded lids, were searching her face. A dirt-stained gnarled hand, the long fingers loaded with silver rings, was held out to her. "What does she want, Ahmed? What is she saying?"

"She want aspirin, white pain pills. She say legs much pain in night, no sleep."

"Fetch me the little case on the table by my bed, Ahmed."

Leah opened the round leather case, which had once been Geoffrey's collar box, on her lap. In it she kept her sewing things and what she considered a few essentials, such as senna pods, aspirin, sticking plaster. She counted out six tablets and, leaning forward, dropped them into the outstretched hand.

"Tell her not to take them all at once."

"She know. Doctor Miss Sahib been here."

Phoebe had advised Leah against giving these people any medicine at all: "If anyone is ill next day, you will be blamed." Surely there could be no harm in a few aspirin? Leah knew what it was to wake with cramp in the night; or those pains could be rheumatism, although there was no dampness in this air, only a sunny brightness. She watched as the tablets were carefully knotted into a corner of the black veil.

The woman, with a sudden crablike movement, came closer until she was sitting at Leah's feet and, turning her head, spoke briefly to the other women. They rose at once and, with many backward glances, went away.

"Old one stay," Ahmed announced unnecessarily. "Want to talk to Memsahib." He glanced a little uneasily at Nabir and said, "Shall Nabir tell her go?"

"No. Of course not. What is she saying?"

"She ask how old is Memsahib."

Leah laughed. "Ask her how old she is."

"She say not know. She ask how many children Memsahib got, how many grandchildren."

It was a strange conversation, if conversation it could be called, her voice following the old woman's, Ahmed's voice, and Nabir's adding a few words. With those intent dark eyes on her, Leah answered as best she could. At her admission that her only son had died long ago and that her one grandson was far away at the war, the old woman shook her head in disapproval, or was it commiseration?

"She say have six sons, four daughters, and many many grandchildren, she forget how many."

Leah could think of nothing to say to that, and the next question came almost at once.

"She say where Memsahib going?"

As she had answered once before, Leah said, "As far as I can."

There was a pause while they looked at each other, a long look. The old woman nodded and it seemed to Leah that at last she was understood.

The far-seeing wise old eyes were slowly withdrawn, were no longer searching her face. The woman leaned forward and fingered the edge of Leah's skirt, as any ordinary woman might have done, apprizing the material. Then the gnarled hand was lifted to point past her at the tents—or was it at Leah's white hat? A loud, disconcerting cackle, more like a crow than a laugh, made Leah jump.

"What does she want, Ahmed?" she asked, drawing back in her chair.

"She look at blue pin in hat, Memsahib. She want see, she want touch."

Leah put her hand up and fumbled for the hatpin. She hesitated for a moment and held it out; the blue enamel wings were brilliant in the sunshine. The old woman turned the pin this way and that, holding it by the end of the long shaft; it seemed to amuse her; the disconcerting cackle came again before she handed it back—reluctantly, Leah feared.

I can't let her keep it, Leah thought. Hugh had chosen it himself for her birthday when he was six years old. She would like to give the old woman something, though, to remind her of this meeting. She looked down at the box in her lap and saw her small sewing scissors that were shaped like a stork. Would they do?

Ahmed protested, "No need, Memsahib!" and Nabir shook his head. Both women ignored them. The scissors were examined gravely, turned over and over, held up, the stork's beak that were the blades opening and shutting. The old woman gave her slow nod again and stowed the scissors away somewhere in her clothes. Fumbling in the open neck of her tunic, she drew out a silver amulet attached to a red cord and held it out to Leah. As Leah took the still warm silver thing, worn almost shapeless with age, her hand was closed down over it, pressed down by the other's hard brown fingers.

"She say wear always," came Ahmed's voice. "She say lucky charm, keep Memsahib safe."

The woman stood up and, without any farewell, turned away. As she passed him, she looked at Ahmed and laughed, that witch-like laugh again. What she said to him in a sudden spate of shrill words, Leah, of course, could not understand. Ahmed evidently understood; he smiled uneasily, tried to look nonchalant and superior, and made what was probably a rude retort before Nabir, grinning broadly, intervened. Nabir signed to the woman to go, and then, grave again, turned on Ahmed and spoke sharply and at some length to him. Ahmed looked furious, and for a moment Leah thought there was going to be trouble, but Ahmed controlled himself, shrugged his shoulders, and walked away. As he went, Leah, watching uneasily, saw him make the age-old sign known the world over, two fingers crossed and pointing stiffly at the old woman's back, the sign to avert the evil eye.

Leah looked down at the amulet, her lucky charm, shaped like a small barrel, the silver carving almost obliterated and made smooth by constant contact with human skin; the red cord was filthy. 'I will wash it,' she thought. 'I'll go now and ask Ahmed for some hot water.' She would wear the charm always, round her neck, under her clothes, as the old woman had done, and she thought, 'It will go with me all the way.' Leah stood up and carried the leather case back to her tent.

Ahmed went straight to the cook tent and, squatting down, began to rattle the cooking pots about as he snarled at Gaffur to light the fire. What the old crone had said to him still rang in his ears: "What have we here? A pretty little cockerel strutting about and preening, making eyes at other men's hens. Keep away, cockerel! Our men have sharp knives."

He had tried to laugh it off, to make a gay and salacious retort. Nabir should have laughed, too, not turned on him. The old hag was only joking—or was she? Unless she had eyes in the back of her head, she could not have seen him look at that girl. Nabir had seen. Could Nabir have known about the girl in the willow grove or, if not known, suspected? All the same, it had been foolish to have looked at the Gujar girl at all, but she was such a beautiful little creature under all that grease and dirt, and if the look she had given him back meant anything . . . Would he never learn to leave all women alone? Now, because of his fatal weakness, there was more trouble between him and Nabir, who was against him anyway.

The memsahib's voice calling, "Ahmed. Ahmed," roused him. What did the old one want now? It was not nearly time for luncheon. Was he never to have any peace?

.   .   .

After Leah had hung the red cord up to dry, she sat for a few moments on her bed, gazing round the tent that Phoebe had lent her for this journey. It was not a climber's tent, not a true alpine tent, but far smaller and lighter than the one she had lived in for the last weeks. "I use it on all my treks into the mountains," Phoebe had said. "Leave it with Nabir when you come back."

Once Phoebe and the Johnstons had realised that nothing could stop Leah from leaving for the lakes that day, how kind and helpful they had been! Phoebe had gone down to the village herself to make the necessary arrangements with Nabir, and Eric had gone with her to buy extra supplies for Leah. "You must take all the food you can," he had said. "There will be nothing to be had up there." As they left, Phoebe had said, "You had better hurry with your packing —it's a three-hour climb to the Gujar encampment and you must be there before dark."

It had been a rush, but Ahmed, who had seemed as eager as Leah to get away, had worked with a will, and Iris Johnston had tried to help. "Travel light," Phoebe had advised and Leah had tried to follow this advice, but almost everything she put to one side to be left behind, Ahmed had put back. Not a knife or fork, not a cooking pot, it seemed, could be spared.

To do without the sweeper boy had not been her decision. Because of Ahmed's beating, perhaps, or because of the leopard, the boy had refused to go any further, to the lakes or anywhere else, and had begged to be sent back to Srinagar with Phoebe and the Johnstons. "What Memsahib do?" Ahmed had wailed. "No can get sweeper here." She had told him not to make such a fuss, that they could manage quite well without the boy. "See that at every camp a hole is dug in the bathroom," she had said. "A hole with a pile of earth and some kind of spade beside it. I'll manage." Ahmed had at last agreed that this should be done; such a rough-and-ready solution had apparently been the rule in his sahib's fishing camps. When it came to it, there was little, for moderate comfort, that Leah could do with-

out, and comfort both Ahmed and Nabir insisted she must
have.

By mid-afternoon all had been ready, and Nabir was
seeing to the loading of the ponies when Phoebe and the
Johnstons had come again to say good-bye. Iris Johnston
had given her binoculars to Leah. "Consider them lent, if
you would rather, like Phoebe's tent," Iris had said; "they
will bring nearer what is far, without you going *too* far. I
should have thought of it before, instead of at the eleventh
hour, but you know what I am!" And to think that she had
often laughed at Iris Johnston. . . . Why should they be so
kind, why should they worry about an obstinate old woman
who only wanted her own way? She did not deserve such
consideration.

Now, looking out from the small shelter of the tent at
the huge panorama of mountain and sky, Leah felt suddenly very much alone. Would it have been wiser to put off
this expedition until Phoebe could come with her? Even as
she asked herself this question, Leah knew the answer, as
she had known it when Phoebe first made the suggestion.
She remembered that her instinctive reaction then had
been one of dismay. She wanted to make this journey alone,
to be free to go where she wanted, to do as she liked. If
Phoebe were with her, Phoebe would be the leader, the
organiser, as she, Leah, now was. Nabir might think himself
the leader, but in fact, the decisions, the responsibility
would be hers.

Standing outside in the sunlight, she surveyed her
camp. Smoke was rising from Ahmed's cooking fire. He,
Gaffur, and a few ponymen were sitting round a steaming
samovar drinking their salt tea—she saw the bowl being
passed from hand to hand. Tonight the whole camp would
feast on a kid bought by Nabir from the Gujars, and Ahmed
was to make a meat stew for her that would last for days.
"Tomorrow long way to Pass, then Ahmed too tired to
cook," he had said. A group of ponymen, making the most
of a day's rest, were lounging in front of their tent. It all
looked peaceful and domestic, too comfortable.

If only she were a strong young man, Leah thought, she could have done without even a tent, have travelled really light and free, covering great distances. That old Gujar woman probably carried all she needed on her own head and back and at night slept under the stars. . . . What was the use of wishing? She was lucky to have got as far as this and she was going further, further and higher. Behind the tents, dark firs climbed the hill towards the sky; these would be the last trees she would see for some time, as tomorrow they would be above the tree line. Firewood would have to be carried and made to last for as long as possible—no more camp-fires or baths after tonight, and when it was finished they would burn juniper, which, she had been told, they would find growing in dark green clumps and bushes among the rocks.

Too high for trees . . . above the tree line; that was an exciting thought. Tomorrow they would camp at the foot of the Pass, which she saw plainly with her mind's eye—a naked rock saddle against a clear sky. Somewhere beyond it lay the lakes. . . .

A furious barking down by the huts made Leah look round. Just such a chorus had greeted her own arrival last evening, and, to her dismay, she saw that two people were climbing the ridge towards the camp: a man, no Gujar but, from his clothes and skull-cap, a villager or a ponyman, who beat off the advancing dogs with a stick as Nabir had done and, striding ahead, a small, purposeful figure. Phoebe! What was Phoebe doing here? Why had she come?

Phoebe Warren wasted no time in greetings or explanations. She pulled her hat off, wiped the sweat from her forehead, and, sinking down in the chair Leah offered her, said, "I must talk to you, now, at once, where no one can hear us."

"Surely after that climb you'll rest first and have something to drink?"

"A glass of water, please, and perhaps Nabir could give my man some tea."

"Doctor! What is the matter? You sound so—so **grim**,"

Leah cried. "You know that you can have anything you want—I'll call Ahmed," but Ahmed was already there, hovering close behind them. He fetched Leah's camp-stool for her and darted off to return almost at once with a glass of water on a tray.

"Nabir here, Miss Sahib," he volunteered as Phoebe, without looking at him, took the glass.

Leah saw that Nabir was waiting a little way off, as if for orders, and that a group of women had gathered in front of the huts to look up at the camp. Phoebe frowned and stood up. "I'll have a word with Nabir if I may," she said. "I don't want those women, or anyone else, to interrupt us. There isn't much time, as I must get back as soon as I can; the Johnstons and I are leaving very early tomorrow."

"Where is your pony?"

"I thought that I would manage the climb more quickly on my own feet, and a pony would be no help downhill on the way back, it's too steep."

"You must have something to eat before you go. I'll tell Ahmed."

"Hear what I have to say first. You won't like it."

It seemed to Leah that Phoebe was taking unnecessary precautions when she moved chair and camp-stool to the far end of the level ground, well away from the tents.

"Who is there to hear us?" Leah asked.

"Ahmed, of course. He's always snooping—haven't you noticed?"

"Then what you have to tell me is about Ahmed?"

"It may be."

"I don't understand."

Phoebe said gently, "You will, but let me say all I have to say before you get angry and refuse to listen. You remember how Ahmed behaved when you opened his letter from Pratapur and when we asked him about the mission?"

Leah nodded.

"Well, that afternoon after I left you, I went down to the post office and put a call through to Pratapur. It took hours and hours, as I had to get enquiries at Srinagar first, but at long last, after it was dark, I spoke to Dr. Macleod at the mission and managed to make him understand what I wanted."

"And what did you want?"

"I wanted to know if he remembered any important and very possibly unsolved crime that had happened in the last six months or even more in Pratapur or the surrounding district, and if he would contact the local superintendent of police and ask him the same question."

Leah stared at Phoebe in astonishment. "Dr. Macleod must have thought that a very odd request," she said. "What an extraordinary thing to do! Did you tell Eric?"

"I told the Johnstons as little as possible. I didn't want Eric to interfere. And was it such an extraordinary thing to do? You see, Ahmed had been so frightened, so obviously terrified at the mention of Pratapur, that I felt there must be a reason."

"What did Dr. Macleod say?"

"That he vaguely remembered reading in the papers months ago about a rather sensational murder, and he very kindly agreed to contact the police and find out what he could. We arranged that I should telephone him again the next evening, yesterday. I had booked a call, but I had to wait hours again."

"So that was why you wanted me to stay at the Meadow another day? It would have saved you toiling all the way up here. Dr. Warren, why have you come all this way after me?"

"Because I didn't want you to set out for those lonely lakes with someone who is possibly a murderer."

"A *murderer*? Ahmed? That's ridiculous. What are you talking about?"

"I'm trying to tell you."

Phoebe moved closer and put her hand on Leah's knee. "Mrs. Harding, about six months ago, an old market gardener and his young wife were found dead in an isolated homestead some miles from Pratapur. According to the

superintendent of police, it was first thought that they had
killed each other, the old man in a jealous rage, the woman
defending herself, but when it was found that they had
been robbed, it was declared a murder. One of the man's
sons was arrested but later released for lack of evidence.
The woman was known to have had lovers and it was believed that one of these was the killer."

"What has this to do with Ahmed?"

"Wait, I haven't finished. The superintendent told Dr.
Macleod that recently there had been new evidence, that a
woman from a nearby village had come forward with information about her husband. What this was, the superintendent would not say, but Dr. Macleod gathered that this
husband had not been seen for months and that no one
knew where he was."

"And you think that he is here, that he is Ahmed? What
nonsense!"

"I don't think that it is nonsense, and I beg you to think
—think dispassionately if you can. You don't want to believe it because you so much want to go to those lakes, but
it fits, doesn't it? The time Ahmed came to Kashmir, the
letter, Ahmed's fear."

For a few moments Leah was silent. Then she pushed
Phoebe's hand away and said, "I think you are making a
far-fetched and unwarranted assumption, a wild guess."

"Perhaps I am, but it's not a risk worth taking. Give up
this journey."

"Go back? Not go to the lakes? Of course I'm going."

Leah turned to face Phoebe and said, "I suppose I
should be grateful to you. I am grateful—of course I am.
You have spent the last two days of your holiday in that
stuffy little post office, worrying about me, and then coming
here."

"All for nothing," Phoebe said. "I can see from your
face that your mind is made up. You won't believe anything
against Ahmed."

"I didn't say that, but even if Ahmed has done this
terrible thing, I know that he must have had a reason, that

he did it without meaning to, to defend himself, or because he was afraid. I know Ahmed."

As Phoebe gave an exasperated sigh, Leah said, "I'll talk to Ahmed, ask him straight out."

"No!" Phoebe cried. "No, Mrs. Harding, you mustn't do that. It would be dangerous."

"Dangerous? What do you mean?"

"Dangerous for you. If Ahmed did kill that old man, he must be terrified of being found out, of anyone knowing or even guessing. He might kill again; the second time is always easier."

"Ahmed would never harm me, I know that."

"How can you be sure? But I see it's hopeless—nothing I can say will make you change your mind. Promise me, though, if you are determined to go on with this expedition, that you will say nothing to him, at least until you are back in Srinagar."

"Very well, I promise, if it will make you any easier," and Leah said slowly, looking out over the Gujar encampment at the distant mountains, "You are cross with me, Phoebe. You think that I'm being just obstinate, set on what I want to do. It's not only that. You are a strong, self-sufficient person, but Ahmed is not. He needs me, perhaps more than ever now. Leave Ahmed to me."

"Don't play at being God, Mrs. Harding," Phoebe said with a flash of temper. "Yes, I am angry, and disappointed. I may as well tell you that when I get back to my mission, I'll follow this up, perhaps go to the police."

"You must do what you think right, I suppose. If Ahmed is ever in trouble, he will have me to help him."

Phoebe got to her feet. "I see that I can do no more," she said. "At least Nabir will be with you. You should be safe while he is there."

Leah caught hold of Phoebe's hand. "You won't say anything to Nabir?"

"No, I won't. It wouldn't be fair. I've no proof."

"And you'll stay a little longer, rest and have something to eat?"

Phoebe hesitated, looking down at Leah. "I'm sorry, but I would rather not. No, I won't stay. I have some sandwiches with me and I'll go at once."

Leah watched Phoebe walk away down the ridge. Although their real farewells had been said down at the Meadow, she hoped that her friend might turn for a last look, perhaps wave, but Phoebe did not turn.

II

THE SUN beat down on the stony valley from a sky of unalloyed blue. To Leah, it seemed that she had been toiling up this path that was often more like the boulder-strewn bed of a dried-up stream, as perhaps it was, for so many hours that she had begun to lose track of time. A cloud, a cloud shadow racing over the valley would have been a relief, but today there were no clouds.

At first, in the freshness of early morning, the way had been pleasant and comparatively easy. Grazing flocks were dotted over the steep hillsides, which were still green, at least on their lower slopes, and for the first time, she had heard the herdsmen's high, fluting cry, a wild, sweet, unearthly sound. Her pony, with Gaffur at its head, jogged along, picking its way with its usual cleverness among the loose stones, and the pack-ponies, strung out behind them, made good progress. Ahmed and a ponyman carrying her picnic basket were walking together, and Nabir, as usual, brought up the rear.

As the valley closed in, the grass vanished and there was nothing under the sky except rock, jumbled boulders, and a few high patches of scree, and yet this inhospitable place had its own inhabitants, as Leah now saw. Marmots, engaging small brown creatures, stood up at the mouth of their burrows, whistling in alarm as she passed, and there were small birds she could not identify, flitting among the rocks.

The Pass came into view, sooner than she had expected yet just as she had imagined it, an abrupt saddle against the sky. It looked close, only a few miles away, but as they toiled on, up and up, it seemed to come no nearer. "A long

march," Nabir had told Ahmed, and Leah realised now that
he counted the way not in miles but in the hours it took to
cover those miles.

The path became too rough and she had to dismount;
Gaffur handed her her stick and took the bridle. It was
impossible, she soon found, to walk at more than a snail's
pace and she signed to Gaffur to go on in front; not only
did she have to pick her way, stumbling over boulders,
slipping on loose stones as the pony ahead of her was
doing, but she soon found that she was breathless. 'We are
climbing all the time,' she thought. 'We must be really high
by now.' After all, the Meadow, now far below, was over
nine thousand feet above sea level. The thought cheered
her but she longed to sit down somewhere for a good rest
and a drink; she felt as if the sun were drawing the moisture
out of her very bones and she was parched with thirst;
Ahmed, who was carrying her water-bottle, should have
been close behind instead of dawdling with the ponymen.
'What kind of an explorer would you have made, Leah,
when you wilt at the first touch of discomfort?' she asked
herself and struggled on.

Gaffur turned his head to grin at her and said something
she could not understand as he pointed ahead. Lallah came
to so sudden a halt that Leah bumped into the pony's
shaggy hindquarters. Flowing across the path, trickling in
and out of the stones, was a shallow stream; where it had
sprung from, where it was going in this arid waste, she
could not imagine, but there it was, running water, clear
and clean, an answer to a prayer.

Lallah lowered her head and drank deeply while Gaffur
crouched and did the same. Leah, leaving the path, followed the water a few yards upstream and, kneeling down,
used the palm of her hand as a cup. It was a laborious way
of drinking, but what did that matter when the water, surprisingly cold under the hot sunshine, tasted like nectar?
When she had drunk all she could, she sat down on a
boulder and looked at her watch: half past eleven; they had

been four hours on the march. Nabir had said that they would reach the foot of the Pass early in the afternoon, so it could not be much further.

From where she sat, Leah watched the head of her cavalcade arrive. There was much pushing and jostling as the ponies tried to get at the water. Ahmed knelt down for a quick drink, then came bounding over the rocky ground towards her, the water-bottle, slung over his shoulder, bumping as he came.

"Bit late in the day," she said in her most disagreeable voice, but he was not abashed; unslinging the bottle, he laid it in her lap and beckoned to the man with the picnic basket.

"Memsahib rest, eat something."

"I don't want anything."

"Long time since breakfast."

Ahmed, kneeling down, opened the basket at her feet and took out the packet of sandwiches that he had made last night. Leah looked down at him, searching his face, and he looked back, his yellow-brown eyes wide and candid, unconcerned. 'It can't be true—how could it be true? There would be something to show, some sign,' she thought, and yet yesterday, after Phoebe had gone, Leah had sat for a long time going over in her mind all that Phoebe had said, and considering all she knew, or thought she knew, of Ahmed. He had come to stand beside her chair, fidgeting a little when she had ignored him and at last asking, "What Doctor Miss Sahib want?" He had said it lightly, quite naturally, and when she had answered, "That's none of your business, Ahmed," he had accepted the rebuke with his usual cheerfulness and had only said, "Memsahib ready for lunch. Is getting late."

'I won't think about it any more, anyway not until I get back,' Leah now decided, as she had decided last night. 'I won't let it spoil the lakes,' and Ahmed, jumping up, said, "Memsahib eat and have little rest. Ahmed come back for basket. Plenty time—not much further now."

The Pass, waiting ahead, certainly loomed larger; now Leah could make out the path they would take tomorrow,

zigzagging up the almost vertical hill. Ahmed was not looking towards the Pass; shading his eyes with his hand against
the glare, he was staring back the way they had come, down
the empty, desolate valley.

"Nothing there, no one is coming," she said before she
could stop herself. Ahmed gave her a startled glance, and
turned away.

Leah sat on the boulder eating her sandwiches and trying to think of nothing at all. From the group of men and
ponies resting by the stream came a murmur of voices and
a whiff of cheap country cigarettes. She watched the laden
ponies slowly get under way again, urged on by the ponymen; after a few moments, Nabir got up and followed them;
now only Ahmed and Gaffur were left. Leaving the basket
for Ahmed to collect, Leah wandered further up the
stream.

Tufts of coarse grass were growing among the stones
beside the water, and there were other plants, one with
yellow flowers—a kind of stonewort, she thought. Suddenly
she stood still. There, growing apparently out of the rock
in this seeming wilderness, was a clump of poppies, poppies of an exquisite azure blue. Leah, staring, entranced,
remembered the Baxters telling her of the flowers she
might find growing at high altitudes. "Gentians," they had
said, "meums, primulas, edelweiss." Those she had expected to find growing near the lakes, but a poppy, here of
all places . . . and yet the Colonel had mentioned a blue
poppy. As Leah stretched out her hand to touch that blue,
she thought, 'Miracles do happen, even to me. It's a sign
I was right to go on.'

When she came back to the boulder, she saw that
Ahmed had left the water-bottle for her and the basket was
gone. Downstream, only Gaffur and the pony were waiting;
she could see the others moving slowly up the valley, growing smaller and smaller. 'Let them go,' she thought. She
would sit here a little longer, in the shade of her hat, as
there was no other shade. Perhaps from now on she would
be able to ride; perhaps when she reached the foot of the

Pass, Nabir would have made camp and her tent would be waiting for her. . . .

The tents were pitched on almost flat ground close under the abrupt rise of the Pass and facing the way they had come. From a distance, as Leah rode towards them, they looked like huge mushrooms springing up suddenly where nothing had been before. She could see busy little figures moving round this new camp, and soon a plume of smoke went up in the still air.

It was not quite three o'clock when Lallah splashed through yet another stream, the third they had crossed— or was it always the same stream, twisting and turning on its way down the valley, coming to the surface for short stretches and then burrowing underground again, as Phoebe had told her was the way of streams in these parts? On the further bank, the stony ground gave way to turf, close-cropped grass where the hobbled ponies were grazing; this green oasis filled the narrow head of the valley and, extending a short way up the slope of the hill, made a green background for the tents.

It was a strange, high, lonely place. Perhaps it was the height, over thirteen thousand feet, that made Leah feel all the short time she was there that she was in a dream, and she felt not so much giddy as floating. Nabir and the pony-men were apparently not affected, but Ahmed had a bad headache. Having made up her bed, he brought the usual tray of tea, then asked for aspirin and retired to the cook tent. It was Gaffur who came to take the tray away and Gaffur, later, who put a tin of hot water in the bathroom of her tent.

While Leah was in the tent, getting out of the clothes she had worn on the march and putting on the housecoat she wore every evening, she found that she was listening— for what she did not know. A pony was cropping the grass close behind the tent, but the usual camp sounds were oddly muted, as though they came from a long way off or as if no one cared to raise his voice here or to disturb the singing silence.

The singing, of course, was in her head. She was over-tired; every movement was an effort; perhaps she had sat too long over her tea, gazing down the valley; she was stiff and ached in every muscle and it needed an effort of will to unpack the few necessities for one night. If Ahmed could not bestir himself, she would probably have to go to the cook tent herself to warm up yesterday's stew. She would have dinner early, soon after it grew dark, and then go to bed after writing the third instalment of the letter to Hugh that she had planned to write every day of this journey. It would grow very cold up here as soon as the sun set, and there would be no fire to sit by. A long night's sleep would help her to be at her best tomorrow, the day on which she would see the lakes.

Leah found it difficult to sleep; she dozed for a while, was jerked awake—not by any sound or movement, she was sure—and lay listening to the silence in which she could hear the beating of her heart, dozed, and woke again. Her legs were aching, and she thought of the old Gujar woman; was she, too, lying awake in spite of the aspirin? Leah's mind was heavy with doubts and foreboding; try as she might, she could not put what Phoebe had told her out of her mind. She saw again Ahmed's face as he opened his letter, and she could not help remembering the bitterness in Ahmed's voice as, squatting by the camp-fire, he had talked about his wife. The bitterness and resentment, which had surprised her then, were easy to understand if the letter had warned him of his wife's betrayal. . . .

Turning restlessly on the narrow camp-bed, Leah told herself she had always known that Ahmed had his dark side, something hidden, but she had never suspected that it could be anything as dark as this. It could be true—did she believe in her heart that it was true? As Leah asked herself this question, she saw Ahmed as he had been yesterday when the Gujar children had come to sell her wild raspberries.

The two small bare-legged ragged girls and their brother had huddled together, as if for mutual protection, staring at her with round bright black eyes, like the eyes of small wary animals. The boy held out his wooden bowl of fruit, but at every movement Leah had made, they had retreated until Ahmed appeared, as he always managed to do when children were about, to shepherd them towards her, encircling them with his arms. "Goat children," he had announced, looking down at them fondly; "all same little goats," and they had certainly seemed to her as agile and packed with energy and innocent wickedness as the flocks they guarded all day.

Ahmed had been horrified when she had told him to give the children two annas each. "Much too much—empty tins what they come for." Ahmed's attitude to money had always amused her. Prodigal in many ways, encouraging her to spend extravagantly on herself—and on him—he would argue hotly if told to give a few pice to a beggar; charity, for Ahmed, certainly began, and ended, at home. The smaller girl, as they had scampered off clutching their treasure, had fallen over a tent rope and lay howling until Ahmed had picked her up, cradled her in his arms, and rocked her till the tears ceased and she was quiet, gazing up at him. Could anyone who had such love, such a gentle way with children, kill an old man with a knife?

Then Nabir had come, Leah remembered, his plaid flying, his face set, to take the child from Ahmed and, after a few sharp words, carry her down to the Gujar encampment where a group of women had gathered again. The animosity between Ahmed and Nabir was growing—she had feared that there would be a scene. Why had Ahmed made no retort? It was not like him to give way so easily.

Towards midnight Leah switched on her torch and looked at the clock; she had told Ahmed to bring her tea at five; how could she lie here sleepless until then? Getting out of bed, she put on her dressing-gown, socks, and slippers, then put the heavy cloak over her shoulders, for it was bitingly cold, and went outside.

Never before, not even from the Gujar encampment, had she seen such a blaze of stars, or stars so huge and brilliant. The heavens wheeled in cold, shining splendour above her as she began to walk up and down in front of the tent. The camp cooking fires were out long ago, yet a faint scent of woodsmoke lingered on the night air, the pure, thin air of high places. There was a line of light showing under the closed flaps of the cook tent. Ahmed was awake. She could go to him, or call him to come to her, and ask him if there was any truth in Phoebe's story. That he would tell the truth when so confronted she did not doubt, and it would be better to know, once for all—but she had promised Phoebe.

In the starlight Leah could make out the crouched shapes of surrounding hills, and behind the cook tent the Pass rose up, a dark mass against the stars. Once over the Pass, she would, Leah felt, be committed, but now she could still draw back, do as Phoebe had asked and tomorrow give the order to return the way they had come. Now was the time to make up her mind.

As she looked up at the Pass, the last barrier between her and her Promised Land, Leah knew that she would go on, come what might, that nothing could stop her, and that Ahmed would go with her. Burying her cold hands in the pockets of her cloak, lifting her head to the stars, she took a few more turns up and down, then went back to bed and fell asleep at once.

Ahmed, too, had lain awake for a long time. The pain in his head had gone, but he felt sick and wretched. He hated this godforsaken place—and what lay ahead, what waited for him? He had tried all that day to ingratiate himself with Nabir and to find out more about the country that lay beyond those lakes, but Nabir had been unforthcoming, had made it clear that he did not relish Ahmed's company and preferred to walk alone. Later, in camp, Nabir had jeered at him for giving in to a headache, for lying in the cook tent instead of getting on with the memsahib's dinner. Nabir had stood over him until he struggled up and produced some sort of meal.

As he lay staring into the darkness, Ahmed cursed Nabir and he cursed that interfering doctor miss sahib. Why had she come to the Gujar encampment? Why had she and the mem talked for so long together where he could not overhear them? Was it anything to do with him? The doctor knew something, he was sure; she had talked of Pratapur, asked him questions. What had she told his old memsahib?

He closed his eyes and, at once he was back in that hut, standing in the golden light, his shirt stained with blood, the knife still in his hand. The woman's red scarf caught the light; the old man's turban had fallen off, showing a head as bald as a gourd. The smell Ahmed would never forget was in his nostrils, a smell of coconut oil, sweat, and blood. . . .

Why must he see the hut again, why must he think of what had happened there? What was the use? But he could not help going over and over it, seeing the mistakes he had made. He should not have taken the money, yet without it there would have been no chits, no Kashmir, no chance, and he had thought himself safe after so many months until the letter came. By this time, for lack of evidence, the case would have been shelved, forgotten, if it had not been for that slut, his wife.

Ahmed sat up and lit the lantern and, with his blanket wrapped round his shoulders, read his mother's letter through again. The light was dim—he had not wanted Nabir or anyone else to know that he was awake—and he had to hold the thin sheets with their spidery writing close to the glass shade. Difficult as the letter was to decipher, there was no mistaking his mother's meaning; but he could not understand, could not begin to imagine, what, after all this time, had driven his wife, that timid, silent creature, to do what she had done. Jasmilla was used to being bullied, ordered about, and to being beaten now and then. What could Mouj have done to her, what word or act that had proved too much?

Alone, in the middle of the night, crouching by the lantern with the letter in his hand, Ahmed knew, or guessed, what it had been. Jasmilla must have had another miscarriage—no, a too premature birth—and Mouj, disappointed once again, exasperated past endurance, had spat out the word "divorce," divorce so easy for a Muslim, and had probably talked of a new wife. That was the only possible explanation, and it was a relief to know—not that it mattered now. Ahmed sighed and, folding the letter, put it back into his wallet.

For the first time, he wondered what had happened to his mother. Could she have been arrested as an accomplice? Had she been taken to the jail, held for questioning? It was Jasmilla's word against hers, and he could trust his Mouj not to weaken, never to give in. If he managed to get right away, as he had every intention of doing, he would never know what had become of her.

In his childhood and youth, he had often seen the outside of the jail, an ugly red brick building, and he had seen the convicts working on the roads, guarded by a jailer in uniform and carrying a gun; there was usually a cart full of picks and shovels drawn by the men, and once, from the bus, Ahmed had seen the jailer lying asleep in the cart with his gun beside him while the men joked and laughed among themselves. For a moment Ahmed saw himself among them, wearing the convict clothes, his head shaved. What was he thinking of? If he was caught, he would not be there—he would be hanged.

The thought almost brought him to his feet and sent him rushing out of the tent. With an effort, he calmed and forced himself to sit still. He did not believe that such a thing could happen to him, not to Ahmed, and he told himself that there was no reason to panic, that he was safe for a time at least. Soon he turned the lantern out and lay down, huddled in his blankets, but he was afraid that if he closed his eyes he would dream again. When dawn came, he struggled up and forced himself to light the fire. Tea must be ready at five, and everything, Nabir had warned him, would take a long time to cook at this altitude.

III

CLEAR, ICY WATER lapped the green turf. Leah was standing on the brink of the first lake at last. It was a small lake, smaller than she had imagined and, from its colour, far deeper than it was broad. The calm, intensely blue water, aquamarine darkening to deepest sapphire, stretched away from her to an almost sheer, snow-streaked, unapproachable rock face. A true mountain lake, it lay in its deep cup under the bare mountain, rising from hidden springs in the rock, fed by melting snow. Even in the mid-day sunshine and seen from this level, flowery sward, it was withdrawn, austere, beautiful, and strange. A cold breath rose to Leah from the surface and she saw the icebergs—yes, the promised icebergs were there—gleaming blocks of ice like two huge swans transfixed in the blue water.

When Leah had crossed the packed snow and ice of the glacier and stood on the far side of the Pass above the steep descent, there had been no sign of the lakes. She had looked down at a wide lush green valley; there were no trees and the mountains that rose up on either side were bare, but between them, instead of yesterday's stony waste, the rich grass went on for miles and miles, seemingly for ever. Gaffur had handed her the binoculars, and through them she had seen that down on the valley floor ponies—wild mares, perhaps—and their foals were grazing beside a stream that flowed from the glacier's piled-up moraine and reflected the sky in its gentle curves; even from that height, she had seen that the grass was full of flowers.

Here at last was her Promised Land, flowing with milk and honey, and Leah had wished that she had wings and could soar out and down on the limpid air, but the path down had not been as awe-inspiring as she had feared. Gaffur and the ponyman had led the way with Lallah, while she had followed cautiously, trying not to look down the sheer drop. It was only when she reached the bottom and looked back, following the line of the path to the summit, that she had realised how precarious the descent would be for laden ponies. Standing on the packed snow below the moraine, which soon gave way to grass, she had asked herself if she ought to wait until all the ponies were safely down. Leah had not wanted to wait; Nabir knew his own business; what help could she be? And when she had turned her back on the Pass she forgot all about Nabir and the ponies. All round her, the flowers she had been promised starred the grass; Phoebe's magenta primulas were everywhere and, at Leah's feet, deep purple primulas with almost black buds and long stalks grew out of the snow.

The sun had been warm on her back when she rode on, eager to see what other delights this green valley had to offer; the scent of grass and flowers had flowed over her and the long-maned mares, unafraid, had lifted their heads to gaze at her as she passed. The valley had opened up to become a grassy mountain-ringed plateau, stretching into the hazy distance, and Leah had thought that a long ride still lay before her until Gaffur ran up to turn Lallah towards the range of rocky hills on their left. The pony, as if she knew that the end of the journey was near, had pricked her ears and quickened her pace. As the scent of sun-warmed thyme came to meet them, Leah had seen the gleam of water. . . .

Gaffur unsaddled the pony and put the picnic basket and her folded cloak on the grass beside Leah. She had been too eager to set out to waste time on breakfast and she now realised how hungry she was. As she ate, she looked back the way they had come. Gaffur and the ponyman were sitting some way off with their backs turned to her, but there was no sign of the rest of her cavalcade; surely it should have been in sight by now?

The other lake must be somewhere close, hidden by the

rise of hill behind her, for she saw that an overspill, which could only be from one lake to another, was falling over a rock ledge in a gentle cascade that made no ripple or disturbance on the still water that received it. When she had finished her picnic, she would wander along the water's edge to find this second lake, but first she must decide exactly where her tent should be pitched when the ponies arrived, as they must do soon. Leah wondered vaguely why they were so long.

Just about the time Leah reached the lakes, a drama was being enacted at the Pass many grassy miles away. Ahmed was in trouble, but it was not really his fault, though Nabir insisted it was. Of course he, Ahmed, had had to let the pony go at the last second—surely no one expected him to go over the edge with the wretched animal! That the load, which included his bedding roll and most of his pots and pans, had begun to slip, upsetting the pony's balance on the worst stretch of the path, was not his fault either. He had not loaded the pony, or seen to the ropes; let Nabir blame one of his own men instead of railing at him in front of everyone.

Nothing had gone right for Ahmed that morning. He had been unable to shake off the effects of his sleepless night and he was slow and clumsy, unlike his usual quick deft self. The old mem had been cross when he was late waking her with the early tea—as if half an hour mattered either way. Then he had burnt his hand while getting her breakfast, a breakfast that she had left half eaten. Gaffur, usually stupidly amiable, had answered him impertinently when he tried to impress on that oaf that he must take good care of the memsahib, who could be so rash and self-willed. Nabir, instead of rebuking Gaffur, as he should have done, had stood there looking amused, and then had told—no, ordered—him, Ahmed, to hurry up with the packing and to lend a hand with the tents.

It was unfortunate that Nabir had taken against him.

They had got on well enough together at first, although, when they had met, way back at the suspension bridge, it had been necessary to make it clear that Ahmed was of some importance, that the memsahib could only be approached through him. Here, in this wild and lonely place, he was one against many—there was no one to support him against the ponymen. The only thing to do was to bear with Nabir, to laugh and shrug it off, to bide his time and give way as gracefully as he could and allow this arrogant ponyman to think himself the king of the expedition, the one whose word was law.

The path up had been steeper than Ahmed had expected and he had found himself short of breath; when he had to rest for a moment every few yards, the ponymen, who were as tough as goats and used to these heights, had laughed at him. Arriving at last at the top, he had found that Nabir was giving the ponies a rest before they faced the descent. It would have been a relief to sit down himself and ease his aching legs—he was, after all, a plainsman, not used to glaciers and mountain passes—but he had not cared to join the group of men who sat smoking and chatting in the sunlight, and he had walked on over the ice, ignoring them when they called out to him. Knowing her as he did, he had not really expected the memsahib to wait for him as he had begged her to do, yet when there was no sign of her ahead, he had felt aggrieved and anxious. If anything went wrong at this stage, if she had an accident, it would be disastrous to his plans.

As Leah had done, Ahmed paused when he reached the far side of the Pass. He had no eyes for the view, only for the path down. It was steep, narrow, with sharp turns above an unpleasant sheer drop, and he saw that in wet weather the red exposed soil of much of its surface would indeed be slippery, if not impassable. What could the doctor miss sahib have been thinking of? This was a dangerous place. He sat down to wait for the others to catch up with him.

Then, far away, vanishing into the green distance below him, he saw small moving figures that grew smaller as he watched them—that spot of white could only be his mem's hat. His relief at knowing that she was safe was mixed with annoyance; there she went, riding away without a thought for him. She had refused to wait until the camp was dismantled and the ponies loaded, and he could not let the pony-men pack her personal belongings or his stores and cooking things. Why she had been in such a hurry he could not imagine—those lakes would not disappear. The sound of voices roused him. Ahmed stood up and moved back from the brink.

He had meant to let the ponies and everyone else go first and to bring up the rear. Nabir, of course, had other ideas and Ahmed had been told to lead one of the ponies. He had thought it better not to refuse, though this was hardly his work. "Take good care of it," Nabir had said. "Remember that your bedding roll and cooking pots are on its back."

Luckily they were more than halfway down when the pony stumbled. Ahmed had done his best to keep it on the path, hanging on to the rope in spite of the pain in his hand. The load must have begun to slip without his noticing it, and as the pony struggled to keep its footing, the pots and pans had rattled in their sack, terrifying the already terrified creature. Ahmed had stood there as it fell, watching his precious dekchis and frying pan burst loose and bounce on the rocks below.

To everyone's astonishment, the animal was not only alive when they reached it but able to struggle to its feet. The bedding roll, cushioning its fall, had saved it, or so Nabir had declared. No bones were broken, it seemed, but blood, from which Ahmed had averted his eyes, streamed from a bad cut down one leg. It had taken a long time to stop the bleeding and to get the pony over the rocks and snow onto the grass, where it had stood, trembling and shivering, with hanging head.

While this was being done, Ahmed had clambered over the rocks himself to retrieve his cooking pots; several of these would never be fit for use again. It was when he bewailed this fact, asking how they thought he was going to cook for the memsahib, that Nabir turned on him, calling him an incompetent, useless, bungling coward, and much beside, in front of the grinning ponymen.

Although Ahmed trembled with anger, there was no point in answering back. Again, he was one against many, and the only thing to do was shrug it off, to look unconcerned and to try later to ingratiate himself. Later still, when he had learned all he wanted to learn from Nabir, he would find a way of getting even with him. As the pony's load was being distributed among the other ponies, he kept in the background, and he did not protest even when the torn sack was flung at him and he was told that he could carry his battered pots himself. Removing himself a little way off, avoiding the patches of snow, he sat down on the grass and, while the others were still milling round the ponies, arranged the sack as best he could.

Nabir was making a ridiculous fuss over the pony. It was very lame but it could walk, if slowly. Surely it was time that they moved on? The memsahib would be wondering what had happened to them. Meanwhile it was pleasant sitting here in the sunshine. Looking down the valley, which promised an easy way from now on over the flower-studded grass, Ahmed began to feel better. He might have no eye for landscape but flowers—flowers and women, provided the women were young and the flowers brightly coloured —always caught his attention, and when he saw the deep purple primulas that had so delighted Leah standing on their long stalks in the melting snow, he almost forgot Nabir's insults. His first thought was to pick a bunch for his mem's tent—it would be as well to please her, to have her on his side if Nabir intended to make an unpleasantness about the pony, but he did not know how long a march still lay before them and the flowers would soon wilt in this strong sunshine. He contented himself with one flower head, which he placed behind his ear and adjusted his black hat over it. This done, he felt his self-respect almost restored.

The ponies were moving off, passing him in single file;

Nabir and one ponyman were to stay with the damaged pony, it seemed, and would bring it along as best they could. Jumping up, Ahmed shouldered his load, which, as soon as Nabir was at a safe distance, he meant to transfer to one of the ponies. As he fell in with the men, he made a joke against himself that set them all laughing. His spirits rose a little, and soon, as he walked over the springing grass, he managed to hum his favourite little nasal love song, usually a sign with him that all was going well.

When Leah came back to the camp-site from her first visit to the upper lake, she was surprised to find that there was still no sign of Ahmed or the ponies. She had spent some time near the overspill, sitting on a boulder at the water's edge, but she had been too tired to take in more than a hazy impression of a great, mountain-ringed mysterious pool, which faithfully reflected every rock face and streak of snow. There were no icebergs and yet she was sure that this second lake was even colder than the first, perhaps because at this time of the day it lay in deep shadow. 'I will come back tomorrow,' she had thought. 'Perhaps I will spend a whole day here and explore as far as I can.'

As she wandered back, she had thought comfortably of her tent, ready and waiting, and of her chair. Before long, Ahmed would bring tea. . . .

Gaffur and the ponyman were standing together, gazing in the direction of the hidden Pass. As she approached, they turned anxious faces to her. "What's the matter?" she asked. "Where is everybody?" They did not understand her, and she realised she should not have spoken sharply just because she was chilled, and suddenly anxious, too. Gaffur hung his head and mumbled something. If anything had happened, if there had been an accident back there on the Pass, it was not poor Gaffur's fault. 'An accident?' Leah thought. 'Oh, no. Not now—nothing must happen to spoil this place.'

She was wondering if she should send Gaffur back on her pony to find out what had happened when the ponyman gave an exclamation and pointed. There they were at last —a line of ponies and men, still far off, mere specks in the distance. When they came nearer, advancing with what seemed to her incredible slowness, she saw that Ahmed was a short way ahead; he must have seen the three of them standing there, for he lifted his arm in salutation. Leah looked for Nabir's red plaid, and when she could not find it, her relief changed to apprehension. Gaffur and the ponyman were chattering excitedly together. Something must be wrong.

Straining her eyes, she counted the approaching ponies again and again. There could be no mistake; one was missing. With her mind's eye she saw that path again, she saw a pony plunge and fall. Could it have taken Nabir with it? Was Nabir hurt—or worse? And if anything terrible had happened, it was largely her fault.

Leah began to shiver with cold and dread. The sun was now behind the hill and shadows were engulfing them where they stood. She tried to calm herself, to tell herself that there must be some other explanation for Nabir's absence, that he must have gone up and down that path many times, that for him it was all in the day's work, that accidents can happen without its being anyone's fault, and yet her cold sense of guilt persisted. She should have listened to Phoebe, done as everyone advised and contented herself with the Meadow. Even as she told herself this, even as tears of contrition filled her eyes, a small obstinate voice somewhere within her, in her mind or heart, said, "You know that you are still glad you came."

The ponyman was pointing again, and there, far behind the rest, still so far away that she could hardly see them, came three dark specks—surely two men and a pony? Had she imagined that she could see a glimpse of red? Gaffur must have seen it, too. His round hairy face split into a wide happy grin and he cried, "Nabir!"

PART FOUR

At the Lakes

I

Everyone, including Leah, slept late the next morning; the sun was well up, shining down on the tents, before Ahmed arrived with her tea. Half asleep, thinking that she was still at the Meadow, she sat up in bed, pulling her shawl round her shoulders, and looked out through the wide-open tent flaps expecting to see the familiar sun-striped pines, not this spread of cold blue, backed by rock and snow. For a moment she was bewildered; then she lay back on the pillows, smiling to herself, content and triumphant. She had done what she wanted to do and, whatever happened in the future, nothing could alter that fact. Here she was at the lakes and while she was here she would forget all that Phoebe had said, and would refuse to worry, or even to think, about Ahmed.

Leah planned the day. After breakfast, eaten in the sunlight by the water and before exploring the upper lake, she would check the stores with Ahmed and calculate how many days they could spend here without running too short of food. Then she would make sure that a deep pit had been dug in which all rubbish—even ashes—must be dumped; the thought of this bare, clean place being in any way desecrated through her fault was distasteful. Luckily the lake was so cold that no one would dare to profane its virgin blue with soapsuds or, worse, the touch of a sweaty body. To bathe, she was sure, would not occur to anyone, even to Ahmed, who had once assured her that he could swim "like fish," adding that all the little boys of his village swam in their river as naturally as small animals, not needing to learn. Ahmed had often given her small vivid pictures of his childhood, had talked of his tribulations in the mission, and even of the idiosyncrasies of the sahibs he had worked for, but she had found that he disliked being questioned and could be suddenly vague.

He had been vague yesterday when she tried to find out exactly what had happened at the Pass. While he was still some way off, she had known from the droop of his shoulders, the way he dragged his feet, from his hat, which he had allowed to slip to the back of his head, that something was wrong; the wilting primula stuck behind his ear had not reassured her.

Leah put her cup down and pushed the blankets back. How could she have forgotten that pony even for a moment? She must dress at once and then, before she did anything else, send for Nabir and find out how it was. The animal had been very lame when Nabir and the ponyman had at last brought it into camp, and she had gone to meet them over the grass, unable to stand and watch that agonisingly slow progress. When she had suggested washing the wound and had offered iodine and a bandage, Nabir had waved them aside and she had had to stand there and watch him plaster the wound with steaming dung, but perhaps her concern had pleased Nabir, for his grim face had relaxed into a smile. Later, he had told her that the pony would recover; he had told her so himself in halting but intelligible English. Why had he never spoken to her before in anything except Urdu, which she found difficult to understand? Did he consider it disrespectful to speak to her in her own language? Colonel Baxter had told her that well-trained servants never spoke to their employers in English if they could help it, adding that Ahmed should not be encouraged to show off. Ahmed had always interpreted for Nabir, showing himself only too willing, but this time he had been ignored.

When the camp had at last been pitched, the fire lighted, and Ahmed, though it was almost dark by then, had brought her the tea she longed for, she had tried to question him about the accident. He had shrugged his shoulders and, busying himself with pouring out, managing not to meet her eyes, had said that the pony had slipped—and no wonder on that path: "Much dangerous, much steep." He had assured her, without being asked, that he and Nabir were "verree good friends." This, she feared, was not true; for some time she had sensed the hostility between them. Before she could ask him anything else, Ahmed had hurried off to fetch his ruined saucepans to show her. All the same, she was convinced, from Nabir's manner, that Ahmed must in some way or other be responsible for the pony's fall, and she, of course, was responsible for Ahmed. She must offer to buy a new pony for Nabir.

Leah, when she had finished dressing, felt under her pillow for the amulet, the lucky charm the old Gujar woman had given her. As she put the red cord over her head, she wondered if it was going to be as lucky as she had thought. Already there had been one accident, but an accident that could have been far worse; Nabir had implied that the pony could easily have been killed. Perhaps the charm was working after all. . . . She gave the small silver thing a polish with her handkerchief and slipped it under her blouse.

It was some time before Leah left the camp and, following the shore-line, made for the upper lake. She was wearing her white hat, for the sun was strong—the butterfly-wing hatpin was the exact blue of the water beside her—and she carried her binoculars and small satchel. Gaffur had run after her with her stick and had followed until she waved him back. Gaffur was an unexacting companion, almost as silent and unobtrusive as her shadow, but today she wanted to be alone. She was weary of all of them, of Ahmed and Nabir and even Gaffur, still upset about the pony. A few hours of solitude with only the lakes for company would be a relief.

Ahmed had protested when she said that she intended to go alone: "Nabir not like, Nabir be angry," and she had been forced to be quite cross with him before he gave in. "If Memsahib not back tea-time, Ahmed come to look for

Memsahib," he had said. Luckily Nabir had not been present or he, in his bland way, might have pretended not to understand and have sent Gaffur after her. Long before she had finished checking the stores with Ahmed, Nabir had ridden off on one of the ponies to look for a party of Gujars who were usually to be found grazing their flocks far down the grassy valley. Gujars, it seemed, were specialists in the treatment of injured animals and he hoped to get some healing ointment from them.

Leah climbed over the low rocks beside the overspill, looked back briefly at the sparkling blue water behind her, noting that the icebergs had drifted further away in the night, and turned her attention to the second lake, which she now saw was a little smaller than the first. Her hazy impressions of yesterday were confirmed; the still water reflected an upside-down faithful reproduction of the opposite mountains, with their streaks and gullies of snow. The silence, except for the faint murmur of the overspill, was complete; her busy camp might have been miles away instead of just round the corner. The deep, still lake was indeed mysterious and withdrawn, almost entirely surrounded by the bare mountains, unapproachable on all sides except this. To her right, the rock on which she stood gave way to grass, a strip of emerald green as smooth as a lawn between the lake and the hill that hid the camp. Leah roused herself from what was almost a trance induced by the dreaming silence and went on, her feet in their well-worn chappals making no sound on the short turf.

The grass verge ended at a trickle of a stream that spent itself in the lake; if she crossed it, stepping on the stones in its shallow bed, she could easily climb a sloping ledge in the rock and look down into the still water below, which, from its colour, a green-blue that was almost black, must be very deep; but the ledge, after a few yards, ended abruptly at a sheer rock face and it would be impossible to go any further round the lake.

To her right the hillside sloped back, forming a narrow, sunny, boulder-strewn gully down which the stream ran, and she thought that she could make out a suggestion of a path winding up to the skyline; if she followed it, what would she see? A wide spread of new country? A line of snow peaks—or only another hill to cross? Not today, Leah thought; perhaps tomorrow. Meanwhile, here at the gully's foot was a perfect resting place, a level stretch of ground raised a few feet above the lake. Leah sat down on the grass and gazed about her.

From where she sat, the reflections were broken by bands of changing colours that perhaps marked the course of hidden currents; the water was gently moving, not flowing so much as stirring, breathing. . . . She must ask Nabir if there were any legends about this lake. It was easy to believe that something, some huge silver-scaled fish or a sacred serpent, lived down there and might, on moonlit nights, rise briefly to the surface—a benign something, surely? There was nothing sinister about the lake in spite of the frowning precipices that hemmed it in. Presently she took up the binoculars and turned them on the opposite mountains, searching the rock ledges. She might see an ibex, a mountain sheep, perhaps; there should have been marmots; but nothing moved, not even the flicker of a bird's wing. If there was any form of life in this enchanted place, it must be in the water below her. Leah put the binoculars down.

There would be room on the grass below the gully for a tent, pitched facing the lake and the morning sunshine. She felt that she was becoming quite a connoisseur of camp-sites: this one would be the most beautiful and unusual so far, and hidden, absolutely private, but the sunshine would vanish in the early afternoon, the shadows grow quickly, the silence and the sense of mystery perhaps become overpowering, the mountains seem too close. There would be room, too, for the cook tent, and water could easily be carried from the stream, but did she want to bring Ahmed or anyone else here? Anyway, Nabir would be certain to object.

Dismissing the thought from her mind, Leah opened

her satchel to see what Ahmed had provided for luncheon. After it, she would have a short sleep, using the satchel and her folded waistcoat as a pillow. Then, if she felt like it, she might climb a short way up the gully and look down at the lakes from a greater height before wandering back to camp.

Leah would have been vexed if she had known that while she slept Ahmed had followed in her footsteps along the shore of the lake and had stood only a few feet away, looking down at her. He had been resting in the cook tent when Nabir had ridden into camp, and Nabir had asked at once where the memsahib was, had reproached him for letting the old lady go alone to the upper lake—a place, according to Nabir, where no one should linger—and he, Ahmed, had been peremptorily sent off to see that no harm had come to her. Smarting from Nabir's words, Ahmed had crossed the rocks by the overspill and, as Leah had done, followed the grass verge, but he skipped easily over the stream and climbed the gently sloping rock ledge.

The wild beauty of lake and mountain meant nothing to him; he thought it a gloomy and depressing place, but as he paused on the ledge above the lake, he could not help being a little awed: the still water lying a few feet below him seemed unnaturally frightening and deep. Ahmed drew back, pressing himself against the rock wall behind him and turned to look up the gully, wondering where the memsahib could be. Before he had time to be anxious, he saw her lying on her back on the grass with her hat over her face.

Ahmed knew better than to wake her. He withdrew cautiously and walked the short distance back to the camp to report to Nabir that all was well. The two lakes, so different, were yet so close. . . . If the memsahib wanted anything, if she called out, Ahmed was sure that even in the cook tent he would hear her. It seemed to him that Nabir had been not only unduly anxious, but officious, and he had a good mind to tell him so.

.   .   .

Leah stood still, grasping her stick and frowning. She
had slept a long time, and when she woke, the far side of
the lake and the head of the gully still caught the sunlight,
but the grass she was lying on was in deep shadow and she
had hurried as quickly as she could back to camp. But what
was this? Another tent was pitched not far from her own
and facing the lake and behind it was another cook tent. A
group of men were milling round and it looked as if most
of her own ponymen must be fraternising with these newcomers; Nabir was among them, but at first she could not
see Ahmed, and then she spotted him in his pink shirt
sleeves and black hat, squatting in front of his own cook
fire, his back turned to her, and talking to a stranger. Far
from worrying about her, there he was, gossiping.

As she advanced slowly, she saw a solitary figure at the
edge of the water, a tall man wearing shorts and a bush
shirt, standing with his arms folded and staring in an entranced way at the icebergs, her icebergs, which had moved
again and were now floating side by side in the centre of
the lake; in the evening sunlight they shone and sparkled
like two immense diamonds. She could not see the man's
face but she was sure that he was white—one of her own
kind, unfortunately—a holiday-maker, another missionary,
or a service man on leave. Phoebe had said that there would
be no one, but even here . . . Leah gritted her teeth with
annoyance.

She kept a wary eye on the stranger as she walked to her
tent. There was a chance that he might not turn round
before she reached it—not that there was much hope of
avoiding an encounter sooner or later without being rude.
Before she could slip into the shelter of her tent, he swung
round, stood staring in what she thought was an almost
discourteous way, and then strolled over the grass towards
her.

"How do you do, Mrs. Livingstone."

He could not have shaved for days and his beard—or,

rather, stubble—was gingery, the same colour as the too long, unsoldierly hair that touched the back of his collar. His bush shirt was stained and crumpled, his boots dusty and worn, and the tweed hat, of the kind bought by tourists in Srinagar, had a hole in the crown, as she saw when he took it off to her, but there was about him a look, or air, that was carelessly lordly. His blue eyes, as blue as her own, were looking at her with incredulous amusement.

Leah drew herself up and said in what she hoped was a severe voice, "You seem surprised to see me."

He laughed, a pleasant, easy laugh and said, "Well, I must admit I am. I've been nearly two weeks in these mountains, crossed two ranges and had begun to think I'd reached the back of beyond."

"Only to find an old woman here before you. That must be a shock."

"Most disconcerting! When I came over that hill and saw your tents, I was put out, to say the least. You see, I've seen no one except a few nomads, and when I learnt from your ponyman that a memsahib was camping here I would have run away if it had not been for this lake—amazing, isn't it?—and that my men and ponies have had a long hard day."

"There's room for us both, I suppose," Leah said. "It's a recognised camping site, after all. Will you be staying long?"

His face was solemn now, but she knew from his eyes that he was still laughing at her as he said, "Only for tonight. Don't worry, I'll be off at dawn. My leave is nearly up and I'm on my way back to civilisation, so called."

"You are not a missionary, are you?"

"A missionary? Good God, no! Do I look like one?"

"Missionaries are not different from anyone else, only kinder," Leah told him. "That's something I've learnt lately. A soldier, then? A soldier on leave? Forgive me—since I came here, although my grandson is a soldier, too, I sometimes forget there's a war on. It was unpardonable of me to have been so rude and unwelcoming, but I, too, thought that at last I had reached the back of beyond."

His expression changed and he said gently, "I understand. I'll make myself scarce, keep out of your way while I'm here."

Leah took a step towards him. "Oh, no! I didn't mean—" she cried, incoherent in her annoyance with herself. "Won't you have tea with me? I was about to call Ahmed, my servant, to bring me some. I should like to hear about your travels."

"That's kind of you, but I must wash and brush up a bit first; I'm in no fit state for a tea-party, and it would be a party with such an unusual and charming lady."

"You must be Irish," Leah said, smiling and at ease again.

"English. Boyd Summers is the name. Tim Boyd Summers."

"And I am Leah Harding. Would you please shout for Ahmed? He's so engrossed gossiping with your man that he won't hear me."

Ahmed was not gossiping; he was listening while the other man talked, and he did not at once hear the shouting. The man sitting opposite him on the other side of the fire, holding in his mittened hands a mug of tea that Ahmed had given him, broke off what he was saying in the middle of a sentence, cocked his head—a middle-aged ugly head with grizzled hair under a round black hat, not unlike Ahmed's own, and sharp bright eyes in one of which was a pronounced squint—and said, "That's my sahib calling. You say that your name is Ahmed these days—yes, yes, I know, only because of the bother over your chits; great misfortune to lose one's chits, so expensive to buy new ones. . . . I wonder how you managed it? Well, Ahmed, don't you recognise your name when you hear it? Better hurry, he's easy-going but he doesn't like to be kept waiting."

As Ahmed stubbed out his cigarette, putting the butt into his waistcoat pocket, and scrambled to his feet, Dost Mohammed said, "Why should the sahib call you, not me? Your mem must be back."

For the last hour, at least, Ahmed had forgotten all about Leah. When the newcomers arrived, he had been busy making a curry of potatoes and dried beans—he had no meat or fish—a meal that would also do for himself. One of the ponymen, seeing a cavalcade coming over the hill from the mountainous country beyond, had called out, and Ahmed, looking up, had seen the line of men and ponies descending the winding track that Nabir had said was seldom used. His first instinct had been to hide, but almost at once, even before he noticed the tall sahib walking ahead, he had realised that these strangers were not looking for him. They were coming from the wrong direction, for one thing; anyone following his trail would come from the Meadow.

Nabir had gone to meet the sahib and his head ponyman, and the three of them had stood talking together. Ahmed, watching from a distance, had seen Nabir gesticulate towards the lake, perhaps advising on a suitable campsite. When the weary ponies had been unloaded and the tents had been pitched, the ponymen from both camps had foregathered to drink tea and exchange news. Ahmed, listening on the outskirts, his cooking forgotten, had soon learned that the strangers had travelled far and were now on their way back to Srinagar by way of the Pass and the Meadow. When he tried to insinuate himself into their circle, he had been ignored, and when he asked a few questions, they had pretended not to understand. Discouraged, he had withdrawn and, on the way back to his own fire, had passed close to the other cook tent, where a small shabby man he had not noticed before, perhaps because he must be the sahib's personal servant and had been busy in the tent, looked up from the fire he was trying to light.

Ahmed stared back unbelievingly. That Dost Mohammed, who knew so much about the former Aziz, should

turn up again—here, of all places—was a great shock, far
worse than the doctor miss sahib's visit to the Gujar encampment. It was too late to retreat. The only thing to do
was to try and show only a natural surprise. "Old Two-
Ways!" he cried with unnatural heartiness. "Old Two-
Ways! What are you doing here? I thought you were going
back to Delhi."

"So did I."

"What happened?"

"I got the sack, that's all. My memsahib, may she rot,
lost a brooch. I hadn't touched it, of course, but she had
taken a dislike to me and had been trying to get me out. It
was an excuse."

"Too bad." Ahmed squatted down and gave a hand
with the fire. The juniper was green and inclined to smoke.
When at last there was a flicker of flame, Dost Mohammed
said, "When my own sahib went off to this war, about the
same time as yours, he got me that job. He meant well, but
I should have known better than to take it. I've always made
it a rule not to work for a memsahib. It's different for you
—memsahibs don't like my ugly mug."

Dost Mohammed was ugly indeed, Ahmed thought, but
there was an air of cheerful willingness about him, which
perhaps explained why his former sahib had employed him
for years. His grey tweed jacket was worn and shabby, his
white pantaloons grey with dirt; the red mittens he wore on
his dark knotted hands seemed to add the last touch of
decrepitude but he had, of course, been leading an arduous
life in these mountains.

"They must have given you at least a month's wages.
Why didn't you go back to Delhi?"

Dost Mohammed snorted. "They gave me as little as
they could, said I was lucky they didn't hand me over to the
police. As I was broke, I hung around the hotels until this
Commander sahib took me on; he wanted a man who spoke
English. When he goes back to the war—he's an officer on
some ship or other; a fighting ship, I think—I'll go back for
a rest. I need one after clambering round these mountains

like a goat. He pays me well, far more than he need, being one who knows nothing, and of course I can't spend it in this wilderness."

As he listened, Ahmed was trying to remember what in the past he had told Dost Mohammed about himself, if he had ever mentioned his village or Pratapur. He feared that it was very likely, but did it matter? He would be far away before Dost Mohammed got back to Srinagar, let alone Delhi. The old memsahib could not stay many days at the lakes; supplies would run short before long. Soon she would say, "Ahmed, we go back tomorrow," and that very night, while it was dark, he would take the path over the hill. To his surprise, the thought of leaving the old lady to journey back without him gave Ahmed a pang, which was foolish. She was quite capable of cooking for herself, and Nabir would look after her. Ahmed gave an almost imperceptible shrug, dismissing all thought of Leah from his mind, and concentrated on Dost Mohammed again.

"Well, that's my news," Dost Mohammed was saying. "What about you? How has the world been treating you since we met? I was looking forward to that good long yarn; why didn't you get in touch with me again as you promised?"

As Ahmed began an excuse, Dost Mohammed cut him short. "Never mind that now. Tell me, have you achieved that longed-for son yet? What's the news from Pratapur?"

"Pratapur? Where is that?" Ahmed said, too quickly, and knew at once that he had made a mistake, which was a pity for until then he had not done badly; his change of name had been explained quite plausibly—it was, after all, the truth, or part of the truth. Now, at the mere name of Pratapur, he had lost his head and told a foolish, useless lie.

Dost Mohammed gave him a sharp look and said, "Odd —I could have sworn you told me your village was only a few miles from Pratapur. I seem to remember. . . ."

It would be worse than useless now to retreat, and Ahmed said, as nonchalantly as he could, "Oh, no—my village is near Lucknow."

It was high time to change the subject and to avoid any more awkward questions. Dost Mohammed must be made to talk about his journey with the sahib, as Ahmed himself would soon be setting out across those very mountains. Ahmed jumped up and said, "Now that your fire is going well, you will need some water. I'll get those tins filled for you."

Although it was beneath his dignity, he would have to fill the tins himself, for Gaffur was lost among the crowd of ponymen, but it would be worth it to create a diversion. When one tin was safely on the fire, he offered to make tea for Dost Mohammed and himself in his own cook tent, an invitation that was accepted with alacrity.

There was no difficulty in getting the man to talk. For weeks Dost Mohammed, like Ahmed, had probably been made to feel an outsider among the ponymen, and now that he had a civilised person to talk to, one of his own kind, words flowed from him. All Ahmed had to do was to keep him on the subject of his travels, to ask, "Did you see many Gujars? Were you able to buy anything from them—goats' milk, for instance," and to refill the mugs and listen.

"What about your sahib?" he interrupted when he had found out all he needed to know. "Won't he be wanting something?"

"He's settled for the time being. The tent is ready and so is his chair. He's got a glass and an opener, and I've put a bottle of beer to cool in that lake; he'll help himself when he feels like it, he prefers it that way. It's always the same, every day when we get in, he sits drinking beer and looking about him. He's a great one for sitting, or standing and just looking, at what only Allah knows. Eventually he'll call for hot water. Until then we can forget him. Your memsahib must give you far more trouble. Memsahibs are the very devil. I could tell you—"

Dost Mohammed's good eye looked past Ahmed to the tents and he exclaimed, "That's my sahib calling!" For the rest of the evening there had been little time for conversation, which was just as well.

.   .   .

Dinner was nearly over. Leah looked across the table—
two small camp tables, one from each tent, joined together
for what had become almost a festive occasion, and covered
with her checked travelling rug, as she had no cloth. In the
light of the lantern standing between them on the table, she
saw that her companion was leaning back contentedly in his
chair. As their glances met, he smiled at her, a warm affec-
tionate smile as if he had known her for years instead of for
a few hours.

It had been a surprisingly successful dinner in more
ways than one. Tim—it was impossible to call him Lieutenant-Commander Boyd Summers—and she had decided,
while they were sitting outside her tent talking in an easy,
desultory way and watching evening fall over the lake, that
they would have dinner together, pooling their resources,
each contributing from their remaining stores. This, they
both had felt, must be a special dinner, a celebration. What
they wanted to celebrate, Leah was not sure. A happy encounter? The flowering of a brief and unlikely friendship?
Who could say if they would ever meet again?

Ahmed and Dost Mohammed when summoned had
seemed eager to contrive as good a dinner as they could
conjure up between them, although it meant more work for
them. When Ahmed said that he had a vegetable curry
already half made, Dost Mohammed suggested making another curry to go with it as he still had some meat left over
from the kid he had managed to buy from a party of Gujars.
Leah had agreed and had decided on apricots for dessert.
Ahmed had become quite excited, as he so easily did: his
eyes had shone, his teeth had flashed in a smile, and, not
to be outdone by Dost Mohammed, he had declared that he
would make an apricot soufflé; he still had a tin of cream,
a little gelatine, and three eggs left. The eggs he had saved
for the Memsahib's breakfasts, but since this was to be a
party . . .

Leah had laughed at this ambitious plan, but Ahmed

was not to be deterred and had hurried off to begin his preparations.

"He'll manage it somehow," Leah had told Tim. "Put the soufflé in the lake to set, I expect. I believe that Ahmed can do anything if he's interested."

"Has he been with you long?"

Could it really be only a few months? Sometimes it seemed to Leah that Ahmed had been a part of her life for a long time, that her first glimpse of him on the hotel verandah was years away. Tim had engaged Dost Mohammed at the same hotel in much the same way, which made another small bond between them. Now she looked at Tim again, at his sunburnt, freshly shaved face glowing in the lamplight; he was apparently without a care in the world, completely relaxed. It had done him good, she thought, to talk as he had done. He had told her, in as few words as possible, how he came to be in Kashmir, and then, this once told, they had agreed not to mention the war again.

Tim had lost his ship, been wounded and, after hours in the water, strafed by enemy planes, had spent three months in hospital until, apparently recovered, he had been posted to a naval base in India. It was soon realised that all was not well with him. "Nerves," Tim had said scornfully, but the doctors had sent him off on a holiday. "To cure myself, I suppose. I had always wanted to see Kashmir and it seemed too good a chance to miss." He and a brother officer, deciding on a fishing and shooting holiday, had taken a beat on a river a long way from Srinagar and engaged a shikari to organise their camp for them. "I didn't need a servant, everything had been arranged, but Dost Mohammed was such an ugly little devil, so obviously on his beam ends, that I hadn't the heart," and that, as it turned out, was lucky for Tim. When he soon discovered that he did not want to spend his leave fishing or shooting ibex, that he did not want to kill anything, only to wander off into the mountains by himself, "just looking," Dost Mohammed had proved invaluable. "As I never had been out East before, I needed someone who could speak English, and although he's no oil painting like your Ahmed, Dost Mohammed is a good little chap."

"I wonder if he was mission-trained, like Ahmed."

"No idea. I don't talk to him much, or he to me, thank goodness. Ours is a strictly business arrangement. He suits me and I suit him—or the wages I pay suit him!"

'All the same, this is a kind man,' Leah thought. 'He wouldn't worry with an old woman like me if he weren't kind. Yes, he has a heart, cares, uses his imagination.' It had been difficult to persuade him to have even one small drink of her whisky. "You may need it all before you are finished," he had said. How strange it was that she felt closer to this unknown young man than she had ever been to her own dead son, or to her beloved grandson, who had nothing in common with her. How strange that in this remote unlikely place she should meet another human being she had warmed to at once and truly liked. How fortunate I am, she thought, as she had thought before. Phoebe, Tim Boyd Summers, and Ahmed. Yes, Ahmed . . .

At dinner, when she had been thinking how good the curry was and listening to Tim as he talked of his leisurely wanderings among the mountains and of a great lonely snow peak he had seen one day at sunset, hanging like a huge gleaming pearl in the sky, she had looked up suddenly to see Ahmed standing behind Tim, about to offer him another helping. Ahmed had been listening so earnestly that the dish had begun to tilt and only a nudge from Dost Mohammed, bringing Ahmed back to himself, had prevented the rich brown sauce from spilling. Why should Ahmed be so interested? Why should he hang on Tim's words? In a few days, Ahmed and she would be on their way back to the Meadow. Dost Mohammed had taken the dish from Ahmed; the lantern had lit the little man's wrinkled face as he offered the curry to his sahib. It was a dark, ugly face, but there was something cheerful and disarming about it.

Now both Ahmed and Dost Mohammed, having put the coffee tray on the table, had gone. There was only Tim and herself facing each other in the circle of lamplight. Above their heads, an awning had been stretched in front of the tents to protect them from the heavy dew. Leah had put on her thick tweed cloak, as it was cold; her rings sparkled in the light. Tim had tidied up; he was wearing a clean shirt under the sheepskin-lined, heavily embroidered waistcoat he had found in a shop below the Third Bridge, a shop she knew well. The two of them, sitting together, were lit up like a small scene on a stage, against the dim back-cloth of the night.

"Coffee, the right ending to a good dinner," Tim said. "I'm glad I had some left to share with you. Do you know, my friend suggested that we should take only army rations with us, K rations—to save time and money, he said. I refused, point-blank. Even if we managed to supplement them with trout, that wasn't my idea of a holiday. I like my comforts."

"So do I, as a rule," Leah said. "But I would be willing to do without them if only I could stay here a little longer. Tim, if I climbed the hill behind the camp and followed the way you came, would I be able to see that snow peak of yours?"

Tim, watching her face, leaned forward and, to Leah's surprise, put his hand over hers. "Don't try to go too far, Mrs. H.," he said. "And don't stay here too long. Promise me you'll go back to that Meadow of yours when your ponyman—Nabir, isn't it?—tells you that it's time to go. Don't be headstrong. . . ."

"Now you sound like my doctor friend," Leah said. "Why must everyone try to take care of me, to prevent me? Is it because I am old? How silly!"

"Perhaps it's because we like you and don't want any harm to come to you."

"Harm, what harm? Have another cup of coffee, Tim. I wanted to bring only one of these cups with me on this expedition, but Ahmed insisted on two. Lucky, wasn't it?''

Tim sat back in his chair again. "I won't say any more. No use—you'll go your own way, I can see."

"And you'll go yours. Must you really go back tomorrow? We could have gone to the other lake again together. You know, I very nearly didn't tell you about it. I wanted to keep it to myself."

"I don't wonder."

"Are you really hoping to get as far as the Meadow in a day and a half? I should have thought that was impossible; I took three."

"After the Pass, it's all downhill, I'm told, and I want to spend a night at the Meadow, having heard so much about it from you."

"I think that after you have gone I'll move my camp to the other lake; there's a perfect site. I don't want anyone else, some stranger I wouldn't like, to come over that hill to camp beside me."

"That's not likely, and anyway would it be worth it for such a short time?"

Leah looked at him, her blue eyes twinkling, and he put back his head and laughed. "You are an obstinate woman, Mrs. H.," he said, "but don't try your luck too far. Well, I had better say good night. It's late and I must make an early start."

As he stood up, Leah felt in the pocket of her cloak and took out a fat envelope. After tea, when Tim had hurried off to see the upper lake while there was still a little light in the sky, she had gone to her tent and, after lighting the lamp, had finished the last instalment of her letter to Hugh. She had meant to post it herself when she got back to the Meadow, but this seemed too good a chance to miss.

"Will you please post this for me when you reach the Meadow? I have stamped it but if that is not enough . . ."

"Leave it to me."

"I'll repay you when we meet again."

He smiled down at her. "Take care of yourself and thank you for everything." He hesitated and then said, "I feel I should tell you that I'm cured, completely cured, of whatever the trouble was. The mountains did it, but you put the finishing touch. Well, I'm off and I won't say good-bye."

"Shall I get up tomorrow to see you go?"

"Certainly not, that would spoil it. Good night."

Leah stayed where she was a little longer, looking out at the faintly gleaming lake until Ahmed appeared suddenly at her side; she stood up to let him clear the table and then walked a short way along the edge of the water. When, shivering in the cold night air, she turned and walked back, she saw that both awning and tables had been removed. Ahmed had gone and the lantern was shining in her tent.

It was still dark, the stars shining, although dawn was not far away when Leah was woken by a pony's neigh. Tim's camp was already rousing; soon it would be gone, leaving only another black scar on the ground where the cook tent had been and a few holes, made by tent-pegs, that would soon disappear. 'Poor Tim—having to go back,' Leah thought drowsily. She would miss Lieutenant-Commander Boyd Summers, but she would have the lakes to herself again, and today she would be busy moving her own camp to the upper lake.

Warm and comfortable under her blankets, Leah lay waiting for the familiar sounds of a camp on the move: the crackle of a fire being lit (everyone must have a drink of strong tea before setting out); a tent coming down, the heavy canvas being folded and tied; ponies being loaded, with jingle of harness. Tim had promised that his departure would be as quiet as possible and she was surprised to hear, instead of the sounds she expected, raised voices, someone shouting, answering cries. Now it sounded as if her camp, too, had been alerted. Everyone seemed to be talking loudly at once; she heard Tim's voice and she thought she heard Ahmed.

Something is wrong, Leah thought as she sat up and

reached for her dressing-gown. What can have happened?

She was fumbling on the bedside table for matches when a torch shone at the entrance to her tent and, from the darkness, Tim asked, "Are you all right, Mrs. Harding? Has anyone been in here? Have you seen anyone? Sorry to disturb you like this, but there's trouble. Dost Mohammed has disappeared—vamoosed, it seems, taking my wallet with him. Better make sure that nothing is missing from your tent."

Ahmed, too, had been robbed while he slept. Instead of leaving his accumulated wages in the village post-office safe, as Leah had advised him to do, he had kept a fat wad of notes in the inner pocket of his waistcoat, which at night he hung up in the cook tent. Dost Mohammed must have drugged him, Ahmed had tearfully declared, must have put something in his food last night, as otherwise no one could have taken his money without his knowing it, and Nabir had admitted that he and Gaffur had been forced to shake Ahmed awake when Tim had roused the camp.

"I can't believe it of Dost Mohammed," Tim said to Leah. "Why now? Why here? He could have taken my wallet any time."

"But not robbed Ahmed any time," she suggested, and Tim reluctantly agreed.

Nabir made it obvious that he shared Tim's disbelief. As soon as it grew light, he organised a quick search, not only of the camps but of the near hillside and the shore-lines of both lakes. It was soon discovered that Dost Mohammed had taken his blankets and all his few belongings with him, as well as some of Tim's remaining stores; even then, Nabir, much to Ahmed's fury, searched Leah's cook tent, for what she could not imagine. "Does Nabir think Ahmed hidden Dost Mohammed under dekchi?" Ahmed sneered. "Perhaps Nabir like to search Ahmed, too, see money really gone and Ahmed not lie?" This, to Leah's surprise and disapproval, Nabir at once did, making Ahmed turn his pockets inside out and take off his hat, even looking in his shoes.

Tim, after asking her permission, questioned Ahmed in front of her, Nabir, and his own head ponyman, as it was at first thought that Ahmed had been the last person to see Dost Mohammed. Ahmed agreed readily that he and Dost Mohammed had cleared dinner away, washed up together, and later eaten together before Dost Mohammed had gone off to his own cook tent, saying that he must get some sleep as the Sahib wanted to be called early. Then one of the ponymen came forward to say that, waking sometime in the night—he could not say when—he had gone outside to relieve himself and had actually seen Dost Mohammed walking towards the Sahib's cook tent; it had been dark, but not too dark in the starlight to see a dim figure that could surely have only been the Sahib's servant. Nabir suggested in his halting English that the Sahib should ask Ahmed if he had met Dost Mohammed before, as he, Nabir, had noticed that the two had seemed friendly and had talked much together. At that, Ahmed, not waiting for Tim to speak, turned on Nabir and said rudely that doubtless Dost Mohammed, on whom he had never set eyes before yesterday, had been as glad as he to talk to someone other than ponymen.

"I can't wait any longer," Tim said finally. "My leave is up and I must get back. If the wretched little man is ahead of us, taking the same way down to Srinagar, we may well catch him up, or hear of him."

Tim's wallet, with all his papers intact and only the money gone, was found lying on the grass behind his tent. Leah offered him enough to see him back to Srinagar, but he assured her that he had arranged for money to await him at the Meadow. It was Dost Mohammed's defection that had upset Tim. "A good little chap," Tim had called him only last night.

Altogether, it was an upsetting and distressing affair for everyone. Even though Leah promised Ahmed to refund the stolen money when they got back to Srinagar, he was still bewailing his loss long after Tim and his entourage had left, and he complained to her about Nabir's overbearing behaviour. She sympathised with Ahmed and snubbed Nabir, but although she had decided that Phoebe's suspicions were unfounded, not to be thought of again, ought she to have wondered about Dost Mohammed—asked herself . . . That was absurd, unthinkable. Ahmed had said that he had never seen the man before, and the money had undoubtedly gone; no trace of it had been found.

A most unpleasant interlude, but only an interlude, Leah decided as, at last, she went to her tent to dress properly—she was wearing her cloak over her dressing-gown and a scarf tied round her hair. She had said good-bye to Tim again after all. "That would spoil it," he had said, but she refused to allow anything to be spoiled, neither their brief friendship nor her few days at the lakes. Leah was determined to forget Dost Mohammed, but as she dressed and did her hair, she saw the grizzled little man again, standing, as he had stood at dinner, behind Tim in the lamplight.

This won't do, Leah told herself crossly. My time here is too precious. Much of the morning was already gone, and today the camp must be moved to the upper lake; now, more than ever, she was determined to move there. After a late breakfast, she must send for Nabir and tell him that she had no intention of leaving the lakes the day after tomorrow as planned. He would probably make objections, try to dissuade her, but he would give in when he saw that she really meant it. Leah told herself that she did not expect much trouble from Nabir.

The argument had been going on for a long time and Leah was growing impatient. She sat in her camp-chair, flushed and cross, confronting Nabir, who stood with the spread of lake behind him, meeting her angry blue eyes calmly, courteous as always, and as firm as a rock. There was no point, he repeated in English—speaking slowly and loudly, as if to a retarded child or, perhaps, to someone slightly deaf—in moving camp to the upper lake, a most unsuitable place anyway, where, as far as he knew, no one had ever camped, when it was imperative that they leave for the Meadow early tomorrow. The Memsahib had engaged him and his men and ponies for nine days, three days each way for the journey and three days at the lakes. As she had spent an extra day at the Gujar encampment . . .

"Only two days here, after coming all this way?" Leah cried. "We have food for at least another week. I want to stay here. I will stay," but Nabir insisted gravely, politely, that they must leave tomorrow. He was booked, it seemed, to take another client down to the suspension bridge, and he had a reputation for reliability to keep up. If the Memsahib thought she could do the journey back in two days, something he did not recommend at her age, she could have her third day at the lakes, but even then it would not be worth while to move the camp. He turned to repeat this in his own language, and from the group of ponymen who had gathered a little way off, drawn there by the sound of raised voices and scenting battle, came murmurs of agreement. Everyone was against Leah; even Ahmed, standing at her side, urged her to listen to Nabir, to do as he said. "Time Memsahib leave. Memsahib seen lakes. What stay for? Top lake not good, cold, dark, no sun. No, no, Memsahib not make camp there."

Surprised at such vehemence, Leah looked up at him. Ahmed did not look well this morning—a bad colour and he seemed tense and on edge. He usually encouraged her to do what she wanted to do; why, then, was he opposing her so fiercely? Had he even seen the upper lake? Ahmed's opposition made her only more determined to have her own way. After a moment's silence, she said, "Nabir must go. I see that. I will stay with Ahmed and Gaffur, and perhaps a couple of ponies, until Nabir can come back for me."

Nabir stared at her as if this reasonable answer to the problem were something outrageous and, flinging his plaid over his shoulder, swung round to let everyone present know what she had said. At once a hubbub of protest broke out. Only Ahmed was silent.

Ahmed was busy calculating. Nabir could be back at the Meadow the day after tomorrow. Three days down to the suspension bridge, three days back, and then there would be the return journey to the lakes. . . . That was far too long a time, the food would run out, and he, Ahmed, could not possibly risk hanging about here for as long as that. The obvious answer was for him to leave this very night; then the memsahib would be forced to go back with Nabir, much the wisest way for her, but not for Ahmed. He would have a far better chance of getting clean away, of not being followed, if Nabir was not here. For him the best plan would be to take the memsahib's side against Nabir, persuade her to stay here by the blue lake, of course—the other lake was out of the question—and then, directly Nabir had gone, to slip away.

To his own surprise, Ahmed found that to leave the old mem alone in this outlandish place with only Gaffur to look after her was something, even now, he was reluctant to do. 'Think, Ahmed,' he told himself. 'There must be another way.'

It was Leah who found it. She lifted her hand to demand attention and said, "Nabir will go tomorrow as planned. When he reaches his village, he can arrange for his brother to come and fetch me. That would give me four or five days more here—there's plenty of food for that, and Nabir's brother can bring fresh supplies for the journey back."

This suggestion was received in silence. Then Nabir said reluctantly that his brother would only just be back from the suspension bridge but that, yes, he supposed that the said brother could be with the Memsahib in five days.

"Well, that's settled," Leah said briskly. "Nabir goes and I stay until his brother comes for me." As she said it, she saw that Nabir had not yet given in. The Doctor Miss Sahib, who had told him to take good care of the Memsahib, would not like it, he said. Suppose his brother was delayed? Suppose it rained?

Everyone looked up at the blue, cloudless sky and Ahmed laughed. He laughed without meaning to, from nervousness, indecision, and, without knowing it, to relieve the tension. Nabir took this innocent laugh as an insult, and advanced on Ahmed, his usually impassive face contorted with rage. Throwing up his hands, stretching his arms wide, as if asking not only the listening men but the wide plain and the sky to witness this affront, Nabir asked how an ignorant, effete plainsman, half his age, dared to question his knowledge of these mountains and their weather, let alone laugh when he—Nabir—the owner of many ponies, the head man of his village, the friend of many sahibs, spoke? Great storms blew up with awful swiftness on this side of the Pass, as he had already warned the memsahib. If she preferred to ignore the best-known and sought-after guide in all the district and to listen to this stripling, this — Words then appeared to fail Nabir.

As Ahmed skipped hastily behind Leah's chair, Nabir controlled himself. He came closer, stood looking down at her.

Leah shrank back, bewildered, even a little afraid. Nabir had been furious with Ahmed and, perhaps, with her, beside himself with anger—there had been specks of foam in his beard. The listening ponymen were muttering uneasily and she knew that Ahmed was trembling.

She had not understood what Nabir had declaimed in his own language, but she understood him now when, coming closer, he spoke gravely, earnestly, and only to her. "Memsahib, listen what Nabir say. Not safe Memsahib stay. Ahmed, he bad, Memsahib. Bad mans, bad."

Leah frowned. She pulled herself straight by the arms of the chair and, looking back at Nabir, said, "I know all about Ahmed, thank you, Nabir, and he is my business."

Her voice trembled slightly, which annoyed her; this was no time to show any weakness. She stood up and told Ahmed curtly to fetch her hat from the tent, an order he obeyed with alacrity. Nabir had retreated a few paces; she walked slowly up to him and said, trying to make her voice sound authoritative and calm yet friendly, to show Nabir that she respected him but that it was she who gave the orders, "You will leave the hurt pony with me, won't you? The animal is still lame and a few more days' rest will help. When we have moved camp, which we had better do at once, perhaps you will give me the Gujars' ointment. I'll see to the pony every day myself."

Nabir did not answer. He gave a mighty shrug that brought his wide shoulders almost to his ears and wrapped his plaid about him. His manner, as he sketched a brief salaam, a grudging acknowledgement of defeat, showed plainly to everyone that he had washed his hands of this affair. Soon the bustle of dismantling the camp and loading the ponies was under way.

No one had time to notice the eagle sailing above the plain in what had been for days an empty sky. From that height, a human would have seen only small moving specks, scattered like confetti on the grass beside the blue eye of the lake. To the eagle, making its tireless, graceful circles, every detail was clear. It watched the laden ponies and men move off in single file, leaving only the ponymen's tent standing; tomorrow this, too, would be gone. It saw the rubbish pit being filled in, the squares of flattened grass where the tents had been, the black marks left by the camp-fires. When Leah, the last to leave, skirted the edge of the lake, moving slowly under the white dot of her hat, the bird watched her go.

Although the cold round eyes noted the new camp be-ing made on the level ground below the gully, they were intent on the rock ledges and bare hillside, searching for any movement that would betray to the always tensed, pow-erful hind claw the possibility of warm live flesh, of par-tridge, pigeon, crow, martin, fox, the rare treat of the lamb of a mountain sheep or, failing these, a mouse, a snake, even a lizard. Human voices, the echo of hammering as the last tent-pegs were driven in broke the silence that had seemed to Leah more profound than silence anywhere else, but they meant nothing to the eagle, enclosed in its own azure sphere. Before long, all the ponies except the lame one and the two riding ponies returned with their drivers the way they had come to the blue lake, leaving only a small group gathered round the newly lit cook fire. When night fell and the fire flickered redly under the dark hillside, the eagle sought some rocky perch, but morning found it wheeling again above the lake.

Leah, standing in the first light at the entrance to her tent, looked up and saw the bird, the broad V of its wings black against the colourless sky, and wondered if this could be the same eagle she had seen in the void above the Gujar encampment. Had that old woman sent it to see that all was well with her and to keep guard over this new and last camp? Leah fingered the lucky charm she could feel through her dressing-gown and smiled at this fantasy, which pleased her. Nabir, with his men and ponies, must at this moment be setting out. Listening, she thought that she could hear a faint jingle and the echo of a neigh.

What did one feel when one's guardian angel went away? Free, but vulnerable? Oughtn't she to be afraid? Mist was rising from the darkness of the lake, veiling the harsh lines of the rocks. At dawn this lake was a place of shadows, of grey half-seen shapes and hidden currents; Leah almost repented leaving the sunny openness of the blue lake. Then she started and shrank back, peering out from the shelter of the tent. What were those dark, humped shapes moving beside the water? Had her imagined monster risen from the depths bringing companions with it? And someone was standing down there by the stream, a dim, motionless figure. For a moment she held her breath.

As soon as it grew light, Ahmed had crept down to the lake. He was haunted by the thought that Dost Mohammed had played yet another trick on him and bobbed up in the night. "How are you down there, Old Two-Ways? Mind you stay there. None of your tricks!" He called it softly, so as not to wake anyone, but still trying to be defiant. His voice, soft as it was, startled him, although he thought there was no one to hear, no living thing to see him, except for the ponies grazing peacefully along the grass verge.

He had not wanted to harm Dost Mohammed—he had not wholly disliked the little man. It had been all Dost Mohammed's fault, but Ahmed was seeing again that hideous congested face with the hanging tongue and his own hands dropping at last from the throat he had squeezed and squeezed. . . . With a shudder of horror, Ahmed ran and hid himself under his blankets in the cook tent.

'Of course it was Ahmed I saw,' Leah thought, although it was not like him to get up so early, and the three dark shapes she had seen were only the ponies tethered on the grass verge below her. As if to confirm this recognition, one of them lifted his head and neighed; the homely sound made her smile. The sun was rising over the mountain. Leah gave herself a shake. She was cold and must go back to bed; soon Ahmed would bring her morning tea. The long day lay before her, without Nabir, and she thought gleefully, 'Now I can do as I like and go where I want to go. Now there is no one to stop me.'

Ahmed stood once again beside the lake. It was the third day since they had moved camp and he was beginning to feel easier and more confident. The old mem and Gaffur had set off early on their ponies and would not be back for hours. He had the camp to himself, but he looked round at the tents and up the sun-filled gully before he bent down to pick up a pebble and send it skimming across the smooth, shining surface; with a last plop it disappeared, leaving only a ring of ripples to break the reflections. There was only stillness; all the same, he crossed the stream, ran up the ledge, and peered down into the deep water to see if there was any sign of the body—this he had not been able to do while the memsahib and Gaffur were in camp. There was no sign.

In the cook tent there had been no sign, either: no blood, no smell of blood, nothing to show. He had made sure, holding the lantern up, moving it to and fro in the small space. Again he had kept his head, been calm, thought of everything. For instance, not only had he collected the scattered cards but he had had the presence of mind to count them, to make sure that they were all there —he might so easily have overlooked one for Nabir to find. Nabir, for all his prying, had found nothing, no trace in either cook tent, and yet Nabir had been suspicious. . . .

Suddenly all the bravado went out of Ahmed. He slunk down from the ledge, splashed through the stream, and sat down abruptly on the stones at its mouth. He was trembling.

It had been growing late, time to get some sleep before the early start next morning, when Dost Mohammed had produced that greasy pack of cards.

"Not now. I don't care to play," he, Ahmed, had said.

"Afraid of Nabir?" Dost Mohammed had sneered. "Fasten the tent flaps, then, and no one will see us. Anyway, everyone is asleep."

It had been a foolish game requiring no skill that they had played in the dim light, sitting cross-legged opposite each other with a small cleared space between them, a game of the wretched little man's own invention, slapping down the cards, one after the other, the highest card winning the stake. Ahmed had soon grown bored, had begun to yawn. Although he had lost at first, it had then seemed that he could not help winning; the pile of notes and silver in front of him had grown bigger and bigger, but Dost Mohammed had refused to stop. Dost Mohammed, although a Mohammedan and so forbidden by his religion, was the kind who would gamble on anything—on a race, a cock-fight, the fall of a card, on which of two cockroaches would cross the floor first—and he had had no chance in the last weeks of indulging this vice.

"I'm cleaned out, Ahmed," he had said, at last. "There go all my wages. No, no, Aziz—sorry, Ahmed—this is no time to stop playing. Wait here, I'll be back in a moment. I know where I can get some more."

What effrontery the man had had! To creep into the sleeping sahib's tent and take his wallet! "The sahib is so careless," Dost Mohammed had explained. "He leaves his wallet in the pocket of his bush shirt and hangs the shirt on the back of his chair. Come on, now. I'll win the whole lot back from you, and then, when I take the sahib his tea, I'll slip the wallet back. Simple, isn't it?"

Dost Mohammed had not won. He had lost steadily and would not stop until every rupee, every anna was gone. Perhaps it would have been wiser to hand over some of the winnings, certainly it would have been prudent, but Ahmed had made no such gesture. Without money he could not set out on his long journey when the time came, and this wind-fall would prove useful indeed; he had only two months' wages with him and there was not much, he knew, in the memsahib's money belt.

As he began to gather up the money, a brief silence had fallen in which he had heard Dost Mohammed's breathing and the tent flaps moving in the cold whispering breeze that blew at night across the lakes. Then Dost Mohammed had laughed, showing his stained teeth in the lamplight as he said, "Well, Aziz, we have had our fun and it's time we got some sleep, but first give the whole lot back to me—yes, every anna of it—or I will go straight to Nabir and tell him you are Aziz, Aziz from Pratapur, Aziz who funked meeting me again in Srinagar. Aziz who is still afraid, who said his village was near Lucknow. Now what can this Aziz be afraid of? Let me think."

Cocking his grizzled head, still grinning, Dost Mohammed had felt in his jacket to produce a scrap of grimy newspaper. "What have we here?" he had asked in mock surprise. "A cutting, only a few lines from a paper I happened to glance at in Srinagar the day before the sahib and I left. I read it with much interest, as I knew it must concern an old friend, so much so that I cut it out and kept it. Apparently new evidence has come to light as to a horrid and unsolved murder committed months ago near Pratapur and the police are searching for one Aziz Hossain. Shall I read it to you?"

Dost Mohammed held the slip of paper near the lantern. He had been playing a cruel, teasing, cat-and-mouse game all this time, pretending, mocking. . . . That was a dangerous thing to do.

There had been no choice. Ahmed had only done what had been forced on him. The little man was wiry and tough but, taken by surprise, as anyone would have been by that swift spring, he had had no chance. There had been astonishingly little noise, only one sharp crack as the grizzled head had met the sharp edge of a store box, and a slight scuffling.

When Ahmed was sure that Dost Mohammed was dead and there was no sound from the camp, he had tried to calm himself, to be cool. The watch that the memsahib had given him had showed that there was not much time. The cards he had collected to put with the silver and copper coins into Dost Mohammed's pockets, but he had set the pile of notes to one side, telling himself that he would find a safe hiding place for them once he had disposed of the body.

Almost the worst part had been the short trip Ahmed made to Dost Mohammed's tent in the starlight, bending low to make himself as small as possible. If he had known then that one of the ponymen had seen him, would he have had the courage to go on? It had been necessary to light the lantern in the tent, as he had to pack all Dost Mohammed's belongings into a satchel, also to roll up the blankets and take some of the sahib's stores—rice and a tin or two. On the way back, he had made a short detour and dropped the sahib's wallet where it would be easily found.

Once he was back in his own tent again, it had taken

Ahmed some time to find the memsahib's clothes-line, unused so far, and he had begun to think that it had been left behind at the Meadow when he found it at the bottom of one of the store kiltas. There he also found an empty canvas bag, which had once held rice and presently would hold large stones or a small boulder. When all was ready, when Dost Mohammed and everything else—satchel, bag, stores—had been wrapped in the blankets and tied into a long bundle with the clothes-line, Ahmed had started out on that nightmare walk in the darkness to the upper lake, staggering under the burden on his shoulders, knowing that he must not make a sound. He had thought, at first, of the overspill; the water there was deep and it was close, but he would have been in view from the tents and a splash might well have been heard.

Luck had been with Ahmed that night. It was lucky that the sweeper boy had been left behind, lucky that Gaffur had elected to sleep in the ponymen's tent, lucky that, long ago, the memsahib had so foolishly brought a clothes-line. Above all, it was lucky that Dost Mohammed was such a small man; even so, it had seemed an interminable way along the path under the hill. Once out of sight of the camp, he had been able to use a torch; what luck again that he had hoarded two batteries for his planned journey.

When, at last, Ahmed reached the stream, he had found plenty of stones there to fill the canvas sack and the satchel. He had taken time to make a secure blanketed parcel, knotting the rope with care, making sure that the weight would not shift and would be sufficient; he had even remembered to roll up his cotton jodhpurs and take off his chappals before hoisting his burden onto his shoulder again and cautiously climbing the ledge. It had been easy, the easiest part of the whole business, to lower Dost Mohammed into the deep water. There had been scarcely a splash.

Ahmed roused himself; it was no use sitting here brooding. What was done was done; nothing could be altered now. He, Ahmed-Aziz, had been forced to do what he had done in self-protection. What else could he have done? He had made no mistake this time, as far as he could see, had been not only quick-witted but clever, although it was undoubtedly strange that Dost Mohammed should choose to decamp from this far-off place. Nabir was suspicious; that was a cause for fear, and what had the doctor miss sahib told the mem? They had taken care that he should not overhear them, but he was sure that it was something to do with him. Since then, he had caught the memsahib looking at him strangely once or twice. That cursed letter—if only it had never been written! As Ahmed got to his feet, a more cheerful thought came to him. True, tomorrow or the next day, Nabir's brother would come, but Gaffur would be posted on the hill above the lakes to watch out for him. When the men and ponies were in sight, Gaffur would be sent to meet them, and he, Ahmed, would leave, well-prepared; soon he would be far away.

Turning his back on the lake, Ahmed went slowly towards the cook tent, which the memsahib had insisted should be moved to this stony patch of ground at the entrance to the gully. Water from that trickle of a stream had now to be carried several yards further, but she, usually considerate of the comfort of those who worked for her, had waved this fact away as of no importance; Gaffur's snores, it seemed, had disturbed her.

Ever since she had overruled Nabir and transferred the camp to this detestable place, the old mem had been even more set on having her own way, even more restless and active, and today she had insisted on leaving soon after dawn to ride with Gaffur over the hills, following the path the Commander sahib had taken on his way down to these lakes; she was set on finding some mountain peak or other. Now it was growing late. The camp was in shadow. Soon it would be dark and they had not come back.

Ahmed began to pace up and down in front of the tents and he scowled at the lake, which, for the last hour, had faithfully reflected the golden evening light that still bathed the opposite mountains. Even as he looked, the gold light faded and a grey stillness slowly descended on the scene. Ahmed swung round and peered up the gully. Clouds, great piles of cloud, were rising and spreading up across the sky.

A few drops of rain fell. Ahmed looked up at the grey cloud now directly overhead and frowned. There was no wind, no thunder, only this light patter of rain, which ceased almost at once. Was this only a passing shower or a foretaste of what was to come? Where was the memsahib? What could have delayed her? Surely she, too, had seen the clouds and would have had the sense to hurry back to camp? Perhaps he ought to climb the gully and look across the hills to see if there was a sign of her and Gaffur.

Ahmed had not gone far when he paused and looked back. The rain had stopped but he did not like this ominous stillness. The lake was a strange livid colour and against it the tents stood out, unnaturally white in the increasing gloom. He remembered what Nabir had said: that if it did rain, they would have to move camp in a hurry or the stream would probably rise and flood this level ground. Ahmed gazed round him, at the steep bare hills, marked by the courses of old landslides, and at the jumbled boulders and stones that filled the gully, bisected by the faint line of the path. The stream was running past him a few feet away; was its murmuring song already louder? If they had to move the tents quickly, where could they go?

An overhang of rock, jutting out from the almost sheer hillside not far above the cook tent, caught Ahmed's eye as he turned to scan the other side of the gully. He picked his way towards it over the loose stones and saw that there was a recess under it, a hollow in the side of the hill that was almost a cave. The roof was high above his head and the floor was reasonably level; they would have to move a few small boulders, but it would be possible, if the worst happened, if the stream did flood, to pitch the memsahib's tent here. There would be no room for the cook tent; that would have to take its chance where it was.

Ahmed hurried back to the camp. He had no eyes for the wild splendour of the view. The towering crags surrounding the dark lake were now almost purple under the stormy sky, the patches and streaks of snow an icy blue. The tent ought to be moved at once, before more rain came, but he could not move it alone and would have to wait for Gaffur and the ponies. Meanwhile, he would try to erect an awning over the cook fire so that he could cook in moderate comfort.

When this had been done—the poles erected with some difficulty, for the ground was stony—Ahmed stood in the open. The light was failing fast. What could the memsahib be thinking of to go so far? If she had met with an accident, surely Gaffur would have come back for help? It was no use staring up the gully, which was too steep for ponies; they would take the hill path down to the lower lake; perhaps they had already reached it. The best thing he could do was to warm up some soup, keep a good fire going, and perhaps put a warmed stone wrapped in a cloth in the old mem's bed—the foolish woman had brought no hot-water bottle with her. . . .

A rumble of distant thunder made him start. He looked up apprehensively at the darkening sky and, as the rain came down in earnest, dived into the shelter of the cook tent.

Leah heard the thunder rolling far off among the hills when she was still miles away from camp and, as Ahmed had done, looked up at the overcast sky; she and Gaffur had started out in brilliant sunshine, riding along the path that followed the contours of the barren hills, dipping and falling across the monotonous landscape. They had met no other traveller, seen no Gujar hut or tent—not that she had wanted to see these signs of humanity, but there was not even a tree to rest the eye in this rocky wilderness. Birds were scarce and marmot burrows few and far between; there was nothing except rock, a few dark clumps of juniper, and the vast sky.

At the top of every rise, Leah had halted Lallah and looked eagerly over the undulating hills towards the horizon where the blue of distant mountain ranges was veiled in clouds. She had known there was little chance of seeing the snow peak that, since Tim's words had fired her imagination, she so much wanted to see, and yet in her heart she had been convinced she would see it if she could ride far enough. When they had paused by the first stream they came across to water the ponies and to eat their lunch, she had allowed Gaffur and the ponies only a short rest. Leah had planned to turn back at midday, the only sensible thing to do if they wanted to be in camp before dark. Sitting on the stony bank of the stream at the bottom of that shallow valley and seeing the path going on, up and up, she had told herself that there would be no harm in going a little further, just to the top of the next rise. Perhaps when they reached the top, the clouds would have lifted from the mountains. . . .

The thunder was an accusing voice in Leah's ears, telling her that she had been foolish, headstrong, and rash. She had gone too far, broken all her good resolutions, refused to listen to Gaffur. Even if the weather had not changed at such alarming speed, she doubted that they would have reached camp before dark. And she would never be sure whether she had seen Tim's snowy mountain or not. The distant rampart of clouds had lifted, as she had thought they might, lifted, parted, and closed again. She had seen a gleaming whiteness, a vague pearly shape hanging between earth and heaven. Was it a great snow peak or only another cloud? As she had stared, the clouds had gathered, formed into towering pinnacles and buttresses, and spread out over the sky.

A light, uncertain rain began to fall and Leah shivered. All that day, riding under the sun, she had been almost too warm; now, with the clouds, had come this sudden chill. She turned and signalled to Gaffur for her cloak, which was fastened into a roll behind his saddle. Her straw hat, hang-

ing by its ribbons from the satchel on his back, had been
replaced by her scarf when the sun went, and Leah was glad
of the warm folds of the cloak and the gloves she found in
its pocket. As she put them on, she looked round at the
desolate hills. It seemed to her that the light was going
unnaturally fast, even under the lowering sky; it was, after
all, still afternoon—or was it? She reached under the cloak
for her watch, pulling the gold chain out of her blouse. The
charm's red cord came with it, tangled in the chain. Leah
gave a dismayed cry as she saw that the cord was frayed and
broken. The silver amulet she so much prized, her luck, was
gone.

It had been there, hanging from its red cord, when she
had looked at her watch by the stream, but it was not there
now, nor was it lodged under her clothes. It must be lying
where she had sat by the stream, or somewhere on the path.
She must go back and look for it, now, at once.

Leah showed Gaffur the broken cord and tried to turn
her pony. Lallah refused to move, planting her hooves
firmly on the path, putting her ears back, and taking no
notice when Leah dug her heels into the rough brown
sides. Leah called to Gaffur, telling him to use his whip, but
Gaffur, for the first time, failed her. He took hold of the
bridle and, ignoring her protests and orders, led Lallah
down the path, with his own pony following after them.
When she shouted at him, even hit him on his broad shoulder with her gloved hand, he only shook his head, gestured
at the clouds above them, and plodded on.

Gaffur, of course, was right. She should be grateful to
the shaggy little ponyman for stopping her, for bringing
her to her senses. It was really raining, raining hard, and
soon it would be dark.

Leah huddled miserably on the saddle, clutching the
wet reins, for what seemed hours. Her luck had gone, no
doubt about that, and she thought of the old Gujar woman
far away on the other side of the Pass. She thought of Nabir
and what he would say if he could see her now.

She did not know where they were, or how far they still

had to go, and she was astonished when she saw that they had reached the top of the hill above the lakes. The plain below was shrouded in gathering darkness, clouds were thick on the mountains, but far away, sharp against a clear sunset sky, she saw the outline of the Pass.

"It's not raining on the Pass," she said to Gaffur as he signed for her to dismount and follow on foot the steep path down to the level ground. She was exhausted, cold, wet, and stiff and yet, as she looked at that distant rift of clear pink sky, her spirits rose and she thought, 'Perhaps I will not be punished after all. Perhaps I will get away with it. All may yet be well.'

It rained on the Pass that night—or, rather, before it was light next morning. The storm that had rumbled far off among the hills, sending advance rain clouds before it, gathered force and became one of the formidable mountain thunderstorms that Nabir had described. The wind rose, lightning flashed; the deluge broke over the lakes, whose rock walls magnified the thunder, and moved on across the plain towards the Pass.

The tumult woke Leah from an uneasy exhausted sleep. She lifted her head from the pillow and saw the lake lit by a fierce, blinding white light in which every detail of the crags was sharp and clear, a light that lasted a few seconds, gave way to inky blackness, and flashed again, as if the shutters of a giant magic lantern, the magic lantern of her childhood magnified alarmingly, were opening and closing, opening and closing. She shut her eyes and listened to the rain drumming on the canvas. This steady downpour was very different from the first light spasmodic rain that had managed to penetrate her heavy cloak, chilling her to the bone before she reached camp.

As they had passed the overspill and turned onto the lake path in the shelter of the hill, now looming above them, her pony had lifted its drooping head and neighed. An answering neigh from Nabir's lame one, tethered not far from the tents, brought Ahmed running to meet them. He was carrying an umbrella and a lantern; its warm light, bobbing towards them in the darkness, had seemed to Leah the most welcome sight she had ever seen. What she would have done without Ahmed she did not know. Expostulating, exclaiming, then falling silent when he realised how wet and tired she was, he had helped her to the tent, holding the umbrella over her, although she could not have been much wetter, and then had shouted for hot water. When she was in bed, huddled into her thick dressing-gown and shawl, he had collected the wet clothes she had struggled out of—how he would dry them she could not imagine —and had brought her a strong whisky; luckily the precious bottle was still half full. She would have liked to give Gaffur a drink, but of course he was a Muslim. Some time later, when she had fallen into a half-doze, Ahmed had loomed up beside her bed, carrying a bowl of lentil soup, and had refused to go away until she sat up and took the bowl from him. Even then he had waited, watching her from the shadows; she had felt his anxious eyes on her and she had said —crossly, she feared—"What's the matter, Ahmed? Do go away. I'm all right now," and had sneezed violently.

"Memsahib got cold," Ahmed had said and, opening her round leather case, pushed it towards her. "Memsahib take two aspirin now," and he had held the glass of whisky to her lips as if she were a child. Gazing up into his face, gilded in the lamplight, and seeing his concerned, worried look, she had done as he asked and, as she lay down again, had whispered, "I'm sorry, Ahmed."

At first, lying in bed, listening to the rain, she had been unable to get warm, and attacks of shivering and cramp had kept her awake. If only she could have had a hot bath; she was sick of washing in that enamel basin. Then she was hot, hot and cold in turns. 'Ahmed is right,' she thought. 'I have caught cold. It's only a chill. I'll be all right tomorrow. I can't be ill here.'

Worry and remorse helped to keep her awake. "Don't try to go too far," Tim had said, and that was what she had done. As she tossed and turned, she heard Phoebe Warren saying, "If you were ill . . . you would cause a lot of trouble and bother." Leah groaned and clenched her hands under the bed-clothes as she thought of Nabir's brother and his men, who would have to wait in cold discomfort on the other side of the Pass, and of Ahmed, Gaffur, of the ponies. . . . 'I should have stayed safely at the Meadow as everyone wanted me to do,' she thought. "I'm sorry," she had said to Ahmed, and now she whispered it again. "I'm sorry," and at once that rebellious inner voice, which could not be quelled, asserted that she was not sorry at all, that she regretted nothing, except perhaps that she had deliberately chosen to go on to look for Tim's snow peak when she had known very well that she ought to turn back.

Whatever happens, it will have been worth it, she told herself, and fell deeply asleep until Ahmed woke her soon after dawn.

Ahmed, too, had spent a restless night. Twice he got up from his blankets and, taking his torch, had gone out to see if the greatly swollen stream had engulfed the danger mark —his stick, stuck upright in the grass a few yards from Leah's tent. He had meant to move the memsahib's tent directly Gaffur came back, but it had been dark by then, and one glance at her face as he had held the lantern up had made him change his mind; it would have to wait until morning unless the stream spilled over in the night.

Even if he had dared to let himself sleep soundly, worry would have kept him awake. Would this sudden rush of water move the body, loosen the rope he had so securely tied—would Dost Mohammed begin to rise? Then, when he had calmed this fear—the lake was surely too deep to be disturbed by any storm—Ahmed began to wonder what he would do if the mem became really ill. 'This rain,' he thought; 'Nabir had wished it on them, because he must always be right.' Ahmed thought of the path leading up to the Pass. It must by now be impossible for laden ponies but, however slippery, perhaps not for a man. Ought he to send Gaffur to find Nabir's brother and tell him to get help from the Meadow? Would Gaffur go? 'Wait until tomorrow,' Ahmed told himself. The mem was tough; perhaps when he took in her tea early in the morning, he would find her sitting up, reading in that Bible of hers as she did every day, none the worse except for a slight cold. On this comforting thought he managed to doze for a while.

Dawn was seeping into the tent when, suddenly wide awake, he flung his blankets off, struggled into his jacket, and, clapping his hat on his head—an automatic gesture—dashed out of the cook tent. The voice of the stream was louder, and he knew, even before he saw, that it had burst its banks and was pouring across the grass towards the tent. He shouted for Gaffur, who lay curled by the dead fire under the awning, turned his collar up, and plunged again into the rain.

Ahmed's urgent voice failed to rouse Leah, and he was forced to touch the mound of her feet to wake her. "Quick, Memsahib, quick!" she heard him say as she opened her eyes.

He flung her dressing-gown on the bed and turned to collect her belongings: shoes, clothes, books, clock—everything was crammed into her bags. "No time dress," he said over his shoulder as she lowered her feet to the ground and groped for her slippers. The shock of cold water running against her ankles made her cry out. She stared round, dazed and stupid, until she realised that the stream, swollen with rain, had flooded the camp as Nabir had said it would.

Ahmed heaved her bags onto the bed, felt under her pillow for her money belt, which she had forgotten, and thrust it into her hands. He bent down and put her socks and chappals onto her feet. "No time, no time," he said when she protested. Gaffur, streaming with rain, was standing just inside the tent holding an umbrella and her cloak; as Ahmed put it round her shoulders, she found it was still damp and smelling of smoke. He tied her shawl over her head and, before she realised what he was doing, picked her up as if she were a tweed-covered bundle and staggered with her through the rain to the cook tent, splashing and cursing, while Gaffur hurried beside them, trying to hold the umbrella over her.

Leah was dumped unceremoniously on the ground under the awning, and Ahmed dashed back to her tent. The fire, quickly tended by Gaffur, was smoking wetly but showing a few tongues of flame. He, too, soon ran out into the rain again, but she was relieved to see that he had managed to balance a saucepan of water on Ahmed's grid. 'When it boils, if it ever boils, I'll make tea for all of us, she thought,' and wondered if she would find the energy to move. Leah felt wretched and her whole body was aching; she sat with her feet drawn up, her arms round her knees, trying to stop shivering.

The rain beat down on the awning as if it would never stop; smoke eddied round her and made her cough. She watched apathetically as Ahmed and Gaffur brought her bedding wrapped in the ground sheet and her folded camp-bed and shoved them into the cook tent, then splashed back to her tent. Gaffur fetched one of the ponies, which stood patiently until they had collapsed the tent, folded it with difficulty, and dragged it onto the poor creature's back. They ran about, collecting the tent-pegs, putting the poles together, and rolling up the wet striped rug, all in inches of water and driving rain, until only the enamel basin and her chamber-pot, sitting forlornly on its box, were left. Her straw hat, she saw, was floating round and round, moving towards the lake. Leah began to laugh, although it hurt her throat and there was really nothing to laugh about, as Gaffur, at a shout from Ahmed, ran to fetch these objects. When Gaffur came back, he held out the blue-winged hat-pin; she took it thankfully, for it would have grieved her to lose it. As she looked up again, she realised that Ahmed and Gaffur, standing beside the pony in the pouring rain, were having an argument; at least, Gaffur was protesting about something, plucking at Ahmed's jacket to get his attention, then pointing up the gully and shaking his shaggy head. Although they were only a few yards from the cook tent, she could not hear what Gaffur was saying through the drumming of the rain, but she thought she heard the word "Nabir" repeated several times. Ahmed shrugged and must have given some sharp retort, for Gaffur gave in, hung his head and took the pony's rope that Ahmed held out to him.

The pony, dragged by Gaffur, pushed from behind by Ahmed, reluctantly began to climb the path up the gully, and disappeared out of her view. "Move the tent," Ahmed had said, but where they would move it to she could not imagine. Poor Ahmed, he must be soaked through, and poor Gaffur—they were working hard, doing all they could for her while she sat here in what shelter and comfort there was. 'I must do something to help,' she thought.

Leah crawled into the cook tent and searched in the store boxes until she had assembled mugs, tea, sugar, a tin of milk, and the only spoon she could find. The water in the pan was steaming and she hoped they would not be too long. She crouched under the awning, watching the rain falling in a slanting curtain across the grey lake. Her heavy eyelids closed; she dozed, roused herself to make up the fire, poking pieces of juniper cautiously under the pan balanced precariously on the grid, and dozed again. She was dimly aware of Ahmed stooping under the awning and of Gaffur going in and out of the cook tent; dimly she heard their voices but made no effort to understand what they were saying. When, after what seemed hours, she roused herself fully, Ahmed was squatting on the other side of the fire looking anxiously at her.

"Where is Gaffur?" she asked, and when she saw that he was crouched in the cook tent, she said, "Tell him to come and sit by the fire; he must be soaked through. I'll make tea for all of us."

Ahmed objected; he was scandalised at the thought of such familiarity, even at such a time. The memsahib to sit side by side, cheek by jowl, with an uncouth ponyman! Leah cut him short, telling him to open the tin of condensed milk while she threw spoonfuls of tea onto the now boiling water. It was a strange way of making tea, 'And a strange tea-party,' she thought, 'the strangest she had ever attended.' She saw a clear picture of the three of them, huddled under the awning, united in damp discomfort round the smoking fire, she in her cloak and shawl, her white hair escaping from under its net, Ahmed unshaven and sullen, Gaffur grinning in an embarrassed way and giving out a strong ripe smell, and each holding a mug of hot strong tea, which she at least found comforting. She thought suddenly, 'What would Geoffrey say if he could see me now?' She had not given his memory a thought for weeks, yet there he was, staring at her disapprovingly, shaking his head at her, as he had often done. It was Ahmed, of course, who sat opposite her, looking down his nose, pursing his lips. Was she becoming light-headed? No, her body might fail her but her mind was as clear as ever. . . .

Ahmed took the empty mug from her and made a sign to Gaffur. She was pulled gently to her feet, supported from under the awning and out into the rain. Ahmed and Gaffur between them were carrying her over the stones and up the gully; she was sitting on their crossed hands, her arms clutching their shoulders. "I can walk," she heard herself say. "Put me down at once."

"Nearly there," Ahmed panted. "Memsahib soon back in bed. Best place till rain goes."

Through the falling rain she saw her tent, standing a little askew on the rough ground in the mouth of what looked like a cave; the tent flaps were turned back to show her bed ready and waiting for her. Everything was in place: her table, her chair, her camp-stool, her bags; even the striped rug was spread over the stones.

When they put her down, she stood holding the tent-pole—her head was swimming again—and said humbly, gratefully, "Thank you, Ahmed—Ahmed, and Gaffur, too."

It rained all that day and the next. The stream roared down the gully, including the grassy terrace in its new course to the lake. Water lapped the stones below the cook tent but spread no further. In the tent, Ahmed and Gaffur existed as best they could and managed somehow to keep the fire going under the awning; the pile of juniper was damp, although they had spread the ground sheet over it, and it had to be dried out. The water Ahmed heated, everything he tried to cook, tasted and smelt of smoke. It was as well, perhaps, that the mem did not want to eat; tea, a little whisky, a spoonful or two of cream cheese was all she had taken in two days. Even then, their supplies were running low. He had laid in a small stock for his own journey, secreting it in his knapsack, which, unknown to Leah, he had hidden under her bed.

The knapsack had been heavy and he had gone through his few belongings to see if there was anything he could leave behind, and when he had come on his little bag of sewing things Ahmed had paused. The memsahib had refused to let him darn her socks—he who had mended and sewn on buttons for all his sahibs—but even she would have had to admit he had made a good job that night in the cook tent, the night that Dost Mohammed had died, when he unpicked the lining of his hat and sewed it up again over the folded notes, the money that had been such a problem to hide. It had taken a long time and he had been afraid that daylight would begin to show under the tent flaps before he had finished.

Ahmed was worried over the shortage of food and he worried about the weather, but most of all he worried about Leah, for her sake and for his own. If she became really ill, he would be in a dilemma. He could not stay here when the rain stopped and Nabir's brother came, and he was reluctant to leave the mem unless she improved. She had a bad cold, coughed a great deal, and, he feared, had some fever; her face was always flushed and looked swollen and he did not like the sound of her breathing, but so far she had managed to look after herself, to totter the few steps to the bathroom, to wash and keep herself tidy. Most of the time she spent staring out at the rain. Often, when he came to have a look at her, as he did from time to time, she would be holding that small black Bible of hers, even if she was not reading it. He disliked seeing it in her hands; the sight of it made him think of his mission days.

To keep warm, Leah stayed in bed, sitting upright against the pillows, under which, to make them higher, she had put all her clothes and her folded cloak; as the days went on, she found it increasingly difficult to breathe. Every four hours, she took an aspirin in a little whisky; there were not many aspirins left and she almost regretted giving six to the old Gujar woman. Leah worried, too, about Ahmed and Gaffur, about the food running out, about the ponies. "Are the ponies safe?" she had asked Ahmed in a painful croak. "Where are the ponies?" And for a time she had refused to believe him when he assured her that the lake had not risen, that the ponies were still grazing in the shelter of the hill.

To occupy her mind, she opened the Bible and turned again to the Psalms. There was no need to read; she knew at least one of them by heart. Her lips moved silently, repeating the words, "I will lift up mine eyes . . ." She lifted her eyes, but the hills were hidden in cloud and rain—no help from them today. "My help cometh from the Lord, which made heaven and earth." Did she really believe that, as Phoebe undoubtedly did? Leah shut the book and turned on her side.

Lying with her eyes closed, she thought, 'I would have been all right, in spite of what everyone said; I would have succeeded if it had not been for the rain. It's unfair, unfair.'

Frustration and annoyance with herself had made her wretched, but now her chest hurt and she feared that she was beginning to be really ill. Presently, she asked herself, 'Can this be pneumonia?' She could not have pneumonia here, without drugs or help—that would be too horrible a way to die. Perhaps, before it came to that, God—Phoebe Warren's compassionate God—would intervene, find some other way out for her. Why should He? In life, she had given Him little thought. And it was God, she supposed, who had sent the rain—she would ask no favours of Him. . . .

Ahmed, coming quietly at midday with a bowl of soup, found Leah sleeping. He listened for a few moments to her heavy breathing and, leaving the bowl on the table beside her, went away.

The rain stopped early in the morning four days after it had begun; it thinned to a light drizzle and then ceased. Clouds hung for a time over the hills and lifted slowly; soon the sun shone; mist, whorls, and drifting scarves of vapour still hid the lake. The eagle reappeared.

Leah saw the sunlight on the opposite wall of the gully and roused herself from a half-dream. The time had passed for her in a daze of pain and discomfort; now, as she sat up against the pillows, she knew that she was better; she felt less ill, and far more hopeful. The rain had stopped and the sun was shining; the path down from the Pass would soon dry and Nabir's brother, who must have been waiting for days on the other side of the glacier, would be able to get here before all the food was finished. If she was still ill when he arrived, they would arrange for her to be carried back to the Meadow where there might be a doctor or a nurse among the campers. But she would not be ill; she was improving every minute; she no longer even contemplated leaving this world, where there was still so much to do and see. 'I must get up,' Leah thought. 'At least I can sit outside in the sunshine,' and she called for Ahmed.

Her voice was still feeble but Ahmed must have heard it. There he was by her bedside, holding a cup of milk.

"Memsahib better!" he exclaimed as he bent over her.

His relief and pleasure touched her. Leah looked up into his face, seeing the dark, curling eyelashes, the thin cheeks, the slightly hooked nose, the face she knew so well. She not only liked and relied on Ahmed, he had become dear to her—whatever Phoebe had said, whatever he had done.

"I'm much better, Ahmed," she told him. "Give me my

dressing-gown and then put my chair outside the tent. I'll sit there for a bit; the sunshine will do me good."

Ahmed protested, begging her to wait until she was stronger, at least to drink the milk first, which, to please him, she did.

"Who is the old woman, you or me?" she said as she gave him the empty cup. "Of course I won't get another chill, and it's weakening to lie long in bed. Nabir's brother will soon be here and I must be well by then."

"Gaffur say if sun shine all day on Pass, path dry. Nabir's brother come perhaps tomorrow in evening."

"Then there's no time to waste. Please go and make me some good strong soup. I'll call out if I need you."

Having installed Leah in her chair with a rug wrapped round her knees and the binoculars and writing-case she had asked for in her lap, Ahmed hurried back to the cook tent to tell Gaffur, who was busy spreading their blankets on the sunlit stones to dry, that the memsahib was better, that it looked as if she would soon be well. It was certain that the sun was shining, that the grey misery of the last days had gone. Although it was unlikely that Nabir's brother could arrive until late tomorrow at the earliest, perhaps—if the mem continued to improve and was more herself this evening—he, Ahmed, would retrieve his knapsack and slip quietly away at dawn. As Ahmed squatted by the fire, stirring his last spoonful of Bovril in boiling water, the sound of his favourite song floated out over the lake.

The sun, now directly overhead, shone down on the gully, penetrating, Leah felt, into her bones; it was comforting, healing, almost too warm; soon she threw the rug off. The soup had strengthened her and she felt less weak, but she made no attempt to begin another letter to Hugh, as she had meant to do. It was enough to bask in the sunshine and to feel confidence and well-being slowly return. Below her, Ahmed and Gaffur were sitting by the fire in front of the cook tent eating their midday rice, and she could see the ponies, their wet coats steaming as they moved along the grass verge. The mist was rising, drifting away from the lake, and the opposite mountains were again taking on their clear, strong colours; soon it would be as if it had never rained.

It pleased Leah to see that the eagle was back. Through half-closed eyes she watched the great bird as it circled above the lake, soaring on dark tilted wings into the sky but always returning. Its shadow passed over the camp as it swooped lower and Leah, suddenly wide awake, sat up.

The eagle had seen something strange on the smooth expanse of water, had made a brief, swooping inspection, and, having decided that what was there could only be of use or interest to a carrion-eater, had spiralled back into the blue. Leah frowned as she stared down at the lake. There was something, a floating dark shape just breaking the surface; her hands trembled as she tried to focus the binoculars.

Her cry brought Ahmed and Gaffur to their feet. When they reached her, Leah could not speak; she huddled in her chair and, in answer to Ahmed's alarmed questions, could only point.

Ahmed slowly straightened; he stood silent, holding on to the back of Leah's chair, as Gaffur cried out hoarsely and rushed down to the lake verge.

Leah struggled up and looked at Ahmed. She offered the binoculars to him but he did not take them. Until that moment, she had held on to the hope that the hideous bloated thing she had glimpsed was someone, or something, else, not Dost Mohammed, or, if it must be he, that on the dark night when he had fled from the camp he must have slipped and fallen, drowned. . . . That hope died as she saw Ahmed's face. She had seen him afraid once before, grey-green with fear, but now she saw guilt and naked terror. He was staring in front of him, yet she was sure that he saw nothing of the sunlit scene, not even the floating horror down there; he was back in some hell of his own. She put out a hand towards him and said, "Ahmed?"

As he turned slowly to face her, the thudding of hooves on grass made her swing round in time to see that Gaffur, astride one pony and leading the other, was fleeing towards the blue lake with the lame pony limping after them. Silence fell again. She and Ahmed were alone.

In the stillness, she heard the stream running in its stony bed, the only sound. The mountains hemmed them in. Through her own choice, she was in this wild, lonely place where there was no one to help her, nowhere to turn. And the time for doubts and evasions was over; it was no use now to shut her eyes and refuse to see what she did not want to see. This man standing so close to her that she could feel his warmth and hear his breathing was dangerous, violent, a murderer. Leah took a deep breath and lifted her head. He was also Ahmed.

Suddenly he fell on his knees and clutched her feet. He was weeping, not his usual easy tears, but a rasping ugly crying that filled her with revulsion and with pity. She tried to draw back; her knees were shaking and, groping for the chair behind her, she managed to free herself and sit down.

He followed her, still on his knees, his hands stretched out to her, and she said, "Ahmed, Ahmed, what are we to do?"

When at last the weeping stopped, Leah looked down at his bowed head and said, "Control yourself, Ahmed. Sit up and tell me why, why you did it. Nabir was right, wasn't he? You knew Dost Mohammed."

Still kneeling at her feet and clutching a fold of her dressing-gown, Ahmed gazed into her face as words poured from him. It was as if floodgates had been opened or a dam had burst; cards, money, a staircase in Delhi, Dost Mohammed's threats, the lamplit cook tent, the walk along the dark lake—it all came tumbling out. Leah listened with horror and strained attention. She did not understand half he said, but she understood enough.

"And that other time?" she interrupted at last. "What about that old man and his wife?"

"How Memsahib know?"

"The Doctor Miss Sahib told me. She telephoned to Pratapur. You killed them, too, didn't you?"

Ahmed sat back on his heels. "Doctor Miss Sahib know nothing," he cried. "How she know? That dead woman, she bad, deserve to die, but Ahmed not kill her. The old man kill her, and he try to kill Ahmed, with knife."

"So it was in self-defence," Leah whispered, and now she no longer listened to Ahmed. A great weariness had come over her. Her head was swimming and she could not breathe. The shock had been too much. Forcing herself to make a last effort, she sat up and said, "That's enough, Ahmed. Now listen to me. When Nabir's brother comes, we will go straight back to Srinagar. I'll find you a good lawyer."

Ahmed jumped up. "No!" he cried. "No! Ahmed not go back. Never! Memsahib want Ahmed hang?"

"Then what will you do?" she managed to say.

"Ahmed made plan. Knapsack ready. Take path over hills, Commander Sahib's path. When Nabir's brother come, Ahmed be far, far away."

"You had better go now, then, while you have the chance," Leah said, and closed her eyes. She did not hear his answer. A dark wave was engulfing her and sweeping her away.

For most of the afternoon, Ahmed kept watch at the entrance to Leah's tent. Often when he came softly to have a closer look at her, she did not know he was there, but in her lucid intervals, which came and went, she would call out to him.

Once, she had opened her eyes and, looking up into his face, had said distinctly, "Have you come to kill me, too, Ahmed?" He had thrown himself down on his knees by her bed and had cried out, "Memsahib, don't say that—never, never!" He had been so shaken that he had run out of the tent, and it was some time before he had crept back.

"You still here?" she had said then, drowsily, rousing

herself again. "Why haven't you gone?" And, not waiting to hear him say, "Memsahib ill. How Ahmed go," she had drifted away again. Her mind wandered, nothing was real. At times she had realised that she was worse, and once she had thought wearily, feeling too ill to care, 'Well, death has to come, sometime, somewhere.'

Ahmed knew that he ought to go as far away as possible before Nabir's brother came, and he longed to put a great distance between himself and that thing floating far out in the lake, about which he could do nothing except avert his eyes. Twice in that long afternoon, he climbed the gully and, standing on the hill above the blue lake, looked towards the Pass. There had been no sign of Gaffur or the ponies. Would Gaffur wait at the foot of the Pass that night or, leaving the ponies, would he try to claw his way up the still dangerous path to tell his news and fetch help? Ahmed resolved that before dark he would go up the gully again. He did not think that Nabir's brother would attempt to reach the lakes before daylight tomorrow, but he must make sure that no one was advancing over the plain; he did not intend to be caught here like a rat in a trap. Meanwhile, he would make his preparations, retrieve his knapsack, of course, but first try to take the mem's money belt without disturbing her.

Leah turned restlessly as he felt under the pillows and gently withdrew the belt, but she did not wake. He was feeling in the belt's inner pocket for the wad of rupee notes when she said, startling him into dropping the belt, "You needn't steal, Ahmed. If you want money, you have only to ask."

Her voice was surprisingly strong, if hoarse, and she was trying to sit up. Ahmed put his hand under her arm to help her; through the thin sleeve of her nightgown he felt the heat of her body.

"Memsahib got much fever!" he exclaimed before he could stop himself.

"I have a little fever," she corrected him. "We mustn't exaggerate."

He put a shawl round her shoulders and arranged the blankets over her as gently and carefully as any woman could have done. "You are as good as a nurse, Ahmed," she whispered. "Now please bring me some tea. I'm terribly thirsty."

Thankful that she was herself again, Ahmed laid the belt on the bed and hurried to the cook tent. As he went, he touched the notes in his pocket. If he felt a slight qualm, he quietened it by telling himself that he needed the money more than the memsahib, that there would be another registered letter waiting for her at the Meadow when she got back.

The sunshine had gone from the gully and the shadow of the hill stretched across the camp when Ahmed brought Leah her tea. He saw at once that her brief moment of strength and sanity was over. She did not recognise or even see him. She sat upright, moving her hands and arms in vague gestures, and talked to herself in a meaningless babble of which he could make nothing. He backed away, unnerved and trembling, but once outside the tent, he controlled himself, put the tray down, and stood in the entrance watching her.

Sometimes she smiled and held her hand out, as if in greeting, but not to him. Her blue gaze, moving round the tent, passed blindly over him and yet saw what he could not see. Once she nodded and gave the low chuckle he knew so well, and Ahmed's eyes filled with tears. He stayed where he was, waiting. He did not believe, as Gaffur would have done, that the memsahib was possessed of devils; this confusion, this witlessness would soon pass. . . .

Although Ahmed did not know it, Leah was entertaining visitors. The first to arrive were Colonel and Mrs. Baxter—so kind of them to have come all the way from Gulmarg; they did not stay long and their place was taken by the Johnstons, who stood side by side, looking down at her; they were too tall, their heads touched the canvas, and she was glad when they moved to let Phoebe, in her white coat, slip between them to take the hand Leah held out so gladly.

Tim was there, too, somewhere in the background, with the three missionaries she had met on the road so long ago. She looked for Geoffrey; suddenly she longed to see him again, not as he had been that last dreadful day, but in his tweed jacket and soft hat, all set to go fishing. Geoffrey, of course, could not be there because he was dead, but where was Hugh? Surely her own grandson should have taken the trouble to come when everyone else was gathering round her? Even the old Gujar woman was sitting in a corner, with Nabir, in his red plaid, beside her; even the lovely girl of the willow grove made a brief, flashing appearance. It was confusing, the way they all came and went. She put her head back on the pillows and shut her eyes. When she opened them, only Ahmed was there. It was evening and he had lit the lantern.

The moon shone down in splendour on the lakes, turning the world to silver, paling the lantern set outside the entrance to Leah's tent where Ahmed crouched, wrapped in his blanket, fast asleep.

The knapsack was ready and waiting at his side; he had crept into the tent to retrieve it hours ago. The mem had not woken when he had stood by the bed, listening to her breathing. She was, he had thought as he looked down at her, so old and ill. If she had to die, why could it not be now, at once? There would be nothing then to hold him back; he would be free to go. The mem should not have said, "Have you come to kill me, too, Ahmed," putting what he had not even imagined into his mind. It would be easy, so very easy, to stop that painful breathing. . . .

Ahmed, bending over Leah, had found that he could not do it. Twice he had held his hands over her, and had drawn them back; he had known then that this was something he would never bring himself to do. Picking up the knapsack, he had backed hastily out of the tent to begin his long, cold vigil.

As he sat with his arms wrapped round his knees trying

to keep warm, staring with unseeing eyes at the shining lake below him and wrestling with his thoughts, he had heard her stirring and, once or twice, talking to herself. It had been a disturbing, eerie sound in the stillness of the night. The silence that had followed had been even more unnerving and the cold, steady, relentless light had worried him; it had pierced through layers of cloth and flesh into his bones, into his heart and brain, distorting his thoughts, exaggerating his fears. Dost Mohammed's body must have drifted out of sight into the shadows, but he had known that it was there, accusing him as the memory of that hut still did. Then the thought had come to him that Nabir's brother and his men, helped by the moon, had already braved the descent from the Pass and were coming nearer and nearer, that at any moment he would be surrounded. Although he had known that this was unlikely, that they would be bound to wait until daylight, unreasoning panic had seized Ahmed. He had thrown the blanket off and started up, convinced that if he wanted to save his skin he must go at once.

Ahmed had not gone. Exhausted sleep had ended his long wrestling with himself. Every instinct had told him to go, told him not to be a fool. The mem had not moved when he had stood by her bed, or when he had groped under it for the knapsack. She had not whispered, "Don't leave me alone, Ahmed." He had only known—though the way up the gully was clear and bright, easy in the moonlight —he could not bring himself to leave her.

Ahmed woke with painful suddenness, jerked awake by what he did not know, unless it was a sense of urgency, an awareness. . . . Had he imagined, or had he dreamt that in his sleep something had brushed past him where he crouched, his head on his folded arms? At first, as he gazed round, holding his breath, afraid of what he might see, it seemed that nothing had changed. The silver lake lay below him, the silvered hills looked down on him, the black shadow of the cook tent was sharp on the moon-washed stones.

A sound, faint, some way off, the sound of a dislodged stone falling, made him turn his head sharply to look up the gully. He gasped, froze in terror—he could feel the hairs rising on his head. Far up the gully was a moving white shape, indeterminate, wavering. . . . A ghost, or an evil spirit, conjured up by the moonlight? Spirits move silently, making no sound. Ahmed sprang up and, seizing the lantern, looked into the tent. The bed was empty, the blankets thrown back.

When he reached Leah, she had fallen on her knees, but before he could touch her, she struggled up and tried to move away from him up the path. Her white hair was wild, and he saw with dismay that she wore only a nightgown and her feet were bare. How could anyone so ill have gone so far, climbed so high up this steep channel of stones? How could her old heart stand it? He could feel his own, after his frenzied haste, pumping furiously in his breast.

"Memsahib! Memsahib!" he gasped. "What Memsahib doing?"

He hesitated to touch her, although he knew that he must. She shrugged his hand off and muttered, not to him but to herself, "I can't breathe here. I can't. I must go higher. It will be all right when I reach the snowline."

At first he thought that she knew what she was saying, that he could reason with her, but she did not answer when he spoke, and he saw that she did not know he was there. Ahmed took off his jacket, put it round her shoulders, and, dreading a struggle, managed to turn her back the way she had come. To his surprise, she did not resist again and, silent now, allowed him to support her over the stones, half carrying her as he tried to spare her bare feet. She was shivering although her body, even through his jacket, felt hot. A plump pigeon, he had thought once, and now she was almost as thin, as sharp-boned, as his mother and far more insubstantial and frail.

As they made the slow descent, Ahmed saw that the

moonlight was paling. Over the hills, a warmer light showed faintly in the sky. Dawn was not far off, a dawn that should have found him setting out, his knapsack on his back, swinging along towards a future that now might never be. He sighed and Leah murmured, "The sun, the moon . . . he that keepeth thee . . . from this time forth . . ." The words came disjointedly in a jumble, and he could make nothing of them.

Suddenly she stood still and, looking up into his face, said distinctly in a strong loud voice, "The sun shall not smite thee by day, nor the moon by night. The Lord shall preserve thee."

"No, no!" Ahmed pleaded. "That bad luck, that mission talk."

In the tent, he lowered her gently onto the bed. She collapsed for a moment against the pillows, and struggled up again. Ahmed tried to put her into her dressing-gown as she stood swaying and staring round her as if she had no idea where she was; his hands were shaking and she would not, or could not, help him. Her blue eyes, now bloodshot between their swollen lids, which had looked at him unseeingly, suddenly focussed. She seized her dressing-gown from him and cried, "What *are* you doing, Ahmed? Give that to me at once."

Tears of relief filled his eyes as he backed hastily away and bent to pick up his jacket. Her voice was the husky, difficult voice of the last days, but her own; this madness, this possession came and went. She looked incredibly old and shrunken and ill, yet he knew she was herself once more.

"It's morning," Leah announced. "Help me into the bathroom, Ahmed, and then bring me some tea. I don't feel well, I'm tired. I shall wash later."

As he put his hand out to help her, he saw her eyes widen into a stare. They were fixed on his face, as if asking a question. Her clenched hands went up to her chest and she gave a cry.

Ahmed caught her as she fell and laid her back on the

pillows. It took him a few moments to realise that she was dead.

It was too sudden. He could not believe it. He only knew that she would hate anyone to see her lying as she was, and he hastily pulled her nightgown down over her legs and drew the blankets up, expecting that she would wake and resent the familiarity, saying again, "What *are* you doing, Ahmed?" He knelt down by the bed, gazing into her face, took her hand in his, and whispered, "Memsahib? Memsahib?"

Suddenly he jumped up and recoiled until his back was against the canvas. Her mouth had fallen open, her eyes still stared. Ahmed gave a loud cry and rushed out of the tent.

The sun had risen above the mountains before he came back. At dawn, when he had fled in panic from the tent, he had clambered wildly up the gully, certain that Nabir's men were coming. There had been nothing moving on the shadowy plain or, as far as he could see, on the Pass, and as he stood on the hilltop shivering with cold and fear, he had grown calmer. They would wait until the sun had dried the night dew from that path, and he must climb the gully again when the sun was up, and bring the mem's binoculars with him.

Ahmed had been sure that when Nabir's men came they would think that he was in some way responsible for the memsahib's death, but they could not be here for hours and he would be far away by then. As his panic slowly subsided, he had climbed down to the cook tent and taken time to light a fire and brew himself some tea. It had been impossible to swallow anything solid, not even a mouthful of cold rice, although he knew that it would be wise to eat before setting out.

Never in his life had Ahmed felt so alone. A silent world of rock, water, and sky stretched round him, vast, uncaring, implacable, showing no sign of life except for the eagle circling far above him, a mere speck in the blue, and the eagle meant nothing to him. He was afraid of the lake and of this lonely echoing place, and even more afraid of the tent and what it held, but he needed the binoculars.

He half expected to find the mem sitting up, neat and tidy, with the small black book in her hands, as he had so often seen her. The tent was dim after the sunshine of the outside world. Ahmed paused on the threshold, then forced himself forward and knelt by the bed. He looked once at her face and looked away. The pale blue eyes were regarding him; she was frowning, as if forbidding him to do what he must do.

'A dead old woman,' he told himself. 'She can't hurt you'; and, gritting his teeth, stifling the frightened sob that rose in his throat, he picked up her hand. She had not yet begun to stiffen, but it took him what seemed a long time to pull the two rings from her fingers—the gold band of her wedding ring was embedded in the cold flesh and he left it where it was. When it was done, he sat back on his heels and put the rings and her gold watch carefully into the wallet she had given him. He thought of taking the red leather belt, but nothing would have induced him to feel for it under the pillows.

He stood up cautiously, as if he feared that she would wake and ask him in that gruff, offended voice what he was doing. It cost him an effort not to dash out of the tent into the sunshine, and he had to force himself again to bend over the bed and lay her blue scarf gently over her face. Gingerly, averting his head, he placed the Bible on her breast and crossed her hands over it, murmuring, as he did this, what was meant as a farewell and an apology, although he did not know what words he used.

Ahmed picked up the binoculars and glanced round the tent. There was no point in leaving the little travelling clock for Nabir's men, and he slipped it into his pocket. He would have liked to take the leather collar-box but that would be too bulky. He could do with the good warm cloak; she would have no use for it now and it would be cold sleeping out in the open.

The sun was warm on his shoulders, as he knelt on the stones outside the tent to roll up the cloak and stow it among his blankets; it was time, more than time, to climb the gully again. Ahmed hurried to the viewpoint, stumbling up the gully, and cursing himself for lingering in the tent.

His hands were unsteady from the speed of the climb when he stood for the last time high above the blue lake, and he had difficulty in focusing the binoculars.

Ahmed saw what he had dreaded: men and ponies, minute in the distance, were moving slowly down from the Pass. He caught his breath; nearer, much nearer on the plain, was a group of men on foot, an advance party who must have left the ponies to take the dangerous path more slowly. For a moment Ahmed panicked, and then told himself that they were still a long way off and could not reach the lakes for several hours, perhaps two or three.

The thought that Nabir was one of those men flashed through Ahmed's mind. He lifted the binoculars again, but now his hands were trembling uncontrollably and he could not look for the red plaid. If Nabir was there, which was possible—if, down in the Meadow, he had heard of the rain on the Pass and had hurried to join his brother—Ahmed knew that he could expect no mercy, that men would be sent riding after him to hound him down. He lowered the binoculars and, crouching as if he feared to be seen exposed on the hilltop, he fled down the gully, sliding on the loose stones.

Ahmed knelt by the knapsack, trying to fasten the roll of blankets securely; his fingers were cold and clumsy, although he was sweating with fear, and he felt strangely weak. He made himself rest for a few moments with the pack beside him and then got to his feet. There was one more thing he had to do.

As he put out his hand to close the tent flaps, a gleam

of blue in the dimness within caught his eye. The butterfly-pin still held the straw hat to the inner lining of the tent, as it had done for days. How could he have forgotten it, even in his haste? It was, he suspected, of little value, but it meant more to him than any of the mem's other posses-sions; he would only have to look at it to see her again.

To leave the winged pin for Nabir's men to find and paw over would be sacrilege, yet it took all his nerve to go into the tent. The straw hat fell to the ground with a rustling sigh that startled him as he withdrew the pin and with trembling haste stuck it through the lapel of his jacket. Later, he would hide it in his knapsack.

It did not take him long to close the tent flaps, lacing the cord tightly through the eyeholes, and to move some large stones to seal up the crack below the flaps. There was nothing more he could do for her and he hoisted the pack on his back, and picked up his stick.

Ahmed was half way up the gully when a sound behind him made him swing round. He was in time to see a small boulder fall from the steep hillside above the overhang and bounce on the stones below; it was followed by a shower of stones and earth. He stared up at the hill, remembering Gaffur's muttered warnings. There was nothing unusual to be seen, no crack, no fissure. The hill seemed as it had always been. No more stones fell and he went on, climbing more quickly now, although he told himself there was no need to hurry. The sun was hot on his back, and in the gully that morning, it was strangely airless.

He had almost reached the top, a few more steps and he would have been on the path that he could see winding over bare, undulating country, when the side of the hill collapsed behind him. A deafening roar filled his ears, a great wind tore at his clothes and plucked the hat from his head. He fell on his knees, and as something struck his back, onto his face, putting up his arms to shield his head.

As he lay with the knapsack weighing him down and a rain of small stones and dust descending on him, he thought his last moment had come.

The din subsided; slowly silence fell again over the lake. Presently, Ahmed rose shakily to his feet and looked back. Half the hillside, it seemed to him at first, had been sliced away, leaving a huge reddish scar. A jumbled heap of rock, stone and earth from which a cloud of dust was rising, lay across the gully, reaching into the stream. Of the rock overhang and the tent under it, there was no sign.

Ahmed sat down abruptly. He was trembling, and although he did not know it, tears were running down his dust-stained cheeks. At first he could think only of the tent and what it held, entombed under that great slide of stone. It took him some time to realise his own escape, and when he did, he began to shake uncontrollably; his whole body twitched and shook. This did not last long, and as he grew calmer, he was able to look more closely at the scene below.

It was not, he saw, a large landslide, but the fall was enough to ensure that the tent would never be unearthed. As far as he could tell, it would take many men weeks—even months—to shift all that rock. He doubted if it would ever be attempted. Let Nabir's brother and his men come—let Nabir come. They would never disturb the mem. Another and even more welcome thought came to Ahmed. No one would ever know that he had escaped the fall, that he had not been in the tent. He could not see the cook tent which must be buried too; being further off, it might have been engulfed more lightly and could perhaps be dug out. When there was no sign of him there, it was bound to be thought that he was buried with the memsahib. Anyone coming to look for him would find that Ahmed—and Aziz for that matter—were no more.

This thought put fresh heart into him. He was able to stand up and brush the dust from his clothes and hair. He took a handkerchief—one of Leah's he had appropriated long ago—from his pocket and wiped his face. His precious hat was a few yards away; he retrieved it, dusted it with care and set it at his favourite angle on his curly black head. It only remained to adjust the straps of the knapsack, pick up his stick again and be off.

When he stood on the path, Ahmed hesitated. The way would be long and difficult, he knew, and he was afraid. He tried to cheer himself up with the assurance that, once across those mountains, whose endless ranges vanished into the hazy distance, he would discover not only villages but towns in whose bazaars there would be food, clothes, women—many, many women. He had money; he would sell the rings, and for a short time at least, be a servant no longer, but his own master, living a life of ease and luxury.

What was the good of standing there, hesitating, when he had no choice? Ahmed walked on, swinging his stick to give himself courage. The sun was shining, the world was before him, the past behind, and he was young. Soon he began to hum his little love song.

It was many miles further on, when he was beginning to feel the weight of the knapsack, that he found he had lost the butterfly-wing hatpin somewhere on the path, or more likely, when he fell in the gully. He had meant to keep the pin always, and it would have reminded him now of the old lady's courage, but to go back to look for it would be madness. He must go on.

A NOTE ABOUT THE AUTHOR

Jon Godden was born in Bengal and is the eldest of four sisters, the second of whom is Rumer Godden. Her parents lived for many years in India, and she herself lived alternately there and in England. She now makes her home in Kent. She began to write in 1938, when she was living in Calcutta, and her novels have received high praise on both sides of the Atlantic. Her novels include *The House by the Sea, The Peacock, The City and the Wave, The Seven Islands, Mrs. Panopoulis, A Winter's Tale,* and *Mrs. Starr Lives Alone.*

A NOTE ON THE TYPE

The text of this book was set by computer
in a type face called Baskerville. The face is a
facsimile reproduction of types cast from
molds made for John Baskerville (1706–75)
from his designs. The punches for the revived
Linotype Baskerville were cut under the
supervision of the English printer George W.
Jones.

John Baskerville's original face was one of the
forerunners of the type style known as
"modern face" to printers—a "modern" of
the period A.D. 1800.

The book was composed at ComCom Inc.,
the Computer Composition Division of Intext,
Allentown, Pennsylvania. It was printed and
bound at The Haddon Craftsmen, Inc.,
Scranton, Pennsylvania. It was designed by
Gwen Townsend.